THE TOUCH OF A STORME

The Storme Brothers
Book Five

Sandra Sookoo

© Copyright 2022 by Sandra Sookoo
Text by Sandra Sookoo

Dragonblade Publishing, Inc. is an imprint of Kathryn Le Veque Novels, Inc.
P.O. Box 23
Moreno Valley, CA 92556
ceo@dragonbladepublishing.com

Produced in the United States of America

First Edition March 2022
Trade Paperback Edition

Reproduction of any kind except where it pertains to short quotes in relation to advertising or promotion is strictly prohibited.

All Rights Reserved.

The characters and events portrayed in this book are fictitious. Any similarity to real persons, living or dead, is purely coincidental and not intended by the author.

ARE YOU SIGNED UP FOR DRAGONBLADE'S BLOG?

You'll get the latest news and information on exclusive giveaways, exclusive excerpts, coming releases, sales, free books, cover reveals and more.

Check out our complete list of authors, too!

No spam, no junk. That's a promise!

Sign Up Here

www.dragonbladepublishing.com

Dearest Reader;

Thank you for your support of a small press. At Dragonblade Publishing, we strive to bring you the highest quality Historical Romance from some of the best authors in the business. Without your support, there is no 'us', so we sincerely hope you adore these stories and find some new favorite authors along the way.

Happy Reading!

CEO, Dragonblade Publishing

Additional Dragonblade books by Author Sandra Sookoo

The Storme Brother Series
The Soul of a Storme (Book 1)
The Heart of a Storme (Book 2)
The Look of a Storme (Book 3)
The Sting of a Storme (Book 4)
The Touch of a Storme (Book 5)
A Storme's Christmas Legacy

CHAPTER ONE

June 10, 1818
London, England

As the Honorable Isobel Storme wiped at the tears on her cheeks, the oval-shaped ruby ring sitting on the middle finger of her right hand winked in the early summer sunlight. Though cheerful, warm illumination streamed through the windows of her mother's bedchamber, it brought anything but that emotion.

The truth of the matter was that her mother—Viscountess Doughton—was dying. It had been a slow, torturous road to arrive at this point, but the disease of her lungs had accelerated. All too soon, she'd leave this mortal coil, and that was an eventuality Isobel wasn't prepared for, no matter how much time she'd had to acclimate.

"Don't cry so, Isobel. You'll ruin your looks," her mother admonished in a whispered voice. At least there was a smile on her wan face. "I didn't give you the ring to make you sad."

"What else am I to think, Mother?" Again, she glanced at the ruby. The facets winked in the sunlight, as did the delicate silver filagree work that held the three-carat stone. "Father gave it to you upon your wedding." And since that union had been fraught with problems and strife, the ring would forever remind Isobel that being wed didn't necessarily mean being in love.

Which suited her mindset regarding matrimony just fine. She'd rather find fun and entertainment with men instead of a gilded cage and the end to her freedom.

"I'm ready to go," her mother continued. "There will be no more pain, or struggle to breathe. Perhaps I can see your father again after all this time." A sigh escaped her. "I only wish I could have lived long enough to see you and Caroline matched and cared for."

From sheer willpower alone, Isobel tamped the urge to point her gaze at the ceiling. "I'm not a marriage-minded lady. You've known this for a long time." As for her older sister Caroline. Well, she couldn't say what her life held in store, for her sister had only just come back into her life from being locked away in an institution for the mentally deficient. "I rather doubt Caroline is looking for a husband either, for different reasons, of course."

"You need someone to take care of you, Isobel."

"I don't." What she needed was for someone to understand her, someone who would pay exclusive attention to her when all she'd ever wanted out of life was to gain the notice of the people she loved. Being the youngest member of the family had assured she'd fallen through the cracks and was ignored.

It was no secret the Storme family had been—and oftentimes still was—embroiled in scandal and upheaval. At times that reputation worked splendidly in her favor, for courting scandal was a favorite way of filling her days, but at others, it grated.

Would she ever have a life removed from the Stormes, to move away from that large and impressive—sometimes oppressive—shadow?

"You're searching for love. I can see it deep down in your eyes," her mother continued. When she coughed, the pristine white handkerchief she dabbed her lips with came away with flecks of blood. "We failed you in that, and I'm heartily sorry." Her laugh was an exhausted sound. "Your father and I failed both you girls, and I fear we passed that trait on to William."

Isobel snorted. "He is a tad overbearing, this is true, but ever since William married Fanny, he's mellowed slightly." Her older brother wed a few weeks ago to a woman nearly ten years his junior, and one of Isobel's friends to boot. While it was exciting having Fanny in the family fold to exchange secrets with, it wasn't the same as having William's full attention any longer. "Every one of the Stormes has their own lives. I'm once again… lost." The last was said on a whisper, and she glanced at the ruby ring her mother had given her.

"But that's all to the good." Her mother rested her tired gaze on Isobel. "Those boys were wild and scattered. Now they're married, which provides a bit of peace for them. Being together last Christmas went a long way to repairing the rift between the Storme branches. I'd hoped it would have helped you as well."

"It didn't. Not truly." In some agitation, Isobel stood up from the chair at her mother's bedside. "I'm not seeking marriage, Mother. I don't want my wings clipped."

"Oh, Isobel." A note of hopelessness lingered in her mother's voice. "If the Storme brothers taught you anything it's that the right man won't stifle the lady they take to wife. Each of those boys has a wonderful helpmeet; they complement each other. There is nothing to say the same won't happen for you."

"I've seen enough men to know those three are an aberration." She shrugged. "Besides, the Stormes are a unique bunch."

"Of course they are, but please promise me you'll consider letting someone court you. I'd like to know that during the time I have left you're making inroads to settle your life."

"Ah. You want me tamed." How disappointing. "I enjoy creating sensations."

"It's scandalous, and if you keep on, no man will have you." Censure had crept into her tones.

"Then I want none of them. If they can't take me on as I am, they're not worthy." Isobel shook her head. At eight and twenty, she'd long been a hoyden and, as her cousin Andrew called her, a problem waiting to happen. There was a reason for that. She adored the control she maintained over her reputation and adored when tongues wagged or heads turned. A demure, proper life had never appealed to her. The attention that came along with aberrant behavior helped to distract her from the turbulence all around her.

"Isobel…"

Suddenly possessed of the need to put distance between her and the inevitable death of her remaining parent, she headed toward the open doorway. "Don't worry, Mother. I won't do anything as rash as you fear."

Much.

No sooner had she stepped one foot into the corridor beyond than Hankins, their butler, entered at the end of the hall.

"Miss Storme, the Earl of Hadleigh is here to see you," the stately man announced in tones he no doubt thought were mysterious and thrilling. "He's waiting in the drawing room, and he's quite in a rush."

What the devil is Cousin Andrew doing here? She sighed. "Very well." As Isobel followed the butler down the stairs, she racked her brain over the events of the last few days to discover what the earl would have had issue with. Then she scrunched up her face. Ah, that bit of scandalous flirting at a ball two days ago. Or was it the handsome groom she stole a kiss from yesterday while visiting with a friend? Obviously, the on-dits had finally made the rounds.

Drat, drat, drat!

Anxiety put knots into her belly as she entered the drawing room. She drew her hands down the front of her jonquil cotton gown, wished she'd worn a color that gave her more of a calm disposition, and then approached her cousin—the Earl of Hadleigh and current head of the Storme family. He stared out one of the windows with his hands clasped behind his back, but from the rigid set of his broad shoulders and the way he held his head, he was already annoyed.

Drat.

"Hullo, Cousin Andrew. How wonderful to see you today." Her attempt to infuse enthusiasm into her voice fell flat. "I assumed your schedule didn't allow for visiting." Two months ago, Andrew's wife was delivered of a baby girl, and the earl's life had been rather hectic since. To say nothing of his duties in Parliament coming to an end for this year's session. According to family gossip, he'd argued a few times on the House of Lords floor but failed to win over older, more traditional peers to his way of thinking. "How does the babe fare?"

"Don't think to distract me, Cousin Isobel." Andrew turned to face her, and even though the afternoon sun backlit him, concern was evident on his face. For two seconds, though, his eyes softened, and he became an entirely different man than the cousin she'd come to know since last Christmastide. "Lady Penelope is a tiny little doll. I still can't believe I have a daughter."

"Yes, she is quite a charming thing." Even though Isobel couldn't imagine settling down enough to have children, her brand-new cousin would soon steal the hearts of everyone. "How is Sarah's health?" It had taken nigh onto two days to bring the babe into the world. The countess had yet to leave the house, and Andrew guarded her health zealously. It was difficult to tell which one he loved more fiercely—his wife or his new child.

"She's well and improving in strength with each passing day. Soon she'll be back to her old self and ready to receive visitors." Then he cleared his throat and the customary mask of irritation slid back into place. "I thank you for your inquiries, but I'm not here to discuss either of them." He gestured to a low sofa. "Please, sit."

Which meant what he had to say would come in the form of a lecture. With a small huff, Isobel marched over to the indicated piece of furniture and flounced onto it.

"Where's William?"

"How should I know?" She shrugged. "I'm not his keeper, and his schedule is too difficult to sort." Even more so since he'd wed. He adored his position as a Principal Officer with Bow

Street, so much so that he'd only taken a week away for his wedding trip.

And of course due to their mother's fragile health.

"He was supposed to be here by now."

Another confirmation that a lecture was in store, if both Andrew and her brother would head this discussion. "I can't imagine what's bothering you, Cousin," she said in a sweet voice and dared to bat her eyelashes at him. It was outrageous enough, but it would either cajole him into a better mood... or infuriate him.

One never knew with Andrew.

"Don't insult my intelligence or yours with that attitude." Andrew once more clasped his hands behind his back as he leveled his angry gaze on her. "These past handful of weeks you've become a veritable powder keg of scandal. Sooner or later, you'll explode into a mess that even my reach won't be able to smooth over."

At least he didn't waste time. "What particular incident have you taken exception to?"

His eyes narrowed and his chest swelled, straining the buttons of his waistcoat. Then, he took a deep breath and let it ease out. "Does it matter? It seems you go out of your way to cause scandal, but if I were to pick something, the most recent of which was the shameful flirting you did at the Waterfords' rout two nights past. I heard you had a bevy of young men fairly eating out of your hand and that you very nearly lured two into an unused parlor."

Well, the gossipmongers hadn't been wrong... Remembering those two men prompted a grin she didn't quite hide quick enough. Twin sons of a viscount and sinfully handsome to boot. A few years older than her, they cared nothing for propriety and were just the sort of men she wished to coerce into illicit embraces.

When she caught Andrew glaring, she sobered. "They were quite insistent." Of course, she encouraged them...

"You cannot continue with that behavior." Her cousin shook his head, and he softened his tones. "I'm not against your having a choice, but please have a care. If you go down this path, you'll be labeled fast or too scandalous for a decent man."

"Piffle." Isobel waved a hand in dismissal. "I never said I wanted a decent man. Where's the fun in that?"

His eyes narrowed. "For God's sake, settle on one." He ran a hand along the side of his face. "Your mother and William are both worried. Poor Aunt Patricia doesn't need her last days on this earth filled with that."

Isobel's chest tightened with the urge to flee, to run through London and far away from this house. Above all, she refused to cry in front of her cousin, let alone show any sort of emotion. That wasn't who the Stormes were. Instead, she drew upon the anger that was all too easy to find these days. "What do you know of my life, Andrew?"

"A fat lot more than you assume." His expression softened. "I know what you're going through, and I'll help if I can. Perhaps if you talked about what's bothering you?"

That didn't sound like her cousin at all, but then, he was still growing since he'd married. She blew out a breath. "Everything is changing. You Storme boys have barely come back into my life, but now you're all married and have your own interests. William just wed. Caroline keeps herself away from everyone. That leaves me alone with Mother." A ball of tears rose in her throat, but she swallowed it down. "And she's dying."

Don't show weakness, Isobel. Women seeking scandal need to be strong.

"I understand."

Isobel snorted, for his compassion felt out of character, which left her even more confused about him. "Obviously, you don't understand that much, for you're anxious and concerned about only your growing little family." She clasped her fingers in her lap. "You have rarely visited Mother; Caroline hasn't. And now William has other duties that take his time."

"I'll try to do better, Cousin." When it appeared he would have taken the spot next to her on the sofa, he held his position, perhaps doubting his reception. "Whether you believe it or not, Aunt Patricia's impending death saddens me."

"Yes, well, it stifles me, presently. Why can I not have a bit of fun before my mother dies and I'm forced into mourning?" She found his gaze with hers. "For so long I've been caught up in the wreck of the Stormes. I need the freedom to find out who I am outside of this family."

That was perhaps the most truth she'd ever shared with him.

Before Andrew could answer, her brother William dashed into the room flushed and looking for all the world as if he'd been involved in wicked, delicious things.

"My apologies for being late. I was on a case," he said, mostly to Andrew, who merely gave him a curt nod.

Isobel rolled her eyes. And he'd no doubt found time along the way to dandle his new wife. "Such gammon, Wills. You look as if you've had a quick tryst. Perhaps in a carriage." It would be all too easy for him since his wife was a journalist and worked with him on his Bow Street cases. "Naughty boy."

Both Andrew and William stared at her with red faces, which prompted a wildly inappropriate laugh from her. They had no clue that some of the literature she'd read was of a more erotic bent than that. To say nothing of the stories she'd heard from some of her married girlfriends or from listening to the maids.

"I don't know how to respond to that," William finally said with a tug to his rumpled cravat, but he couldn't hide the sheepish grin. "Francesca said to give you her regards and that she'd set aside time for you two to talk later."

"All right." Though it was dear that her brother called Fanny by her Christian name, jealousy speared through Isobel's chest at that closeness. Fanny now had more life experience than she did, had been with a man intimately—even if it was Isobel's brother—and that put up yet another barrier between them.

Though she was opposed to marriage, it didn't stop her from wanting a man in her life for companionship or a bit of a toss in the hay every now or again. That wasn't likely to happen any time soon, for once her mother died, a year of mourning would be upon her.

And her life would once again shift into confusion and loneliness.

"Isobel!" The command in her brother's voice brought her out of the maudlin thoughts.

"Yes?" She glanced between the two men, who were so close in looks they could easily pass as twins, if not brothers instead of cousins.

"I've been speaking to you for the past two minutes and you've only looked through me, unhearing." He crossed his arms at his chest. When she raised an eyebrow, he plunged onward. "You need to marry. Settle down, which will go a long way into eliminating the scandal you're fond of courting."

Not only did Wills resemble Cousin Andrew in looks, but his thoughts apparently mirrored the same. Before she could answer, Andrew rushed in.

"Yes, exactly. Perhaps between your brother and I, we can find you a nice, titled man who will catch your fancy."

She groaned. "God save me from that." That last thing she wanted or needed was a gentleman who held a title. If there was something more than spiders she detested in the world, it was anything having to do with the *ton*, titled men especially. Though she'd never shared her thoughts on it, she suspected being part of the *beau monde* and the suffocating responsibilities therein worked to drive the wedge between her father and Andrew's. To say nothing of the fact that had broken both of those men. "I don't want marriage, but I wouldn't say no to a flirtation. The more heated, the better," she couldn't help but add.

Both men protested that statement.

"Absolutely not!"

William shook his head. "No more fuel for the gossipmongers, Isobel!"

"What am I supposed to do instead? I feel like a veritable prisoner here." When they glared at her, she sighed and twisted her mother's ring around her finger.

Andrew rubbed a hand along the side of his face. After a glance at William, he perched on the edge of a delicate chair that faced her sofa. "Listen to me, Cousin." He leaned forward and took possession of one of her hands. Though his tone was well-modulated, there was no mistaking the irritation in his eyes. "You're proving a problem that is rapidly going beyond our means of containing. If you don't desist in causing scandal, I'll have no recourse but to send you to the Derbyshire property."

"Ah, you think to dictate my life like you have Caroline's?" Isobel yanked her hand from his hold. "I think not. However, there are loads of men in the country, so if you go through with that threat, I shall still have company."

Oh, it was horrid of her to bait her cousin when he struggled with controlling his temper, but she couldn't help it.

"For shame, Isobel," her brother said. Mortification lined his face.

Andrew narrowed his eyes. Again, he took a deep breath and let it ease out. Perhaps it was a calming technique he'd come to rely on to master his temper. "If you don't want banishment—with a companion—then you need to find a hobby, a purpose here in London. I care not, but stop putting the Storme name front and center."

"Ha!" Isobel shot from her chair. Restless energy filled her body. She wanted to ride through Hyde Park, or better yet, ride astride in the countryside flying neck or nothing. While wearing breeches. "You tell me to do that when both you and Wills have both caused scandal and rumors to swirl about the family reputation. To say nothing of my other two cousins. How is that fair?"

Sputters emanated from Andrew and William. While they both searched for something to say, Isobel wandered to one of the windows. Outside, the noise from the street wafted to her ears: the *clip clop* of horse hooves as the animals pulled carriages and carts. The hawking cries of vendors selling their wares. Laughter from children having an outing with their governesses.

There was so much life contained within London that she didn't want to be sent to Derbyshire. But even the atmosphere she adored so much couldn't lift her ennui or maudlin mood.

The trouble was, boredom had set in as she waited for her mother's death. Though she was an expert in flirtation, and she enjoyed it heartily, no man had truly caught her fancy since last Christmastide when the whole of the Storme family had come together at Hadleigh Hall. That's when she first met Cousin Finn's surgeon, that redhaired Doctor Marsden.

A small grin curved her lips as she ignored the men in the room. Now *he* would be just the thing to liven up her existence and bring her some cheer as well as a distraction. Handsome and possessing a sense of humor, he'd make a good trysting partner. And those elegant hands with the long fingers! A shiver went down her spine. Did he know how to caress a woman?

But he remained busy with his clinic in the Marylebone neighborhood. Occasionally, she saw him at a society event or family dinner, but that was the depth of their association. With a sigh, Isobel turned, planted her bum against the windowsill and regarded her relatives.

"What would you have me do instead?"

William crossed his arms at his chest. "Sit here and behave like a proper *ton* lady?"

"I'd rather be sent to Derbyshire." She stuck her tongue out at him as she'd done as a small girl. "Might I visit with Jane and Finn?"

Andrew sighed. He stood up from his chair. "If you don't disturb his writing. Or you could assist Jane with her salon."

Though altruistic, the thought of spending long afternoons with women who'd lost children either before or after birth didn't appeal. Not when she was already facing the imminent death of her mother. "I don't need more grief or talk that surrounds it." She blew out a breath. "Might I continue to walk Ivan in Hyde Park?"

"Only if you deport yourself as a lady."

She couldn't promise that, but her cousin didn't need to

know. "I'll visit with Fanny then."

Sudden panic lined William's face. "Uh, her schedule – with the newspaper and my cases – is rather busy. Perhaps she can call on you when she's free."

Oh, dear stupid brother. A huff of frustration escaped her. "Ah, that means you two are copulating like rabbits and don't wish to have visitors hanging about."

Both Andrew and William wore twin expressions of scandalization.

"Isobel!"

"Dear God, Cousin, enough!"

Really, she should make an effort to curb her penchant for plain speaking, but it was too much fun to shock people and cause a sensation. Instead, she grinned like a loon and wished her dog were in the room to add further chaos to this meeting. "Never fear, Wills. I have other friends in London to occupy my time."

He lifted a dark eyebrow. "Female friends?"

"Some, but I have many male friends too, and quite frankly they're more fun."

"Absolutely not." Andrew shook his head. From the flush that raced up his neck and into his cheeks as well as his swelling chest, he was ready to pop. "For the love of all that's holy, please behave yourself and show some decorum."

She batted her eyelashes. "I so adore it when men beg me for something."

William uttered a sound somewhere between a strangled gasp and a cough. Annoyance flashed in his eyes. "Mother doesn't need further heartache in her last weeks. If you can't promise to behave, I'll forbid you from moving within society."

And that would put an end to any entertainment she might glean before going into mourning. "Fine." Isobel heaved a sigh. "I'll adhere as best I can to your rules. For Mother's sake, not yours."

In the meanwhile, she'd try to make certain she attended events where Doctor Marsden might be. After all, a girl had to do *something* to occupy her time, and she *did* need a new challenge.

CHAPTER TWO

June 12, 1818

DOCTOR ROYCE MARSDEN—OLDEST son to the Earl of Worchester—looked about his small clinic for wounded military men with a pleased grin. All ten cots were currently empty, and that meant he and his brother Trey had successfully healed ten soldiers. Hopefully those men were able to acclimate themselves into being back in civilian life and could reinvent themselves.

When his brother came into the large room, Royce raised a hand in greeting. "Good morning. I didn't see you come in."

"You were busy cleaning specimen jars. I had an early patient, so I left you alone."

Trey was his middle sibling. He'd lost his left arm in the Battle of Waterloo, but he never let that bother him or hold him back from chasing his dreams. It was one of the reasons he'd consented to open the clinic with Royce. Additionally, he was quite skilled in assisting wounded military men with the wellbeing of their minds and emotions. Between them, patients at the Marsden Clinic had the best odds of regaining respect for themselves and moving forward in life.

"Ah." Royce took a clean cotton apron from a cupboard, snapped it open, and then fit it around his body, tying the strings about his waist. "It seems I'll have an hour to catch up on my paperwork, then."

"Not quite, Brother. Speaking of patients, Major Storme is here. Says he'd like an examination."

"Oh? That's odd. I'm not scheduled to see him as a patient for another month."

Major Phineas Storme began a relationship with him as a patient with a spinal cord injury. Then, last year, Finn married Royce's sister Jane—a wedding which shocked and delighted both families. To say nothing of the fact the man helped out two days a week in the clinic. Now, whenever a Storme needed the services of a physician or surgeon, they adamantly demanded that he attend them. His friendship with the family had earned him the title of an honorary Storme, and that was about the highest title a man could achieve.

"Who can say? He seemed a trifle worried." Trey waved his hand, presumably to encompass the whole of the clinic. "I told him to wait in one of the exam rooms and that you'd be in directly."

"Thank you. And don't bedevil the nurses while I'm occupied." Trey could play quite the rogue when he wanted to, yet most of his time was devoted to the clinic. It was doubtful he'd ever settle down or marry.

"Can I help it if one of them is gorgeous enough to set London on its ear if she wanted?" he replied with a cheeky grin.

"Behave." Then Royce set his thoughts upon his patient.

Knots of worry formed in his belly as he strode through the room to the short corridor beyond. There was always the chance something had gone wrong with the nerves in Finn's spine, or the original complaint had worsened, which would leave the man in a dire situation. Damn if Finn's life hadn't improved greatly since Royce began treating him, and he'd do everything in his power to keep it that way. Finn deserved everything good.

When he entered one of the two cozy examination rooms, he uttered a sigh of relief. Finn didn't show signs of trauma or emotional distress or even pain. "Good morning. How's my favorite brother-in-law?"

The dark-haired man in the Bath chair snorted but offered a wide grin. "I'm your *only* brother-in-law." Upon closer examination, Royce noted gray feline hairs clinging to Finn's charcoal jacket and gray-and-black striped trousers, for Finn had a rather friendly cat.

"That doesn't mean you can't be my favorite." He ran his gaze over Finn's body. Nothing appeared disturbed. "Trey told me you wished for an examination."

"I did." The peace in his expression soon faded beneath a veil of concern. "I'd like you to take a look at my spine again as well as other portions of my anatomy." There was no embarrassment in his tone or face, for they'd both left that emotion on the wayside long ago.

"Is there a problem?" One never knew when dealing with nerve damage in the spinal column.

"I'm not yet certain."

"Very well. Let me call Miss Clark in to assist with your undressing." Out of the two nurses the clinic employed, she was the one with the most experience, especially in caring for men with Finn's unique wounds.

Thirty minutes later, the major lay on the cot watching as Royce scribbled notes into a notebook that contained everything pertinent about Finn's rehabilitation and injury. A fabric diaper of sorts covered his privates, for he didn't have control over his bowels. As a last matter of course, Royce then held the narrow end of a hollow wooden monaural tube to Finn's chest and placed the funneled side to his own ear. The stethoscope allowed him to listen to a patient's lungs in a process called mediate auscultation. After a few seconds, he nodded and straightened, removing the instrument before laying it on a nearby table.

"There is absolutely nothing untoward I can see. No further nerve damage in your spinal region." He tapped a forefinger to Finn's right knee. "Can you move the leg?"

"There are still limits, of course." An expression of concentration filled the major's face, but his right leg slid a few inches over the cot. "It depends on the day."

Royce nodded. "It's good work, so keep doing the strengthening exercises. You might not walk but using the leg as leverage at times is fantastic. It's enormously more mobile than you had when I first began treating you." Again, he made a notation on his paper. "How is your depression?"

"It's a constant, daily battle. I've found if that's all I focus on, my wellbeing declines, but if I choose to dwell on all the good currently in my life, it's kept at bay." But shadows lingered in his eyes.

"Many soldiers struggle with the same. You're not alone." In any given month, Royce might treat twenty men with various injuries, but the mental toll those wounds left behind were often the most difficult to heal. He and Trey tried, but it depended on the individual. "But if you need someone outside of a blood relation to talk privately and candidly with—as well as a fellow solider—I'm here."

"I appreciate that." The sadness in Finn's eyes intensified. "When my mind plays tricks on me, I bury myself in writing. That helps."

The major's first book with a London publisher came out two months prior to moderate success. It was an adventure novel in a fairy tale setting with a touch of romance. The princess in the story heavily resembled his wife—Royce's sister. From all accounts, the publisher was pleased and asked Finn to write another book, which would be for sale in the shops next spring.

"I'm glad you have that outlet." With a tight chest, Royce threw himself into the only wooden chair in the room. He tossed his notebook onto the table and then gave the major his full attention. "There's something bothering you, though. Something I can't find in an exam." That was one of the most difficult aspects of being a doctor.

Finn nodded. One of his hands fisted at his side. "Is there no chance at all I can father children?"

Ah, so that's what ate at him, and probably had since his marriage. Conveying less than favorable news was another aspect of his profession that made him feel low, but he couldn't lie. Still, poor Finn. Poor Jane. "As I've indicated before, erections and ejaculation are determined by nerves. Yours have been damaged. At this point, I don't know if they need more time to heal or for inflammation to go down, or if they're permanently dead." He rubbed a hand along his jaw. "It's not the best of news, but I refuse to offer you false hope."

"I understand." The major blew out a breath. He stared at the ceiling, but the dismal emotions in his eyes tore at Royce's chest. "During intercourse, I *do* come at times."

"That's all to the good." Royce nodded and wished he could give the other man words of comfort. It must be devastating to want children but to never prove fruitful. "The best advice I can give you is to keep trying."

Finn turned his head and met Royce's gaze. His grin was decidedly cheeky. "We do."

"Ah." As nice as it was to see his friend in a better mood, Royce held up a hand. "Spare me the details. I don't want to hear about how many times you violate my sister."

"Spoil sport." Finn laughed, and it was such an unexpected sound that he joined in on the mirth. Eventually, the major sobered. "I know it weighs on Jane." Sadness pooled in his eyes. "I want so much to give her the secret of her heart, but…"

"I know." Royce leaned forward and laid a hand on Finn's shoulder. "Don't lose hope, my friend. Your body just needs a longer time to work and more chances than the average man's."

"Thank you." When Finn struggled to sit, Royce launched from his chair and assisted him until the major's legs dangled over the side of the cot. "I try to remain strong for her. Writing helps and she has her charity salon. It's enough for now, but every month that goes by, as I hear her crying from in our dressing room when she thinks I'm sleeping, my heart shreds."

I can't even imagine such pain and disappointment.

Royce nodded. "Give it time, Finn."

"I will. It's the only thing I *can* do." With a sigh that signaled the end of the conversation, he accepted the fine lawn shirt Royce handed him, slipped his arms into the sleeves, and then smoothed it down over his torso. "What of you, Doctor? Is there a woman in your life that you might marry soon so you'll enjoy your own set of matrimonial problems? Then you can lament to me, and *I* can give advice."

"Finding a woman who doesn't bore me to tears is the issue currently." Royce snorted. He stood and pulled the chair closer to the small table. "Besides, I'm not compelled to enter the parson's mousetrap. My time is largely spoken for here. The *ton* ladies I know wouldn't stand for my attention being split."

One of Finn's dark eyebrows went up. "Then you're not looking hard enough."

"Perhaps, but to be fair, I have not the inclination, and even less interest."

Unbidden, his mind flashed to that Christmastide house party where the Storme family had gathered in Derbyshire last winter. It was then he'd met Finn's youngest cousin, Isobel. They'd gotten on well together, and unless he'd imagined it, there had been a spark of attraction between them. Nothing that he'd acted upon, for that wouldn't have been wise in the midst of the Storme connection. Since then, they'd seen each other at a handful of family events or society functions, and still the attraction lingered.

Should he try to pursue that? She certainly was more entertaining than other ladies of his acquaintance, and her name had been linked to half a dozen on-dits in the last several weeks alone. From all accounts, she danced attendance on no one and the energy she commanded made her quite the storm, collecting young men in her path.

With a sigh, he came back to the present, and when he glanced at Finn, he started for the other man had tied his cravat and had put his collar into place. "Besides, there's no rush for me to wed. Father is still hale and hearty, even if he's been exhibiting signs of stress and excess drinking."

"That's because he's quite the notable on the floor of the House of Lords." Finn nodded when Royce held out his trousers. With little effort the two of them clothed the major's lower half, and once he'd donned his jacket, Royce ushered Finn into his waiting Bath chair. "Drew often is impressed that your father helped argue one of my brother's points. Eventually, those buffoons in Parliament will cast votes that will benefit the good of all people in England, not just the privileged upper class."

"We can only hope, and that's another aspect of life I'm not looking forward to once the damned title is handed down to me." A shiver of disgust went down his spine. "Let us both hope that's far off in the future."

"Indeed, but back to allowing yourself to be matched," Finn said with a particular twinkle in his eyes. "Don't wait too long, Doctor. I know enough to tell you that life's burdens will run away with you—throw you far afield in some cases—and then you won't have time any longer to set that side of your life into order."

"I appreciate your concern." Royce dropped a hand onto Finn's shoulder. "I enjoy the life I lead now. There will be plenty of days ahead to enter the Marriage Mart." The laugh he uttered sounded a bit hollow to his own ears. "I excel at being a surgeon. Being a suitor? Not so much."

Finn grinned. "I understand, but the clinic cannot offer you comfort, nor can it bolster your confidence when you need it most." Then he winked. "And it certainly cannot offer you a warm place to stick your—"

"Stop." Quickly, Royce held up a hand as he crossed the room and wrenched open the door. "Go." He made a shooing motion. "Take my sister to a society event and treat her like a queen." Wishing to offer hope to his friend turned brother-in-law, he said, "Get into your cups. Indulge in passionate embraces with her, take her to bed, but leave me out of that part of life. It's not for me; I'm certainly not looking for romance."

"Ah." Finn's grin turned entirely too wicked. "There needn't be romance if all you're searching for a is good slap and tickle in someone's garden."

Heat crept up the back of Royce's neck. "Do shut up, Major." He stood aside as Finn wheeled himself from the room. "Women in any capacity require more of a commitment and effort than I'm willing to give. Perhaps I'll revisit this conversation later." Involving himself in a courtship or even an affair was something he couldn't squeeze into his schedule. Truth be told, not even the prospect of a quick shot at release could change his mind. There simply wasn't room in his life for a woman at the moment.

"Fair enough. However, you need to drop by for a visit soon. Jane would enjoy spending an afternoon in your company. She misses her brothers."

"I can't imagine why since she sees us at the clinic twice a week." They'd gained the large patient room, which was still devoid of patients.

"That's in a business capacity and not the same." He eyed Royce askance. "Just come to dinner occasionally. It'll do much to lift her spirits."

"Agreed." Jane had always had a sunny disposition. She carried joy around with her like sunshine, so if her mood was flagging due to her inability to conceive, things must be dire indeed. "Speaking of time spent together, I'm doing a live cadaver exam a few days hence at the Duke of Titterbury's townhouse."

"The devil you say!" Interest lit Finn's expression. "How exciting."

"I thought so too. The duke is paying me a nominal fee to do the thing as a sensation for his friends, but I've agreed to perhaps educate the onlookers regarding medical practices and possible postmortem care." He shrugged. "Will you come?"

"It's quite the morbid prospect." Yet from the flush on his face and the light in his eyes, he was as intrigued with the upcoming spectacle as Royce was.

"Yes, but an interesting study, postmortem, on the cause of death. To say nothing of watching how polite society reacts to it." How many women would faint? How many oh-so-proper men of the *ton* would cast up their accounts?

"Indeed." Finn nodded with enthusiasm. "I'll see if I can coerce Drew or my cousins to join us, for no doubt Jane will come. Ever since she began working in the clinic—since meeting me—she's worked to expand her knowledge of the human body and how it works."

"Yes. She's taken to borrowing my medical books without permission." But that was all to the good. The more knowledgeable she was, the more valuable she was to the clinic, and he could use all the assistance he could muster. He shoved thoughts of Jane out of his mind, for here was the natural opening he'd been waiting for. "Uh, how do your cousins fare? I recently read about William's victory in solving that serial killer case."

"Ah, yes, he and Fanny are still basking in the glow of that." Finn brushed at some of the cat hair stuck to his jacket sleeves. "I've not seen Caroline, of course. She keeps to herself and makes it a point not to linger in our company, which is understandable."

"She'll need to square with those relationships—and her past—soon though."

"I agree, but for now she's safe." Finn shrugged. "Isobel has landed in scandal yet again. Drew and William met with her a couple of days ago with dual fits of outrage, threatened to shuttle her off to the Derbyshire property if she didn't behave."

"That's a bit heavy handed, but then Hadleigh *is* the head of the Storme family now." He chuckled as he remembered how spirited Isobel was during the Christmastide house party. "She's a hoyden to be sure." Then another thought occurred that sent cold streaks down his spine. "Does your brother plan to marry her off?" That would be a shame, for knowing the earl, he'd chose a man entirely too stuffy and unsuitable for Isobel, someone who'd want to clip her wings or tame her spirit.

"Who knows? Drew is quite vexed with her and at loose ends. The other problem is that Cousin Isobel isn't exactly looking for matrimony."

"At least we have that in common." He shared a laugh with Finn. "Does that mean she's fast? I didn't have that impression of her. I rather think she enjoys being entertained as well as the attention." A stab of *something* went through his chest, but he ignored it. The woman meant nothing to him outside of a vague acquaintance.

So why couldn't he completely banish her from his mind? And more importantly, why did the thought of potentially seeing her again set his heartbeat racing?

"Oh, she enjoys the attention. Perhaps too much. Thus the reason for Drew's annoyance." Finn snorted with laughter as if the whole thing were some grand joke. "Isobel is quite popular among the men of the *ton*, men of the merchant class, men who work a trade, servants…"

Royce shook his head. "I have the gist."

"She enjoys attracting men and then dropping them once she loses interest. I've often wondered if she's like a cat, playing with them and abandoning them after she's bored, or once she's been kissed." He shared a look of confusion with Royce. "For whatever reason, my cousin always finds some issue with her suitors, so the relationships don't move past a certain point." He shrugged. "If nothing else, Isobel's mindset would be a good case study for Trey."

"It's certainly interesting." And something he wouldn't mind delving deeper into if she would let him. Something must bother her, and it was showing in her behavior that went beyond wanting attention. "Definitely bring her on Friday night. It'll keep her out of trouble, at least for a few hours."

"And relieve William's mind for a bit." Finn shoved a hand through his hair. "You can ask Isobel to your cadaver exam in person. Jane is having a dinner party tomorrow evening. She's invited a few authors and poets who reside in London for live readings after dinner."

"Oh? How fun." He slid a sly glance at his friend. "Will you read from your book as well?"

"If there is time." The look of satisfaction on his face made Royce grin. It was nice to see Finn coming into his own after battling depression for so long. "By the by, you're invited if you wish to come."

Of course he would, especially if Isobel would be there as well. "It sounds intriguing. I'll bring Trey. Besides, how can I turn down the opportunity to bedevil Jane?" Indeed, since she married, some of the light had been missing from his life.

"Good to hear. I'll let her know." Finn stuck out a hand. "Thank you. For everything, Royce. You have no idea what your friendship and support has meant to me over the years."

Unexpectedly, a wad of emotion stuck in his throat. He shook the offered hand. "You might have started out as a patient, but now you're a friend for life. I don't take that lightly."

"I keep telling you. You're an honorary Storme." Moisture sparkled in Finn's eyes that he rapidly blinked away. "I'm afraid you're stuck with the mess of us from now on."

"There are worse things in the world."

"Ha!" Finn wheeled his chair toward the front door. "So you say now, but you haven't found yourself in the direct path of a Storme. You'll change your mind if one of us flies into a rage at you, I'll wager."

"Surely it can't be as horrid as you make it out to be." Royce escorted him to the door and then held the panel open for Finn to pass over the threshold. A shiny black open carriage waited for him at the curb. "Don't rainbows form once a storm is over?"

"Oh, you poor, disillusioned man." Finn's laughter swept the last vestiges of maudlin emotion from his person. "Anyway, I'll see you tomorrow night. If nothing else, there will be good food and fine spirits, along with gay company. If the readings prove dull, we'll play a few hands of whist against the ladies."

"Now that *is* a good incentive. I'm a smashing success at that game. I look forward to relieving you of a few pounds at the table." He waved and then closed the door. Isobel Storme would be in attendance. What the devil would he say to her?

He couldn't help his grin. It didn't matter. If that low-grade attraction between them was still present and if he could manage to talk with her privately, perhaps he'd have a better idea of how to proceed. No, he didn't want to court a woman, but perhaps a bit of a flirtation wouldn't hurt, especially with a lady who wished for the same.

There was a certain freedom in that.

CHAPTER THREE

June 13, 1818

ISOBEL WAS AT sixes and sevens. She clasped her hands in her lap while she stared at William and Fanny, who sat on the carriage bench opposite her.

"It doesn't feel right."

"What doesn't?" The fierce frown her brother wore didn't bode well for the remainder of the evening. Was he already thinking of a lecture to deliver her way?

"Continuing to socialize while Mother will die soon." Her chest felt too tight, and she could scarcely breathe every time she thought of the death that was so imminent.

"Isn't that what you wished for? To continue entertainment even though you should be at Mother's bedside?" Though he'd couched the words in a low voice, the hypocrisy of the statement sent a wave of hot anger sailing through her being.

"As if I'm the only one of the Stormes that must sit in attendance?" Isobel shook her head. "How dare you assume the whole of the responsibility falls to me." She heaved out a huff of frustration. "Besides, Mother urged me to go. She said there was nothing to be done for her anymore and that she didn't wish to hinder my life."

Yet the possibility of returning to the house only to find her parent had passed on was exceptionally terrifying. Again, when an excess of emotion climbed her throat, she repressed the urge to set it free. Instead, she clasped her hands tighter. The presence of the ruby ring beneath the gloves brought her a modicum of comfort.

To say nothing of the fact that the period of mourning would soon be upon her.

How will I survive with nothing to look forward to?

How would she survive being alone?

"I understand how you feel. It's heartbreaking that Mother must suffer this lingering, horrible illness and that we must bear witness to it." William leaned forward and patted Isobel's knee. "We'll help each other through it."

"Perhaps." For the moment, it was enough that she was able to attend an evening out, even if it was only through the Storme family connections. She craved the mental stimulation as well as the gaiety. It kept sadness and anxiety at bay, at least for a time. When she was dancing and laughing, she didn't have to think about what was to come… or her future.

"However, I must warn you, Isobel, that tonight is not the time for your usual sensations."

Ah, here was the expected lecture. She sighed but kept her attention on the window and the black velvet curtains she'd opened to watch the Mayfair townhouses they passed. "And?"

He heaved a sigh. "Don't dare any of the guests to slide down the bannisters with you. Do not think to dare any young men in attendance to wade in the fountain contained within the square." His tones conveyed doubt she could follow simple instructions. "And please don't encourage anyone at this dinner party to act in any sort of impropriety. We are going at Finn's behest, and he doesn't deserve to have the evening made a mockery or a sensation."

"And it's the first time he and Lady Jane have opened their new house for visitors," Fanny added with excitement in her voice. "I'm so looking forward to a tour. I've heard they've installed an exquisite chandelier in the entry hall. The space can double as a reception hall and makes the townhouse open and airy."

Isobel didn't much care for the architectural wonders the house claimed or how magnificent the chandelier was. Such things didn't fascinate her as they apparently did her friend. Though she doubted Cousin Finn would flaunt his affluence, a stab of envy pierced her chest, but she shoved the feeling aside. "Your rules are stifling, Wills." Finally, she turned her head and met her brother's gaze in the waning light, for the sun had nearly set. "Why ask me to remove any bit of gaiety I might have derived from life?"

He snorted. "Because it's not proper for a grown woman to slide down bannisters, whether in her own house or that of someone else."

"Have you tried it? It's quite fun." She allowed a tiny smile, but it didn't banish the warring emotions building in her person.

"No, and I don't intend to."

Fanny's eyes twinkled as she regarded Isobel. "I think it might be fun. At least once." She leaned slightly forward. "Do you remember when we put the mattresses on the stairs at Hadleigh House and rode them down?"

Isobel snorted. "That made Christmastide truly spectacular." They'd been certain to do so while Cousin Andrew was busy elsewhere, to circumvent the lectures on deportment.

"So that's what that hysterical laughter meant," William said as he glanced at his wife. "We heard it from the drawing room but had no idea what was happening."

"Isobel is quite inventive when it comes to games." Fanny patted his hand. "Don't worry. I'm all that is proper now... to an extent." She followed the statement with a wink, which caused William to lean closer to her.

"Do stop. Please. I do not wish to see a display of affection by my brother." Isobel held up a hand. Both William and Fanny wore twin expressions of embarrassment. "Regardless, your rules and dictates chafe. I'm certain tonight will prove dull. And long." She crossed her arms at her chest and once more contemplated the scenery past the window.

Her brother snorted. "If those rules curb your penchant for causing scandal, that's all to the good. Andrew will flay me alive if the Storme name features into the gossip mills again."

"If that's the only way my family will take notice of me, what am I to do?" she asked softly without looking at them.

"What the devil are you talking about?" She heard rather than saw the frown in William's voice.

Drat. I shouldn't have said that aloud.

With a sigh, Isobel met her brother's gaze. "You've left me with the responsibility of Mother." Not for worlds would she share her innermost concerns. Her father had detested emotions and had said women who showed them—especially with tears— were hysterical, unreasonable creatures. Her mother had always trained her to act like a lady in all circumstances. Those early teachings had left deep wounds that still hadn't healed.

"Poppycock. I haven't gone anywhere. In fact, Francesca and I are still underfoot."

"Perhaps, but you have your work at Bow Street, and you have Fanny." Isobel peered at her friend turned sister-in-law. "The two of you are married, and that's lovely of course, but I miss you—both of you—and how things used to be. I miss Caroline too, yet she holds herself out of reach. I fear she's lost to me, to all of us, really."

Her family, though constantly changing, had shifted again, thus leaving her behind. They'd closed ranks, so to speak, and now she was on the outside looking in.

"I had no idea you felt this way." Concern wrinkled William's brow. "I'm in the middle of an intense case—"

Isobel waved a hand. "You always are." If her tone sounded overly waspish, she couldn't help it. "I'm... lonely." Shock from the admission moved through her chest and sent the ball of unshed tears once more into her throat. All her life she'd always had *someone* around her, but it was different when she wanted family now over friends.

"Oh, Isobel, you should have told me." Fanny quickly switched benches to sit beside her. "I'm so sorry for neglecting you. I had no idea how much being married or delving into journalism would take up my time." She linked one of her arms with Isobel's. It provided a modicum of comfort but didn't take away the emptiness prowling through her chest. "I'll make more of an effort at being in your company."

"Thank you."

Fanny babbled on about making plans for a host of things. Her eyes twinkled with mischief. "We should have a day to ourselves, to do anything we want. I can introduce you to a few male acquaintances—"

"Is that absolutely necessary? My sister doesn't need more would-be suitors for greater scandal." William's frown was as fierce as she'd ever seen it.

"Yes, he's right. I have enough of them." She suspected they merely hung around for the entertainment aspect, to wonder what she'd do next that would shock and astound. It grew… tiresome.

William huffed. "Then choose one of them for a proper courtship."

"So I won't be your responsibility any longer?" Isobel bit off. That prowling heated anger curled through her gut, always there but not quite ready to explode. "You want a man to tame me, don't you?"

"Uh…" His frown deepened and he threw a frantic glance at Fanny. When Isobel glanced into her face, her friend's eyes were wide. Finally, William's sputters coalesced into words. "Is that truly the worst thing that can happen?"

At the moment, yes. She narrowed her eyes on her brother. "I don't want to be tamed." After disentangling her arm from Fanny's, she crossed them at her chest. "I wish to be understood by a man, to fit into his life without conditions or restrictions."

To belong to a man for no other reason than I'm enough.

For the space of long heartbeats, silence reigned in the carriage. Then William stirred. The smile he bestowed upon her was tinged with sadness and perhaps a trace of regret. For what she couldn't say. "I'm merely asking you to behave tonight. We'll continue this discussion later."

"Of course we will." But she knew they wouldn't. No one ever wanted to delve into the woman she was or why she deported herself with scandal. No one ever asked how she liked being a Storme or if she was even happy. "But I want you to know that I *will* live life on my terms. In that you can't stop me."

He very well might once she read snippets from two naughty poems she'd memorized and recalled from her years of being sent to finishing schools. That thought provoked a small smile. After all, a lady had to do *something* to amuse herself.

ISOBEL'S OUTLOOK VASTLY improved when she discovered Doctor Marsden was in attendance. Beside Finn and his wife, there was William and Fanny, Isobel's aunt, Lady Jane's mother, as well as a handful of other guests she didn't immediately recognize. As she came into the drawing room where the bulk of the guests had assembled, she put on her most winning smile, smoothed her hands down the front of her blue-gray gown, and then crossed the floor toward the grouping of furniture where he held court.

"Good evening, Doctor Marsden. It's a happy surprise to see you here."

When he excused himself from his conversation and then glanced at her, recognition and interest lit his moss green eyes as he stood. "Miss Storme! It's been a bit since I last saw you."

"Yes." She roved her gaze over him in blatant regard. "How have you kept yourself?" His long form was clad in the requisite dark evening clothes, but his waistcoat of sky-blue satin embroidered with vines and flower buds spoke to a playful personality.

His red hair, combed into the latest style, had been kept into place with a trace amount of pomade, but it was the tiny twinkle of mischief deep in the depths of his eyes that caught her attention.

Here was an excellent way to pass what was certain to be a monotonous evening. Perhaps she could convince him to slip away for a private conversation.

"Busy at the clinic, I'm afraid." As much as she looked her fill at him, he did the same to her, and when his gaze lingered at her décolletage put on display by the low bodice of her gown, a tiny thrill went down her spine.

She cocked an eyebrow. "All work and no play makes for a very dull boy indeed."

"Mmm. So I've been told recently." He caught one of her hands in his, brought it to his lips, and placed a fleeting kiss on the back, holding her fingers for a fraction of a second longer than was proper. "You look well, but I've heard about your mother's health. You have my sympathies."

"Thank you." For the space of a heartbeat, her chest seized with both confusion and grief. "It's, ah, a trying time." Desperate to return to lighter subject matter, Isobel pasted her grin back into place. "Are you hoping to hear a particular piece tonight?" How would he react when he heard the poems she'd planned to recite?

"I hadn't given it thought." His shrug was an elegant affair. "I merely wished to come and circulate."

From somewhere nearby, Finn's loud laughter caught her attention. She glanced his way, and the genuine fondness in his expression took her aback. "Don't let the doctor fool you. He's only here because I bedeviled him, told him he needed more from life than existing in his clinic."

"Yes, there is that," Doctor Marsden said with narrowed eyes at her cousin in his Bath chair. "So here I am."

"And if I were you, I'd make inroads into leaving reality behind," Finn continued with a wink before training his focus on her. "Good evening, Cousin. I trust you'll find something to amuse yourself with."

What the devil was going on between the two men? "Yes, that is the hope." When one of the guests requested his attention, she was left again with Doctor Marsden. "Never say you're a secret poet, Doctor. There's an elegance about you that might lend itself well to such a thing."

"Such folderol you speak." When he laughed, brown flecks appeared in his eyes. "I wouldn't know the first thing about putting lines of poetry down."

"Ah, neither do I, and I'll tell you another truth." She lowered her voice just enough that he was obliged to step closer to her. "I don't enjoy it. In fact, I find it exceedingly boring."

"Then why are you here tonight, Miss Storme? I was under the impression the major worked hard to put together a guest list that would appeal to all."

Was it too terribly forward to tell him the truth? "Honestly, I wanted a bit of fun before I'm thrust into mourning."

"That is understandable. In fact, I appreciate your candor. You don't seem like the type of woman who will fall to hysterics easily." When he grinned, a shallow dimple in his right cheek flashed. "Honestly, I wouldn't mind seeing some of these stodgy, stuffy people turned on their head by something not quite… proper."

Was that an invitation? Isobel's heartbeat pounded more quickly. "Will you be the man to ensure that happens tonight, Doctor?" As much as she wanted to touch him to further draw him closer, she didn't dare, not while William watched her every movement like a hawk.

"With the right persuasion, perhaps." There was a question in his eyes and the slightest elevation of one of his red eyebrows. Did that mean he waited for her to make the first move? Would he willingly follow?

Before Isobel could respond, the butler appeared at the drawing room doorway and rang a brass bell.

"Ladies and gentlemen, dinner is now served." The middle-aged man glanced about the gathering. "If you'll make your way to the dining room?"

The doctor caught her eye. He offered her his arm, bent at the elbow. "Allow me to escort you into dinner. We might further our acquaintance."

"What an excellent idea." As soon as she laid her fingers upon his sleeve, warmth danced up her arm to her elbow. Oh, there was a distinct connection between them. Now to discover how to draw it out and use it to her advantage. The evening suddenly had improved.

DINNER HAD BEEN a pleasant two hours. She and Doctor Marsden had talked upon a variety of topics, so much so that she'd rather neglected the diner who'd sat on her left. He'd been entertaining enough and quite erudite on each subject introduced, and underlying those conversations, through each different course, frissons of attraction had sparked between them.

Her biggest challenge now was trying not to nod off while various poets and authors read selections from their own works. The only one of any thrill was Finn's reading from his first book. She'd already read the story three times and she guarded her copy with much vigor, for she never loaned it out. The magnitude of having an author in the Storme family wasn't something she took lightly, and within those pages of fantasy and adventure and romance, she'd found an escape of sorts.

Polite clapping wrenched Isobel from her thoughts, and as Lady Jane came to the front of the room, she slowly rose from her spot on the sofa.

"Who's next?" Finn's wife always appeared as if she knew a joke that no one else did. Despite the challenges she and her husband faced, she maintained a sunny disposition.

"I'd like to give it a go," Isobel said.

"You, Cousin Isobel?" Finn asked in some surprise.

"Yes. Do you mind a recitation?"

"No. In fact, I welcome it." He made a shooing motion with a hand. "I can't wait to hear how you'll entertain us." The sparkle in his eyes testified to that fact.

"Oh, I'm quite certain I'll have everyone's attention." As soon as she gained the open spot where all the other poets and authors had stood, her gaze went immediately to Doctor Marsden. "I realize I'm neither a poet nor an author, but I long ago memorized a handful of poems. I thought the gathering tonight would appreciate them."

Would the doctor's notice of her after this reading be piqued or disgusted? Perhaps if all went well, it might spark his attraction.

With flutters in her belly, Isobel cleared her throat. Every eye in the room was trained on her. "This is a poem entitled *To His Mistress Going to Bed* by Anglican priest and later Dean of St. Paul's Cathedral in London, John Donne."

A wave of murmurs went through the company, but she began her recitation before one of her relatives could decide to halt it.

She might have been hesitant at first, for the words were unfamiliar while spoken aloud, but once she'd passed the first stanza or so, Isobel found her confidence. All too soon she reached the end and what was the most erotic words of the piece.

"By this these angels from an evil sprite,

Those set our hairs, but these our flesh upright.

License my roving hands, and let them go

Before, behind, between, above, below."

From the silence billowing through the room, she'd properly shocked the gathering. Isobel bit the inside of her lip to keep from smiling. When she looked at the doctor, he and Finn shared amused grins. Even Lady Jane tried to fight off her own expression of mirth, while Isobel's aunt and William were apparently rendered speechless.

"Perhaps while you're all recovering from that poem, I should recite another."

William slowly stood. "Isobel, I rather think—"

"It's no bother, Wills. I memorized a handful of poems." She gave him a wink and then said, "This next one comes from Ovid. He's long been thought of as one of the best writers in Latin literature. The piece I'll recite is called *In Summer's Heat* from his book of poetry, *Amores*. This is about his love affair with a lady named Corinna."

"Oh, dear God," Finn whispered, but his words were quickly overtaken as Isobel began.

"Stark naked as she stood before mine eye,
Not one wen in her body could I spy.
What arms and shoulders did I touch and see?
How apt her breasts were to be pressed by me?
How smooth a belly under her waist saw I?"

"Damnation, Isobel, stop at once!" William's entreaty echoed through the stunned silence.

But she merely smiled at him and continued,
"How large a leg, and what a lusty thigh?
To leave the rest, all liked me passing well;
I clinged her naked body, down she fell.
Judge you the rest. Being tired, she bade me kiss.
Jove send me more such afternoons as this."

"That's enough!" William strode over to her position and grabbed her upper arm.

"Of course that's enough," she calmly said in the face of his ire. "That's the end of the poem." Deliberately baiting him, she batted her lashes. "Wasn't that romantic, though? Imagine a man having the confidence and freedom to write an erotic poem about one of his lovers."

A scandalized cry issued from her aunt. "Oh, please, you must stop talking." She pressed a hand to her flaming cheek. "This is not right, and in such mixed company. That you'd even know such things…"

"I told you to behave tonight." William renewed his grip on her arm and shuttled her across the floor. "There's no choice now but to inform Andrew about this stunt; he'll hear about it in any event."

Well, drat. "It was all in fun." She wrenched out of her brother's hold. "Why is it that no one in my family can joke about anything?"

"It's all right," Finn interrupted, wheeling his chair over to their location. Amusement danced in his eyes. "You have my respect, Cousin Isobel. I'll need to talk with you later on where you learned such things."

She nodded, but her gaze jogged to Doctor Marsden. When their eyes locked, shock and admiration filled those mossy depths. Elation filtered through her chest before annoyance swept it away. Her attention flicked back to William. "Are we done here?"

"Yes, of course, but don't leave this room."

As if I'm a child of nine instead of a woman grown of eight and twenty. Bitterly disappointed in her family, Isobel flounced across the room and seated herself on the sofa farthest away from the rest of the company. The next poet would have one devil of a time regaining the attention of his audience.

"That was quite bold of you, Miss Storme," Doctor Marsden whispered as he drifted over and stood behind her sofa.

"I had to do something to put life into this evening," she responded in an equally low voice without taking her attention from the speaker.

"That effort is commended, for I nearly fell asleep until you took the stage, so to speak."

She allowed a small grin. "Then it was fortunate I came tonight."

"Indeed." Doctor Marsden leaned his forearms on the back of the sofa and put his lips near her ear but kept his focus on the speaker. "Over the course of my education and the ability to delve into various ancient texts, I've learned a few erotic poems myself."

"Oh?" Her heartbeat accelerated, as much from his words as the warmth of his breath that skated over her cheek. How exciting it must have been to see those aged books and either translate their meanings or have someone there who could.

"Shall I tell you one?" The fine tenor of his voice sent awareness tingling over her skin.

"Yes." She didn't wish to turn her head and look at him for fear William would shuttle her out of the room.

"And that seductive laugh, which sets
the heart to flutter in my chest
For when I glance your way, my words
Dissolve unheard.
Silence breaks my tongue and subtle
fire streams beneath my skin,
I can't see with my eyes, or hear
through buzzing ears.
Sweat runs down, a shiver shakes
Me deep—I feel as pale as grass:
As close to death as that, and green,
Is how I seem."

"It's beautiful." This time she did look at him and caught the wicked glint in his eye. "Who is the poet?"

His quiet laugh echoed in her ear, his breath warmed her neck. "Her name is Sappho. She was a Greek lyrical poet and an aristocrat born between 630 and 612 B.C. It's said that Plato placed Sappho among the divine Muses."

"How interesting." He was so close that she couldn't help but stare at his mouth. What would those sensual lips feel like against hers?

"For many years, intellectuals and poets alike have deliberately—it's assumed—said the speaker in the poem is a man talking of his jealousy while the woman he is enamored with is speaking with another man."

Isobel nodded. "It certainly sounded like it."

"However, there are those in some academic circles now who have put forth the idea that even though Sappho was a female and was married to a rich merchant, she had a female lover, and *that's* who she was speaking of in the poem."

The words were titillating enough and spoken in the doctor's whispered tones they sent shivers down her spine. "Would that I could know more."

"There are many intriguing things life holds if one is but open to receive them." Polite applause went through the room at the conclusion of the next reading. "Next time you think to cause a sensation, Miss Storme, always be aware there are others with more shocking subject matter." With a grin, Royce straightened.

"Touché, Doctor Marsden." She kept her attention on the next reader who stood before the company, but her pulse fairly raced through her veins and excitement buzzed at the base of her spine. "Does this mean you're not averse to creating a bit of scandal?" Though her words were whispered, they sounded overly loud in her ears.

His soft chuckle sent gooseflesh racing over her arms. "That depends."

"On?" She could scarcely breath from waiting for his answer.

"What you have in mind."

Oh, merciful heavens! Without looking at the doctor, she said, "I'll arrange to walk my dog at eight o'clock in Hyde Park tomorrow morning. Meet me?"

"I'd be delighted, Miss Storme. It'll be a pleasant distraction before I go into the clinic." His fingers brushed her shoulder as he moved away. "A morning constitutional is most welcome exercise, don't you agree?"

She absolutely did, especially if she could walk with a handsome man with mischief in his eyes.

CHAPTER FOUR

June 14, 1818

ROYCE SIPPED HIS tea as he stared at nothing in particular. Amusement and excitement twisted together in his gut, for renewing his association with Miss Storme the night before had been thrilling—exactly what he'd needed. Though he'd known of her through their family connections, he wouldn't mind furthering a relationship. For what or how deep he didn't know, but did it matter?

He took another sip as he contemplated an oil painting of an English wildflower meadow. No, it didn't matter overly much, for she was like a fascinating new plaything to a cat. A slow grin tugged at the corners of his mouth. In this instance, he wasn't entirely certain if he was the cat or if she played that role.

It was something he wished to discover.

"What are you so chipper about this morning?" Trey groused as he came into the morning room looking as rumpled as if he'd just strolled in from his club.

"I wasn't aware that I was." Royce regarded his brother with a grin. "And good morning to you. By the way, you look like a dog's breakfast."

"I overslept. Besides, it's not as if I'll see anyone of consequence at the clinic." He straightened his cravat as best he could with his one hand. "You were humming just now when I came in." Apparently, such a sound worked to further aggravate his brother if his scowl was any indication.

"I was not." Royce drained the remainder of the liquid from his cup. "I don't hum."

"Well, you were this morning. Additionally, you're grinning at your reflection."

"What?" He glanced about with a start, for no longer was he peering at the painting. In fact, he'd somehow wandered over to the sideboard and now regarded himself in the rectangular mirror that hung over that piece of furniture. "Not more than usual, surely." He shrugged. "It's no crime if I wished to check my appearance before going out."

"Such gammon you speak." Trey shook his head as he shoved his hand through it in an effort to tame some of the red tresses. "You detest mornings."

"I don't." Calmly, as if he weren't hiding an enormous secret, Royce lifted the teapot from its trivet and poured a measure into his cup.

"You do. Always have." Trey's frown deepened as he roved his gaze up and down Royce's person. "For that matter, where the devil *are* you going? You're dressed too fine for the clinic even if you have rounds this morning."

"Not this morning I don't." He slid his regard to Trey and then saluted him with the teacup. "You and Finn can keep an eye on things for a couple of hours."

"Why?" Trey poured out a cup of coffee for himself and then moved to the round table that sat four, for he and Royce shared a townhouse and rarely had guests.

"I'm going for a walk in Hyde Park." Would Trey read too much into it?

"Again, I ask why." His brother narrowed his eyes.

Apparently, he would. Had Trey always been so annoying? "Why not?" Royce laid his teacup on the sideboard and checked the knot of cravat one last time. Then he turned and faced his brother. "It's good exercise. Fresh air. A good opportunity to clear the mental faculties."

"Ah hmm." Trey slipped into a chair.

Their butler rushed—as quickly as he could with a slight limp—to fill a plate for him, which was funny since Dirkens had been one of Trey's friends during their stint in the military. He, Trey, and Royce were around the same age. One day Dirkens had come into the clinic. His outlook was bleak since he'd been injured at Waterloo, and along with his limp, sometimes his mind wandered, rendering him unemployable for much work. Trey had made the decision to offer him the butler's position, and they'd been getting on well together for the few years since Royce and Trey had taken up their bachelor residence.

"Do you recall that we have a full schedule today at the clinic?" Trey continued once his food had been delivered.

"I'm aware, but my appointment doesn't begin until ten. There's plenty of time for everything."

"You planned it this way?"

"Not quite, but it is rather serendipitous." Royce drifted over and sat beside his brother but declined food. "I'll eat later. Thank you, Dirkens."

Like a dog with a particular toothsome bone, Trey wouldn't let the matter rest. "Explain. You've never taken to walking Hyde Park before."

There was no harm in telling his brother, for he would worm the information from him eventually. There were very close as brothers, with a small age gap separating them. "I have decided to cultivate a bit of my personal life."

"Oh?" Trey's eyebrows shot into his hairline. "What aspects of your personal life?"

The heat of embarrassment crept up the back of Royce's neck. "Uh, finding a companion of sorts."

His brother snorted. Even the butler had a good chuckle. "You're hardly elderly nor do you require friends. Be more specific, please."

Royce drummed his fingers upon the tabletop as Trey shoveled food into his mouth. "Let's just say if I happen to meet an attractive woman during one of these outings, I might wish to see where it leads."

The toast triangle his brother held fell from his fingers to land, butter side down, on the table. "Are you thinking along the lines of courtship?"

"Ha!" Royce waved a hand. "Perish the thought." He laughed, for the very idea of such a thing was ludicrous. "I'm not looking to become leg-shackled. However, if a friendship were proffered, I wouldn't say no." His thoughts jogged to Miss Storme. In his mind's eye he caught her blue eyes that sparkled with boredom and trouble, those pink-hued lips that curved in a grin when he'd recited the bit of erotic poetry. Then he shrugged. "But we shall see what happens."

Trey's eyes narrowed. "Are you meeting someone this morning?"

"I'm afraid that remains a mystery, for I cannot divine the future." He hoped his expression didn't give anything away. "As of yet, a lady hasn't caught my eye enough to portend courtship."

"Gah!" His brother shook his head and exchange a look with the butler. When he gave Royce his full attention, he gestured with his knife. "Then you're failing miserably at interacting or even entertaining the fairer sex."

"How do you mean? I could catch a lady if I put my mind to it."

"Oh, indeed. You're the heir to an earldom. This alone should make your path easier than it would with me." He pointed the knife at the empty spot where his arm should have been. "And you have both arms, so there is no excuse for you not having a match or opportunities."

"Perhaps this is so, but I don't wish to think about those future duties at the moment. It quite ruins the now." For long moments he stared at his brother, nay, his best friend. The man who knew all of his secrets, and he knew that he'd need to keep his interest in Miss Storme clandestine, at least for a little while, until he could determine what role he wished for her to play in his life. "I have my own existence, and the clinic takes up all of my time."

"And?" Again, those damnable eyebrows rose as Trey cut into his hamsteak.

"And what?"

"You don't want an affair, something to occupy your time when you're not engaged at the clinic? For years now you've not allowed yourself a bit of fun. I worry about your mental faculties." He pointed the knife at Royce once more. "Men have needs."

"I'm a doctor, Brother. Spare me the lecture on what a man's body demands." Though it was true he hadn't actively sought out the companionship of a woman in at least a year, it didn't mean he didn't miss certain aspects of such a relationship.

Trey snorted. "You'd best listen to those demands before you find yourself going insane." He shook his head. "One week of high passion won't harm your career, and quite frankly, a toss in the sheets is a better way of clearing one's head than a walk."

Perhaps a tryst *was* in order, but was Miss Storme the right partner?

"By the by, you and Miss Storme seemed quite cozy last night at the poetry reading after she shocked the hell out of the audience." Curiosity and speculation warred for dominance in Trey's expression. "Is there something afoot there?"

"Nothing more than a social connection." At least it was the truth—for now. Royce stood, for the longer he lingered here, the more it cut into the time he'd spend in Miss Storme's company. "Now, if you'll excuse me? I have a walk awaiting me."

Anticipation buzzed at the base of his spine. It would be interesting to see where this one simple walk led.

A QUARTER OF an hour later, Royce meandered along one of the riding paths in Hyde Park. He'd arrived by a hired hackney cab, for there was no need to rouse the lads in the mews merely to accomplish the short trip to the park. Besides, his father had gifted him with a carriage and two horses when he'd moved out of the Worchester townhouse to open his clinic. When at all possible, he tried to distance himself between the trappings of the earl and his everyday life.

That was an eventuality he didn't want to dwell upon. Assuming the title once his father passed would mean too much upheaval... and the end to all of his dreams for the clinic.

"Doctor Marsden!"

He turned about at the sound of the hale. Miss Storme came toward him on the path from the opposite direction, looking for all the world like spring personified in a jonquil dress and matching spencer. Though she wore a simple bonnet decorated with white and yellow flowers and yellow satin ribbons, it was perched upon her upswept hair in such a way that it could tumble off at any time.

"Good morning, Miss Storme." He touched the brim of his beaver felt top hat and then switched his attention to the energetic Corgi straining at the leather lead. "And who is this?"

"His name is Ivan. He's nearly a year old now." She glanced from the dog to Royce's face. "While I do like dogs, I got him mostly to irritate William." When she grinned, his pulse accelerated. "I nearly gave him the name Wills."

"You *do* like to court trouble." Royce kneeled in front of the dog and held out a gloved hand. "Good morning, Ivan. It's been a while since I kept company with a canine." After the dog sniffed his fingers, he gave a soft woof of greeting. "I hope you give your mistress much mischief." He scratched the dog's ears and patted his neck before standing. "If you'd like, I can hold the leash. Ivan seems quite enthusiastic this morning."

"Oh, he's like that all the time." She passed the loop of leather to him and when their fingers brushed, heat ricocheted up his arm to his elbow. "I'm at a loss as to how to keep him engaged and make him tired enough that he'll be docile."

He snorted. "I don't believe it's possible. This breed is rambunctious and demands everyone's attention." Not unlike the dog's mistress. How interesting. "Do you take him walking here every day, Miss Storme?" He offered her his arm, and when she laid her gloved fingers upon his sleeve, a shiver of awareness went down his spine.

A tiny inhalation, barely audible, betrayed that she might have felt the same connection. "I try, but most of the time, he tears about the house like a vengeful spirit until I give him a bone or two from the kitchens." She walked beside him, matching his pace. There were a few men who rode through the park. Each time he led Miss Storme to the side of the path, putting his body between her and the oncoming horses in the event the equines spooked. "I dislike this formality between us, so for the duration, please refer to me as Isobel."

"Such a request is quite bold so early in our association, don't you think, Isobel?" Ah, but her name rolled off his tongue like the grandest of all words.

She turned her head slightly. The glint in her eyes smacked of intrigue and secrets. "Is it, though? We've known each other since last Christmastide. Since then, we've met at a handful of society and familial events." Her fingers tightened on his arm. "I would think that's adequate knowledge to make use of Christian names."

"Since I have no stronger rebuttal, I have no choice but to agree." He smiled and when she did the same, excitement began to build in his chest. The scent of orange blossoms mixed with something slightly spicy wafted to his nose. It further enhanced her allure. "Call me Royce. Not many in my circle do, for everyone prefers the prestige of my doctor status."

Which was nothing to sneeze at, for he'd worked hard, put in many years and long hours in training and beneath a mentor to gain that title. And neither was the near four hundred pounds annually he commanded for that knowledge.

"Oh, I agree that knowing a doctor is quite lofty indeed. However, I don't put much stock in a man's title."

Another interesting bit. "Ah, so if I were a sea captain, that wouldn't impress you either?" When Ivan tugged at the leash, he answered with equal pressure so the dog would know he was in charge. The quack and honking from the geese on the water didn't help to soothe the canine's enthusiasm.

"I rather think not." She shrugged and her arm brushed his. When had she moved so close to him? "The titles men use to differentiate themselves from others hold no sway over me. Those things are merely to fan their egos." Since she stared straight ahead, the edge of the bonnet shielded her eyes from his view. "But what I despise even more than that is the titles found throughout the *ton*, of gentlemen peers, for those men assume they're better than others merely for the sake of those titles."

Royce's eyebrows went up. "Is it all peers you detest or just some?" What had brought her to this pass?

"All." Isobel turned her head and met his gaze. Nothing but honesty shone in those sapphire depths. "I'm convinced the *ton* and its stifling traditions did much to put the fracture in my family."

He scrambled to remember the bloodlines of her father as well as the current Earl of Hadleigh's. "You speak of rift between your father and his brother."

"I do." This time when she put pressure on his arm, he drew them to a halt and led her a bit off the path toward a large boulder. The Serpentine waited beyond, the rising sun sparkling on its surface like a million diamonds. "Had not the demands of my uncle's title—and the prison of society both he and my father were trapped in—come between them, that argument would never have happened, Caroline would never have been sent away, and my life might have turned out much differently than it has."

That was quite a confession from a woman he didn't know all

that well. "I beg your pardon but refresh my memory of who Caroline is."

"She's my older sister, sent away to an institution at the age of twelve because her brain doesn't work normally." A trace of agony lined her face. "Which leads me back to the *ton*. Their impossible images of perfection are distorted and ridiculous. No one can ever achieve them, and Caroline had no chance." She shook her head. "My parents were influenced by my uncle, and it was deemed too scandalous to have a child at home with Caroline's... difficulties." The faint tears that glimmered in her eyes tugged at his chest. "I never had the opportunity to know her, and now she won't see any of us."

Vaguely he remembered the talk during last Christmastide's house party in Derbyshire when the eldest Miss Storme had arrived. She'd kept herself apart from the Storme family, and he supposed she had good reason. "I'm sorry. Life is sometimes complicated and unfair."

"Agreed," she said in a low voice. For the space of a few heartbeats, Isobel gazed at him with speculation. Then she propped herself against the boulder, breaking their tenuous connection. "Caroline isn't accepted for her mind, and I'm not accepted because the matrons who preside over ballrooms have deemed me too wild and improper."

That was a truth, for one couldn't go anywhere in society without hearing some sort of rumor or on-dit regarding the woman before him. "There will never be a shortage of gossiping tabbies, Isobel. One must learn to ignore them, for they look to tear down reputations, so they don't have to realize there is nothing but emptiness in their own lives."

Shock jumped into her eyes. Had no one ever let her speak without handing down lectures? She pressed her lips together, and his gaze temporarily dropped to her mouth. Would those lips feel as soft as they looked? "If it weren't for the *ton*, perhaps my father and uncle wouldn't have succumbed to heart attacks, no doubt brought on by the traditions and dictates put forth in the world they lived in."

Royce frowned. "But you also live in that world. You're the daughter of a viscount, a cousin to the Earl of Hadleigh. Regardless of how you feel about the *ton* as a whole, it's what has guided your life."

"Bah. I want nothing to do with them."

He bit back the urge to grin. "Then you would leave it all behind? Give up your fine clothes and the comforts of the home you live in, merely to prove a point?"

She waved a hand in dismissal while her eyes narrowed. "I didn't have a choice; I was born into it." A sheepish grin overtook her lips. "However, I'll admit I enjoy the comforts that come with that privilege."

At least he'd won that point. "From what I've seen of your family, there was more that drove a wedge between the branches than merely a connection to the *ton*."

"Brought on by the title!" Her voice rose an octave, which startled a few sparrows in a nearby oak tree.

The dog barked once and looked at her.

"Easy, Isobel. I meant no offense." When Ivan strained at the leash, intent on diving headfirst into the Serpentine to chase after a pair of swans, Royce tightened his hold on the leather. Her views on the aristocracy weren't necessarily wrong but they were skewed. "This current generation as well as the last of the Storme family have problems. Do they stem from the *ton*? I can't say without an in-depth evaluation. Yet, I can't help but feel many of those problems and personal failings have much to do with the men—and women—themselves. Birthright aside, it can either make you bitter or make you better."

Those sapphire eyes remained trained on him, and the longer he looked, the more evident the tiny golden flecks in those irises were. Did those flecks only appear with high emotion? "I wonder if that's true."

"Your cousins certainly struggled to find their true identities before they married." Ivan barked and ran in the opposite direction, which twisted the leather lead around Royce's legs. "And consider your brother. He's of the *ton*, but he's one of the most intelligent and unstuffy men I've met."

Isobel rolled her eyes. "Wills has his peccadillos."

"No doubt he does—we all do—but from someone who has had the chance to observe the Storme family, I'm impressed by the progress each of you have made." From their location behind the large boulder that was as tall as he was, his view of the path was obstructed. However, no riders or pedestrians made an appearance.

Surprise flickered over her face. "You've watched me?"

Heat engulfed his nape. "Only as a friend of the family."

"Ah. That's too bad. I'd hoped to gain your notice."

What exactly did that mean?

Ivan wound the leash around his legs another time in his quest to chase a squirrel.

"The Stormes are difficult to ignore."

Her eyes lit with a gleam that would surely spell disaster for someone. "That's quite true." She dared to bat her eyelashes. "I think you'll find I'm even more so."

Oh, dear Lord. There was no doubt in his mind she was experienced in flirting. "Yes, well." His laugh sounded slightly desperate. "In light of what you have shared with me, I shudder to think how you feel about me, the son of an earl, a man who will someday hold that title." Merely uttering that fact aloud sent ice into his veins. Would their budding relationship end before it got started?

"You're not the earl yet."

"No, I am most certainly not." Thank goodness for that.

"And the rest of my opinion largely depends on how you've planned to move forward with our… friendship." One of her dark brown eyebrows inched upward in challenge.

"Clever girl." But before he could say anything else, Ivan darted after one of the swans. Because the leather leash was wound about his legs, when the dog moved, Royce didn't.

Instead, he fell over like a toppled tree with a strangled, "Argh!"

Isobel's laughter tinkled through the air. "Ivan!" She kneeled at Royce's side and tried to disentangle the leather leash from his legs, but the dog thought all the attention should be on him, so he jumped between them both, licking and happily barking, which prevented any work on the lead. "Oh, this is impossible." She held onto Ivan's collar, and with a few tugs undid the leash. "Don't go far."

The dog shot away toward the Serpentine without a moment's hesitation.

"What the devil is wrong with that dog?" Royce struggled into a seated position. He met Isobel's gaze, caught the amusement and perhaps longing in those blue pools, combined with her springtime dress, and it tangled with the growing awareness he had for her. With a stifled groan, he slid a hand to her nape. She looked so innocent yet all too tempting sitting there as cheerful and undeniable as a daffodil. "Forgive the trespass," he murmured and then he claimed her lips, for she'd quite managed to temporarily scramble his brain.

Isobel uttered a quick squeak of surprise. Surely she'd been kissed before; she *was* a practiced flirt after all, but she rested her hands on his shoulders and promptly returned his kiss. While she moved gently over his mouth in exploration, he mimicked her, adding a few nips and licks to the mix. Those petal soft pieces of flesh cradled his, pressed against his with increasing urgency that lit tiny fires in his blood. Certainly, she was no inexperienced miss, at least in kissing, and in many ways, it was refreshing to not need provide instruction. Miss Isobel Storme continued to intrigue the hell out of him. The more the introduction continued, the greater he wanted to deepen the kiss.

But not now, not here. She didn't need the additional scandal, and neither did he even though from all the rumors, she walked the razor's edge of that.

Uttering a groan of regret, Royce pulled away. His pulse raced. When was the last time he'd had such a reaction to a woman? He searched her face for any signs of annoyance or outrage, but there was only amusement and that same mischievous glint, as if she had secret knowledge, she hadn't yet shared... or she'd pull him into something all too wicked. "I—"

"Don't you dare apologize," Isobel said with a grin, yet sadness lurked deep in the depths of her eyes. Why? "I enjoyed that too much for you to attest you didn't mean to."

"Oh, I did indeed intend to kiss you. Absolutely there are no regrets." He shook himself free of the leash and then stood. When he offered her a hand and she slipped her fingers into his palm, he tugged her into a standing position. Would that he could take her properly into his arms and press her against that boulder in a real embrace. Was she as fast and as daring as she wished everyone to think? "I'll tell you this as well. I'll do it again if given half a chance."

Where the devil was his caution and adherence to propriety? He tamped on the urge to laugh. It was gone as if the lady herself had reached into his soul and squashed it.

"That's incentive, indeed, to find myself once more in your company." She set her bonnet more firmly on her head as she moved toward the Serpentine to presumably retrieve her dog.

Slight panic ricocheted through his chest, for he needed more time with her. God only knew why. "Come to the Duke of Titterbury's home tomorrow evening. Nine o'clock. I'm conducting a cadaver exam for his guests and would like it above all things if you'd be in attendance." It was a chance to show off his skill with a scalpel and perhaps find himself alone with her afterward. "Tell the butler you've been invited as my guest. Or better yet, tell William to accompany you. It will look better."

Isobel glanced at him from over her shoulder, more bewitching than demure as she trailed the leash behind her. "Perhaps I shall. Enjoy the remainder of your day, Doctor."

CHAPTER FIVE

June 15, 1818

ISOBEL'S NERVES FELT strung too tight, and knots pulled in her stomach. She clasped her fingers in her lap while the carriage made its ponderous way through Mayfair toward the Duke of Titterbury's home, but she stared unseeing out the window. The one thought circling through her mind was the fact that Doctor Marsden—Royce—had kissed her yesterday in Hyde Park.

It hadn't been chaste; it hadn't been toe-curlingly deep either, but that kiss had ignited tiny fires within her blood. Even now, she felt the press of his lips against hers, and in that one meeting of mouths, there had been the promise of potentially wicked things in the offing. Even after she'd shared with him why she detested the *ton*.

He hadn't lectured her, nor had he launched into an explanation of why her thinking was wrong. The man had merely accepted her explanation and attempted to delve deeper into why that was. Suffice it to say, the doctor intrigued her, presented a challenge she couldn't wait to undertake. Would he be the voice of reason, a moral compass of sorts, to her desire to cause scandal and a sensation? Or would he willingly follow her into trouble?

Oh, she certainly hoped it was the second one.

With a barely tamped sigh, she shifted her position on the

squabbed bench. Before she'd left, Isobel had checked in on her mother, who'd been asleep. More and more, she took refuge in slumber. Was that an indication that her strength waned, and the end was near? Perhaps she should have declined Royce's request to attend this evening. What if her mother called out and she wasn't there in the final moments? Her chest tightened with grief and worry. *I can't think about that right now.* And her mother had already told her not to spend hours at her bedside, waiting for death. So tonight, beyond trying to tempt the good doctor away into an unused room, she would witness Royce examine a dead body, which she assumed meant cutting into the dead flesh to reveal its innards.

She must have uttered a slight moan of dismay, for William's head shot up. "Have you changed your mind about attending tonight?"

"I'm not quite certain. One the one hand, there's a certain element of excitement there, but on the other, just the thought of being in the same room with a nameless, unwanted cadaver leaves me rather unsettled." When she met her brother's gaze across the narrow aisle of the vehicle, she shrugged. "I want to go but I don't. Does that make sense?"

"Absolutely." The juxtaposition of them both decked out in elegant evening clothes to bear witness to the macabre wasn't lost on Isobel. "However, it might prove interesting. For me, I might learn a few things that will help in cases. From what I understand, Doctor Marsden advised the duke to keep the crowd small, for the odor from the body will be quite potent."

The mention of Royce sent tingles of *something* through her lower belly. "Oh, dear. I hadn't thought about that."

"Indeed. I'm quite familiar with that aspect, of course, but in such close quarters as a drawing room, it will be extreme." William shook his head. "I rather think your presence will come as a surprise, for these things are usually conducted in front of a male audience only."

Isobel snorted. "Ah, because women are too delicate and

fragile to think of things like death or the shedding of the corporeal form?" Perhaps there was some truth there, for the thought of looking upon a lifeless body made her shudder. It was one thing to be brave and strong when courting scandal, but quite another when gazing upon someone's remains out of scientific curiosity.

"Of course. Genteel ladies like yourself should be spared the ugliness of life."

"Well, I won't go home, if that's what you're hinting at. Doctor Marsden personally invited me."

"Oh? That's a surprise."

"Why? We're acquaintances within society as well as the Storme family." Did she appear nonchalant enough to not give away her interest in the man? "I have enough curiosity, the same as you, so I'll see it through." Besides, she would be in Royce's company again, and that was more than any discomfort.

William's lips twitched. "I wouldn't dream of ordering you to do so. I'm slowly learning that if I tell you not to do a thing, it's exactly what you'll do." He flicked his gaze over her person. "You look lovely tonight. That color suits you. If one didn't know better, one would think you're every inch the proper *ton* lady."

Isobel pulled a face at him. "Thank you." She brushed at the satin skirts of robin-egg blue. It was one of her favorites. "The color reminds me of spending summers at Hadleigh Hall, and the sky when it wasn't raining." And amidst all the men who'd wear dark suits, she'd stand apart. Hopefully, Royce would notice her, pull her aside afterward to talk… or perhaps steal another kiss.

Those days had been idyllic when she ran about the estate with her siblings and cousins. There were no worries in the world back then, only adventure and freedom. Before everything changed when Caroline was sent away, and she never saw her cousins again.

"I remember those days." His voice had softened. "Life certainly was different, but truth to tell, the life I'm living now isn't horrid."

"Because of Fanny?" Isobel wasn't in the mood to listen to him wax poetic about his wife, even if she was a friend.

"In some ways, yes, but I was speaking about our cousins. It's been nice having family about again and feeling as if I'm a part of a greater whole." He bestowed a look of compassion upon her. "Aunt Lavinia will help fill the void once Mother passes."

"Piffle." Isobel shook her head. She returned her attention to the window. They were nearly to the duke's residence. "No one can take Mother's place." Hurt and slight panic rose in her chest. The edge of a new reality loomed ever closer, and it was terrifying. *Dear Lord, I need a hard distraction, something that will make me forget.* "As much as I like our cousins, they certainly haven't taken time out of their lives to make our mother's last days comforting. She *is* their aunt, for heaven's sake." If she let those emotions out, the anger would take control and she'd turn into a screeching harpy.

"Agreed. I'll talk to Andrew about it. Perhaps we can all take turns holding vigil, though getting Brand here from Ipswich will be a chore, especially when his wife will give birth soon."

Yes, there were certainly no shortage of babies in the Storme family right now. Envy stabbed through her heart. She didn't begrudge the women their infants, but she *did* wish she had that sort of closeness with someone like they enjoyed with their husbands. "That would be nice," she said when she realized William waited for an answer. Though having the extended family around her wasn't all that she needed. Why couldn't her cousins come sit with her, ask after *her* health, wrap their arms around her in solidarity and familial support? Did none of them remember how they'd felt when their father had died? Did none of them see how she was barely holding herself together in the face of this?

With a swallow to keep the unshed tears out of her throat, she asked, "Where is Fanny? I'd think a cadaver exam is the sort of thing she'd find interesting." Her friend was curious about everything, and that was what made her a brilliant journalist.

Concern wrinkled his brow. "She's not feeling well at present. No doubt it was something she ate or exhaustion from the pace of our cases."

"I'm sorry to hear that. I'll check in on her when we return home."

"She'd like that." William leaned forward. He patted her knee. "Are you well? Your color is quite high."

"I'm not certain yet." At least it was honest. If she continued to think about the doctor, she'd burn to death from blushes. Yet that was more acceptable—and fun—than becoming the storm of her namesake and unleashing her ire upon them. Words once said could never be unsaid. *Oh, dear God, I think I'm beginning to understand Cousin Andrew a bit more.* And he wasn't the ogre she'd once thought. "I need more time to wrap my head around things." Least of all what that kiss with Royce meant yesterday when she'd returned his overtures with enthusiasm.

"That's understandable." He sat back while the carriage drew to a stop at the curb. "Perhaps you'll snag a man's notice tonight in that gown." The grin he flashed didn't set her at ease. "I'm sure the duke has invited friends who are high on the instep."

She snorted. "Leave off, William. I already have much on my mind and don't need to worry about men with titles."

No matter what, she would never find herself serious over one of them.

ISOBEL DIDN'T KNOW what to expect when she entered the duke's drawing room, but the powerful aroma of death wasn't one of them. Immediately, her eyes watered, and in some haste, she fished her handkerchief from her reticule. Pressing it to her nose and mouth, she glanced toward the top of the room. Situated before the dormant fireplace was a long wooden table. Atop that piece of furniture was a corpse—she assumed for it was covered with a white sheet. Off to the side was a small occasional table where a battered black bag waited. A group of perhaps fifteen men stood clustered about the table, for the original furniture had been moved to one side of the room to accommodate this most gruesome of activities. Some of them she recognized from previous forays into society; some she'd not seen before. As William had alluded to, there were only two other women present in addition to her—one she assumed was the duchess— and they stood behind the men.

She tightened the fingers of her free hand on William's arm. "At least the windows are open," she whispered. Not only that, but the French-paned doors that led to a small terrace outside had been thrown open too. The murmur of excited talking covered her words, but the bulk of the men held handkerchiefs to their noses too. That putrid smell permeated everything.

I don't think I'll ever be able to remove it from my nose.

"Indeed." His lower jaw hung slightly open. Ah, so that was how he'd learned to tolerate such a gruesome thing; he breathed through his mouth. "I thought I saw a parlor down the corridor as we were escorted in. If you find the need to escape, you can go there and wait for me."

"I'll bear that in mind, but I'm not a shrinking violet." For the moment, she had no intentions of removing herself, especially not since she'd seen the doctor yet. And she did so wish to impress him with her bravery during this event.

"Thank you all for coming."

Everyone in the room turned as the Duke of Titterbury came into the room. Royce followed. Though the older, balding duke was dressed in the requisite dark evening clothes as if this night were an ordinary social engagement, the doctor was in a state of undress that would normally have him tossed from polite society. His jacket was missing, along with a waistcoat. He wore a muslin apron over his remaining clothing. It covered his chest and hung to his knees, and the sleeves of his lawn shirt had been rolled up to the elbow.

"Oh!" Isobel nearly forgot how to breathe as she stared at the naked expanse of his forearms. Red hair lay sprinkled over the pale skin, as did a smattering of freckles. Despite the fact that he made his living as a physician, those forearms weren't weak. Did the rest of his form possess the same lean, banked power? His appearance spoke of quiet strength and a man who wasn't afraid of physical labor.

At her side, William snorted. "Out of all the people in attendance this night, I assumed you wouldn't be the one shocked," he whispered. "I'd imagine the doctor doesn't wish to sully his clothing with entrails."

"Do shut up, Wills." Then her attention went to the duke. He stood to one side of the table with the sheet-covered corpse while Royce paused near what she assumed were the feet.

"I'm glad to see a good crowd tonight. This is Doctor Marsden. He'll be conducting tonight's entertainment, and I'm sure we'll all find it the height of interesting."

Isobel huffed and added in a barely audible voice to her brother. "I don't know that cutting a dead body open is entertainment, but then, the machinations of the *ton* have already struck me as offensive." When she glanced at the doctor, their gazes connected. His lit with pleasure and she couldn't help but offer a smile. Immediately, some of her ire concerning the world she lived in faded.

Then he looked away to assess the guests, and she was able to draw a breath again. "Good evening. Thank you for coming." He made certain to include everyone in his attention. "The Duke of Titterbury has requested that I perform a cadaver exam for you this evening, so if there's no objections, I'd like to get to it straightaway. As you have probably noticed, the smell isn't the most pleasant, and every moment we delay means the body decays all the faster. Already, this fellow is a week past death."

"The floor is yours, Doctor," the duke said. "I look forward to your findings." He came around to stand at the rear of the crowd next to his wife.

"Thank you, Your Grace." Without ceremony, he slipped the sheet from what was indeed a corpse, and one that had seen better days. The man was completely nude except from a length of linen that had been draped over his privates. In places his skin sagged. His face was sunken and hollow.

Murmurs of shock and surprise filtered through the room.

"Oh, my," she uttered in a barely audible whisper.

Beside her, William chuckled. "Didn't you want scandal? Allowing you entry tonight is quite that, and if Andrew ever discovers I allowed it, we'll both feel his wrath."

Isobel shook her head. "I won't tell him." She swallowed a few times in rapid succession to keep the urge to cast up her accounts at bay.

"It's rather ghastly to gaze upon the dead, but this is the state we're all headed toward." Royce cleared his throat. "His Grace has persuaded the Royal College of Surgeons to release into my custody this man whose name was Horace Smythe." As he spoke, he pulled what looked to be a thin knife from the bag along with a pair of silver tongs, similar to what someone would use for sugar cubes but longer and thinner. He laid both instruments on top of the cloth on the body. "Whether it's his real name or a false moniker, we'll never know, but he was convicted of murder and then put to death a week past. He had a long history of violent crimes."

A murmur of interest went through the assembled crowd. One of the men clapped a hand to his mouth and hurried from the room with a decidedly green tinge to his face.

From his bag, Royce removed a stack of folded rags. Though it appeared they'd been freshly laundered and ironed with crisp edges, they were stained, and Isobel shuddered to think upon what made those stains. "What I aim to do tonight is determine not only his cause of death—England has many ways to put down convicted murderers—but also discover what sort of health he might have enjoyed in life and perhaps provide you with a better understanding of anatomy."

Another wave of murmurs went through the assembled company. Isobel rose up on her toes in an effort to better see. When that didn't accomplish much since she was short, she left William to stand off to one side of the knot of men. In this way she could observe but stand further away... as well as watch Royce to full advantage. In profile she was able to appreciate his form as well as the tight curve of his bottom, showed to advantage in the trousers without being covered by a jacket's tails.

"Let's begin." Royce donned a thin pair of kid gloves. "As you can see, there are obvious signs this man was strangled—hung." He moved to the corpse's head. "There is bruising here." As he drew a finger along a purpled line that went across the throat, he used his other hand to pry open one of the body's eyes. "And there is petechiae—or red spots—in the eyes." He gestured to the face. "Further examination shows swollen lips. These are sure signs of strangulation."

A part of her wished she could see what he did, but from her vantage point she couldn't. How fascinating he did the exam without flinching or horror.

Royce then lifted the head with a hand and felt about the neck itself. "Ah, yes. There." He nodded. "Just as I suspected. The second cervical vertebra is broken. This occurs when severe force is applied, such as when a trapdoor opens beneath the condemned man's feet and his weight falls into the noose, snapping the neck." He laid the head back down. "There are no doubt inward compression fractures with outside periosteal tears and sometimes antero-posterior compression fractures with inside periosteal tears."

All of those words were foreign sounding, and she had no idea what they meant, but it was lovely to hear him utter them. How intelligent Royce must be to know the names of bones within the body! How many hours of study he must have completed to gain that information? From his admission of learning that erotic poem, he'd had access to textbooks and treatises done in the original Latin. It was staggering how clever he was.

"Even though it's obvious, an attending physician would check for the broken neck bones even if all the evidence points to strangulation by hanging." Royce took up the knife with its wicked-looking blade. "I'll use a scalpel to cut into the soft tissue of our corpse and we'll see what's to be had inside."

Several of the men strained forward as the doctor inserted the tip of the silver blade into the midsection. The other woman present whimpered with alarm.

Isobel stopped short of rolling her eyes. *Stiff upper lip, madam. It's not as if he's killing the man.*

"As you can see from a visual examination, the abdomen is distended. This could happen over the natural course of a body decaying, but it can also be a sign of malnutrition or starvation."

Isobel kept her handkerchief tightly pressed to her nose and mouth, but her eyes remained glued to the bizarre tableau before her. Royce's hand was steady as he made a long vertical cut on the midsection. Then he made a horizontal cut. Once finished, he used what he called forceps to peel back the skin of the corpse. The stench in the air intensified. Several of the men nearby had perspiration building on their upper lips and foreheads. At that point, the duchess nearly swooned. One of the servants ushered her quickly from the room. The other woman held her ground, but from the way her hand shook as she clutched her handkerchief, it wouldn't be long before she exited as well. Though Isobel's stomach pitched, she ignored the discomfort as best she could, for how often would she see this again in her lifetime?

Once the corpse had been essentially opened, Royce felt around in the cavity. His gloves were hopelessly covered with blood and other disgusting bits. "Ah, yes." He delved his scalpel into the body. Seconds later he hoisted something quite foul out of the remains. Blood and gore clung to his gloves. "This is Mr. Smythe's liver. It's not as exceptional as it could be." He held up the dark red offal organ that resembled a piece of raw meat Isobel had seen once in the country after a hawk had dismembered a rabbit. "During a malnutrition event, every organ in the body shrinks to about half its original size. Every organ except for the brain. That only shrinks by two to four percent."

His knowledge and expertise astounded her. Though she'd rather not look upon the body or its organs, she couldn't tear her gaze away from the man who spoke with such authority and dare she say joy in his work? Her respect and admiration for him went up.

Royce replaced the liver. "Right here is the stomach." He indicated the area with his scalpel, but it was difficult to see from her vantage point. "The reason for the swollen abdomen." He raised his gaze to encompass his audience. "It is important to understand that in malnourishment, the rounded abdomen is not due to fat accumulation, as many physicians insist. I've seen this issue too many times in my patients. Instead, the water retention and fluid buildup in the body cause the abdomen to expand. This results in a bloated, distended stomach or abdominal area." Carefully and methodically, he put the pulled back skin flaps into place. "It's safe to say that Mr. Smythe didn't eat with any regularity. Was this the factor that drove him to a life of violent crime? Only he could tell you, but he is but one story that makes up the layers of London."

How extremely sad, and it drove home the point of the huge class divide that operated throughout England.

Applause echoed through the room as Royce replaced the sheet over the body leaving bloody fingerprints behind on the cloth.

"Well done, Doctor Marsden, and how fascinating." The duke was quite a jovial person as he came back to the front of the room. "Now, perhaps we should let the footmen remove poor Mr. Smythe while we gather in the library and away from the foul odors in here."

As one, the company exited the room with more haste than finesse.

Isobel threw a glance at William, who looked at her with a

frown and speculation. She shrugged and mouthed, "I'll be there in a moment."

He nodded and finally left the drawing room. On his way out, two footmen entered with a wooden ladder between them. As they bundled the body onto the ladder, Royce dropped his instruments into a bucket that rested at his feet. His gloves followed. While the footmen carried the body from the room, the doctor removed his apron, and it too was put into the wooden bucket. A maid darted into the room to take possession of the bucket.

"Please be sure to burn the fabrics and soak the instruments in boiling water for several minutes before cleaning, and then boil them again," he told the young woman.

"Of course, Doctor. I'll tell the housekeeper."

When he glanced up and his gaze alighted upon Isobel, he grinned. "I'm uncommonly happy to see you. What did you think about this evening, Miss Storme?"

"I'll be honest, I hope I'll not have cause to think about what I've seen tonight again." Her laughter sounded forced. She couldn't wrap her brain around the fact the murderer hadn't enough food to eat. Did he have a family? People he cared for? Were they on the verge of starvation too? That last thought brought tears to her eyes, which she quickly blinked away. "That being said, I'm slightly in awe of you."

"Oh? You'll need to tell me more, but please do so outside. I need to give my hands and arms a good washing. A doctor's work is rather messy business." He led the way across the room and through the open doorway to the terrace where yet another wooden bucket waited. "We're finding more and more evidence that keeping one's hands clean while performing surgeries, setting bones, or even general medical tasks cuts down on the patient contracting an infection."

"It's so fascinating, what you do. You're a veritable scientist along with how you save lives."

"I don't know if I'd say that." His humbleness was adorable.

A stab of envy went through her chest while he squatted at the bucket and plunged his hands into the water. "Compared to your skills, I'm quite a superfluous member of society. Nothing that I've done up until this point matters in the grand scheme." It was true. She did absolutely nothing in the way of charitable causes or helping people.

"I wouldn't say that. Everyone on this planet serves a purpose and provides joy for another."

Isobel snorted. She sincerely doubted that, but the longing she'd carried around in her chest for years intensified. "That's sweet of you to say. I couldn't bear to see pain or suffering on a daily basis like you do."

"I agree, it's something not many people wish to do. The education and study alone are staggering, and there's always something new to learn." He grabbed a cake of soap that gave off a strong odor. "I like to think of it as a gift." As he scrubbed the soap over his forearms and hands, he continued to look at her. "Why do you wrinkle your nose like that?"

"What is that smell?" Granted, it was more pleasant than the decaying body, but it was quite pungent.

Royce's laughter reverberated in her chest and set off several flutters in her belly. "It's a mixture of tea tree oil, which was originally discovered in Australia by Captain James Cook and then brought to England for it cleaning properties as well as protecting against infection. It also contains eucalyptus oil for the same." For long moments, he worked at his task. He paid strict attention to his hands and cleaning beneath the nails. Eventually, he washed off the soap and then stood, grabbing a clean rag that rested to one side of the bucket. "I make certain I buy many cakes of the stuff for my clinic and home."

"I don't blame you, and from what little I understand of physicians, that sets you apart from many of them." She didn't know how to explain it, but watching Royce as he'd worked, seeing him take such time and care into cleaning himself, and now talking with him alone on the terrace all worked to send awareness for him trembling over her skin. There was something all too heady about seeing someone excel in their chosen profession.

"Um, what will become of Mr. Smythe's body?"

"The duke's men will transport it to a local graveyard, where it will be buried."

"Did he have family?" Would they even know where he was?

Royce shrugged. "Who can say? No one claimed his body. That's often the case with convicted criminals or those who've lost their way."

"There is so much I don't know about our society, and the more that's uncovered, the greater my disdain grows." Perhaps she could use that as motivation to make a difference. Somehow. "Will you join the others in the library?"

"It would probably be best." He came around the bucket, approached her, and didn't stop until a mere two feet of space separated them. "Unless you had other plans?"

Heat slapped at her cheeks. His blatant flirting yanked her from the maudlin thoughts. "I did, of course, especially after that kiss from yesterday." When he grinned, clearly unrepentant, desire tripped down her spine. "However, I'd rather not get up to mischief with you while you're wearing the same clothes you did to explore that corpse." Despite her hope to remain unaffected, she gave into a shiver. "Additionally, I'm unable to banish the scent of death from my nose. That is not conducive to other more... pleasurable endeavors." And when next she kissed him, she wished to have use of all her senses.

"At least you're honest. I appreciate that." He began the task of rolling down his sleeves, and she frowned from the unfairness of covering up those forearms. "Then that merely gives me an excuse to see you again."

Isobel nodded. Her throat went suddenly dry, and as odd as it was, the lingering scent of the astringent soap left her craving more of him. "When?" The word came out on a squeak. What was wrong with her? She usually had no difficulties flirting with men.

He shrugged. "Surprise me. Isn't that what you excel at?" The delicate skin at the corners of his eyes crinkled with a grin. In the illumination from the drawing room, they'd darkened slightly. From the dimness of the night or from the thought of being with her again? "You should go. It won't do for someone to catch us here alone, and with me in this state of dress."

"Right." That would ruin her plans for the intriguing man. And the last thing she needed was Cousin Andrew's wrath before she'd had a proper scandal with the doctor. "Until the next time, Doctor Marsden." Already her mind spun on how she could come up with an idea to land in his company without doing so in polite society.

Oh, the planning would be so much fun!

CHAPTER SIX

June 17, 1818

ROYCE SHIFTED POSITION in the leather chair he occupied. The library he shared with his brother was small and not stocked with a robust variety of volumes, but the mostly medical journals, texts, and treatises he and Trey used were well-loved and all the more valuable because they pertained to the work at the clinic. Perhaps one day in the future he'd look into acquiring more books on subject matter that had nothing to do with the medical field like what resided in his father's vast library, but today was not that day. There was plenty of time for all of that.

Thinking of his father brought out an indulgent chuckle. Right now, his parent was no doubt arguing on the floor of the House of Lords. He was quite the force to reckon with while in his glory as a member of Parliament. His mother would have been so proud of him had she still been alive. That forthright, determined attitude was one he wished to emulate once it was his turn as earl and to take on the stodgy, unchanging men who made the laws.

Thank goodness that wasn't a worry Royce needed to mull over any time soon.

A cool June breeze came through the open windows. It ruffled his hair and flirted with the pages of the tome that sat open on his lap, but his attention had long ago wandered from the words. All his mind wished to contemplate was Isobel and her reaction to the cadaver exam two days ago.

Oh, she'd been curious, that much had been evident, but as he'd spoken of the life Mr. Smythe had allegedly led, compassion had pooled in her eyes. Emotions had played over her expressive face, and he'd almost been able to hear her thoughts in that moment. No doubt she'd considered the horrific divide between the classes in England, wondered if the man had had a family that had fared equally horridly.

His respect for her had gone up a notch. Yes, she courted scandal almost to the point of harm, but beneath that façade beat a heart for the people. If she'd let herself, she could work toward changing the political and social landscape of London if not England. But that meant she'd need to lower that guard, let people see past the mask of sensation she persisted in living behind.

The question was why she did so. What was driving her to portray herself in such a reckless, shallow light?

It was merely one of the questions he wished to have answered regarding the fascinating Storme. Just like her cousins and brother, Isobel was a creature of high emotion and even higher drama, but if she could harness that power, there'd be no stopping her.

He'd enjoyed having her at the cadaver exam all too much, and it had given him the opportunity to show himself in a more favorable light than she'd seen before. When they'd spoken briefly on the terrace, it had been evident she held him in high esteem and had admired his work. Never had he craved praise like he did in her company. Her regard made him feel more alive as a man—in a different way than helping his patients. And damn his eyes if he didn't want another kiss merely to see if the first one—and his reaction therein—had been an aberration.

With a sigh, Royce gave his head a firm shake and returned his attention to the medical textbook on his lap. There was a particular procedure he'd hoped to learn more about before he needed to perform it upon a patient, but sadly there wasn't much knowledge regarding such surgery. Did he have the bravery to go forward in what was essentially an experiment even if it did manage to heal the patient?

A slight clearing of a masculine throat at the doorway alerted him to the presence of the butler.

"What is it, Dirkens?" He set aside his book. Though the nine o'clock hour had just struck, he hoped there wasn't an emergency. The clinic had remained open until seven that night, but Trey and Finn had manned that particular shift. No doubt they were taking dinner together at their club as was their custom on the late nights.

"There is someone here to see you, Doctor."

Obviously. Tamping on the urge to huff in annoyance, Royce rose from his chair and faced the other man. "Who?"

"A Miss Storme." Dirkens raised a brown eyebrow as if having a woman beneath a bachelor's roof was the height of scandal. He wasn't far off the mark. "Currently, she's in the parlor and quite unescorted. What shall I tell her?"

Royce snorted. "That largely depends on why she's here."

"The lady didn't say."

Of course she didn't. That would be too tame and quite uninspiring. "Very well. I'll attend to her directly."

"Very well, Doctor. Will there be anything else?"

"I can't imagine there would be." Royce waved a hand. "Consider yourself off duty." Once the butler departed, he ran a hand through his hair and then straightened his cravat. What the devil was Isobel doing showing up here at night without an escort or companion? Still, his heartbeat quickened as he made his way through the corridors. At the parlor door, he stopped short, and his breathing temporarily failed him. "Dear God."

She turned at the sound of his voice. Dressed in a gown of silver satin with a gauzy, ethereal overskirt that twinkled and glittered with tiny spangles, Miss Isobel Storme was a vision that had apparently fallen from the heavens to glow with starshine in his parlor. He could easily imagine her as a lost deity of old, and when he peeked at her feet, she wore matching silver sandals whose leather ties crisscrossed up her calves. "Good evening, Doctor." When she bestowed a smile upon him, it held a certain wickedness that spelled disaster for him.

"I, uh..." He cleared his throat. "Good evening. What are you doing here, dressed for a ball, I assume?"

Her dark brown hair had been pinned into a glorious mass high upon her head ala a Greek goddess. A delicate dual band shimmered from those tresses while curls provided temptation at her temples and nape. "When one is going to a ball, one must dress for the occasion. Don't you think?"

"I... suppose." That didn't answer his question. "I mean, if you're going to a ball, why are you *here*?" The spicy, orange blossom scent of her wafted to his nose to further cloud his thinking.

"To ask you to accompany me to the Marquess of Brandenshire's annual midsummer masquerade." She held up a hand. Clutched in her fingers was a domino mask of silver satin and glitter that matched her gown. "Well?"

"I haven't been invited." Never had he been more devastated.

Isobel's tinkling laughter bounced through the room as if she were visiting from fairyland. "Neither have I, which is why it'll be so much fun to crash said ball."

For the second time that evening, Royce was rendered speechless. He stared at her with his lower jaw hanging slightly open. "I... I beg your pardon. You mean to sneak into a society event?"

"Of course." She waved her free hand as if doing such a thing were a paltry feat. Perhaps it was where she was concerned. "Now, don't dawdle. If we're to make a go of it, you'll need to don evening clothes. Preferably a tailcoat, and if you own one, a cloak and domino mask."

This is insane! And the height of scandalous. "That assumes

I'm going to accompany you." He crossed his arms at his chest. "We cannot simply saunter into a ball without someone recognizing us as frauds."

"Oh, my dear doctor, you have much to learn." She crossed the room and once she reached his location, she gave him a little push toward the door. "Go on, now. You *did* promise to land in my company again, so here we are."

"But—"

"No excuses and no thinking about if it's proper. You need fun and excitement in your life to tear you away from all things medical." Again, she gave him a little shove. "Besides, there will be dancing, and I do so adore it."

"Ah." How could he pass on the opportunity to potentially hold her in his arms during a dance? "Very well. Give me twenty minutes to change clothes and I'll be back down."

Amusement filled her eyes. "I thought you might agree."

Never had he exited a room so quickly or at such a run. This stunt was extremely improper and had the power to see them tossed out on their respective arses with gossip in their wake, but damn if he wasn't looking forward to it.

⋙✦⋘

THREE QUARTERS OF an hour later, he and Isobel stood surveying the Brandenshire's ballroom at the posh St. James Place address. Because they'd arrived so late, there was no longer a reception line to pass through nor had there been any questions regarding their invitations. For that matter, a butler hadn't answered their knock, and a footman had shown them in while clearly worried about other duties.

"How did you know we wouldn't have difficulties?" Royce whispered to her as he watched the dancing, swirling couples. The variety of colors put him in mind of a wildflower meadow even though the bulk of the costuming leaned toward Grecianinspired attire, which played into the Midsummer Night's Dream theming throughout the ballroom.

Her eyes sparkled like sapphire gems behind her mask. "This isn't the first time I've slipped in somewhere I haven't been invited." An elusive smile flirted with her lips, and Royce's gaze dropped to her mouth. Damn his eyes but he wanted another kiss, and badly. "Shall we wait for the next set, or should we seek out the refreshment tables?"

"Since you were the one who dragged me here, I'd imagine you already have plans for how we spend the evening." And he wouldn't put it past her to include inappropriate things in that repertoire. Again, he wondered why she continued to hide behind that façade and what it was she continued to run from.

"Ah, you're still reluctant to grasp your full potential." For a handful of seconds, a frown pulled down her perfect lips. "Well, that simply won't do at all." She lowered her voice even further so that he had to lean close to hear. "I want you to be a willing participant in whatever we chose to indulge in tonight."

Oh, dear God! He shuddered to contemplate what that meant even as inappropriate desire shot down his spine. With a healthy dose of wariness mixed with a smidge of anticipation, Royce sighed. "Let's mingle first and then we can dance."

She nodded. "Are we giving our real names if asked?"

And run the risk of being found out? "I shouldn't think so. As long as we're spinning this fiction, we might as well see it through to the end." There was a certain comfort in secrecy though, and he certainly didn't want the Earl of Hadleigh ringing a peal over his head for encouraging Isobel's behavior. As long as they stuck to docile things like dancing, there was no reason for wind of this stunt to reach Andrew's ears.

"I'd hoped you'd agree." Isobel gestured with her head. "Let's test the theory that people don't look too closely and only see what they expect to see."

Please, please don't let anyone recognize me.

There was every chance the guests here were too high on the

instep to move in the same circles he did, but with his red hair and his profession, the risks of being known were high enough to cause knots to form in his belly. But he docilely followed after the lady as if he didn't have a brain in his head.

So easily she drifted over to a knot of women and just as easily outshone them. "Good evening." Then he noticed her voice had changed, as had her accent. No longer was she the Isobel Storme he'd come to know. Now she possessed tones that had a smokey quality and by Jove, she'd somehow adopted an American accent. "I'm Miss Cassandra FitzHerbert of the New York FitzHerberts." She gestured to Royce. "This is the Duke of Thistlewaite, in Town from the Lake District."

How had she managed to assume a whole different persona with such impromptu grace that everyone around her seemed to believe it as truth? Not only that but she'd effortlessly included him in the farce so that it was too late to back out.

"It's a pleasure to meet you, ladies," he said, hoping to God he didn't sound like an utter fool in the attempt to use the correct accent from the region. Good thing he had a close mate in medical school who'd hailed from the area.

Young and old alike tittered and ogled him as if he were a piece of meat to their lionesses. This was the part of being out within society he detested. Most of the time women only paid him attention because he was an eligible bachelor, the son of an earl, which is why he chose to bury himself in his clinic. He wanted a lady to show an interest in him as a man aside from the soon-to-have title.

Isobel shot him a sweet smile that was as powerful as her wicked one. "My father has made his fortunes in coal and textiles, and he graciously sent me to London to visit his aunt. But I'm frightfully bored and in need of entertainment. Thank goodness His Grace came along this evening." A thin rope of pearls and diamonds glittered from her gloved wrist as Royce stared in wonder and a tiny bit of horror. "Might you give some advice on what to do while in London?"

For the next few minutes, the ladies happily chatted with Isobel as if she were suddenly a long-lost sister and they were ever so grateful to have found her again. She was quite animated as she chatted, with sparkling eyes and high color on her cheeks, as if she found amusement at their expense and relished in it.

Then the crowd on the dance floor shifted and string quartet did experimental notes for what sounded like a waltz. Royce's pulse increased. "Terribly sorry to interrupt, Miss FitzHerbert, but they're setting up for a waltz and I believe I've reserved this set from you."

When she glanced at him, the sweetness in her expression had vanished only to be replaced by scandal and sin that had unexpected heat rushing through his blood to concentrate in his shaft. "Of course. How silly of me to forget, Your Grace." She waved a hand to her new friends. "If you'll excuse me? We shall talk later." Then Isobel laid her fingers upon his sleeve and allowed him to lead her to an empty spot on the parquet dance floor. "It's going swimmingly, don't you think?" she asked in a whisper.

"Honestly, I don't know what to think. You've managed to flummox me in many ways this evening." If he weren't careful, he'd be at sixes and sevens because of her, and become lost to her allure. "At least while dancing you can't get up to creating a sensation."

"Oh, you know me not at all, Royce." Her tinkling laughter heightened the awareness he already had for her. "I'm only just starting my evening."

He gaped at her as they assumed the correct position to begin. "Dare I ask what else you've planned?"

"I wouldn't." She winked and he swore he felt the ground beneath his feet shift.

Then the dance was underway. For the first few steps, he concentrated on putting his whole attention on the waltz; it had been some time since he'd last do the pretty like this, but he needn't have worried. The knowledge came back to him as if it had been ingrained. At every dip and swirl, Isobel somehow returned to him closer than before.

How had she managed that without him realizing?

For the moment, Royce didn't care, for she was an engaging bundle. The heat of her seeped through his gloves while her breasts brushed his chest with just enough teasing that he feared the teasing would drive him mad. "What are your plans beyond this dance?"

"That largely depends on how much I can push you past the bounds of your own comfort." The fingers that rested on his shoulder tightened slightly as she cocked an eyebrow. "Have you an objection to that?"

"Not necessarily." When was the last time a woman had affected him on every level as she did now? "However, I *am* curious."

With the simple direction of her fingers on his shoulder, she encouraged him a fraction of an inch closer. As brazen as if she were alone with him instead of in a ballroom full of people, she dropped her gaze to his mouth before meeting his eyes. "Then I'll tell you this. I plan to slip away once this waltz concludes, perhaps find a study or library on this floor. What happens after that is up to fate."

His heartbeat quickened. "I see." The steps of the dance temporarily took her away from him, but when they came back together, he asked, "What about the impending scandal if we're caught?" He would flat out refuse to put himself into a situation in which he might need to ask for her hand in a forced situation. Neither of them needed that. And a bout of heated kissing didn't warrant marriage.

Isobel snorted. "Remember, Doctor, we are not ourselves this evening. That scandal—*if* we're caught—will rest squarely on Miss FitzHerbert as well as the Duke of Thistlewaite." Her eyes twinkled behind her mask as she leaned into him. "Imagine what people will say."

"I don't have to, but I'm certainly glad it's their future to worry about." Feeling more reckless than confident, he twirled her about the floor with grand and sweeping finesse. "You're quite a bad influence."

All too soon the music concluded. The assembled couples drifted to a halt and polite clapping went about the room. Royce escorted her over to the sidelines while another set formed. "Shall I fetch you some punch, Miss FitzHerbert?" he said in a voice louder than usual for the benefit of anyone eavesdropping?

"That would be quite refreshing, Your Grace. While you do that, I'm going into one of the ladies' retiring rooms. I seem to have torn a hem." With an elevated eyebrow, she headed toward one of the doors leading from the ballroom.

Royce exited from a different door. His heart beat so hard he feared someone would hear it as he navigated his way through the corridor and then down another, shorter one. Each time he came to a door, he tried the latch. Some were locked, but some weren't. Finally, he located a dimly lit library, and with his heart in his throat—for the chance of discovery and hitting upon his real identity if he were ordered to unmask was quite high—he entered the room, pausing to check the corridor before closing the door behind him with a soft snick.

"Isobel?" The whispered sound of his inquiry seemed overly loud in the heavy silence.

She came out of the shadows; her shimmering gown reflecting the light from the candelabra burning upon one of the low tables in the center of the room. "There is no one here by that name."

Ah, she would play the role to the hilt. Minx. He grinned. A streak of recklessness went down his spine. "Miss FitzHerbert then?"

"Of course, Your Grace." Before he knew what she was about, Isobel tugged at his cravat, moved him off to the side and into the shadows, and then gave him a shove until his back connected with the wall. "I hope you're here for an erotic interlude. If you're not, I shall have to find some other willing gentleman to relieve certain... needs."

Damnation! I'm in a spot of bother.

Then a stab of *something* went through his chest at the thought of her with another man before he'd ever delved deeper into the real Isobel. "I don't think that will be necessary." He reached for her, sliding a hand about her nape, and hauling her to him. Then, with his other hand at her hip, he claimed her lips with his.

She gave into him with a sigh, but he never expected a complete surrender. Though her lips were as soft and as yielding as they'd been before, there was a certain urgency to this kiss. Perhaps it had been the teasing and flirting they'd already indulged in, but there was something about this woman he couldn't ignore. When she pressed her body into his and angled her head for better access, Royce groaned. The damned masks kept bumping and sticking together, but he refused to stop long enough to remove them. He settled her more comfortably in his arms with the intention of kissing her senseless.

If only to evict her from his mind and cool the ardor in his blood.

When that didn't provide nearly enough, he flipped positions. Holding her captive between his chest and the wall, he moved over her lips, nipped the plumb bottom piece of flesh, nibbled at the corners until she opened for him. The tiny moan she made spurred him onward. Satin slid against silk as their tongues dueled from dominance. With every thrust and parry, she wound her arms more tightly about his shoulders, and he moved his hand upward, dared to brush his fingers along the curve of her breast.

She mewled like a contented kitten. When she sucked on his bottom lip and then released it with a slight *pop*, Royce's hold on control slipped a fraction. His pulse roared in his ears. Hot need rushed through his length, tightening with arousal. He put a knee between her legs, and she moaned again, slightly sliding up his thigh. Did she enjoy the sensation of her skirting, his leg, at the center of her being?

Wanting to give her pleasure and to see how far she was comfortable leading him, he dragged his lips down the column of her neck. The soft, fragrant skin was addicting, as were the soft sounds of encouragement she made. One of her hands burrowed beneath his waistcoat, sliding down, down, down his abdomen toward—

The slight *click* of the door latch echoed in the room. The sound wormed its way through his passion-fogged brain. Royce wrenched away, trying to regulate his labored breathing. "Someone's here," he whispered against the shell of her ear.

Isobel clung to him as they waited. Would scandal chase them from the house?

Slowly, the door swung open. "James?" A woman's soft call sounded directly on the other side of the door from their location. Obviously, her assignation wasn't in this room. Just as slowly and quietly, the panel closed, and Royce breathed a sigh of relief.

He rested his forehead against Isobel's. "We should probably go lest we find ourselves caught."

"But we haven't finished here." The tiny whine in her voice caused him to snicker.

"There will be other times to more fully explore what we've only just discovered." With a kiss to her cheek, he pulled fully away and shoved a hand through his hair. "Go to the refreshment table. I'll join you there in a few minutes."

"Fine." Her kiss-swollen lips turned downward in a pout, but she left the room without further argument.

"Bloody hell." Yet he couldn't hold back his grin. That was, by far, the best evening he'd spent in quite some time. Even if that string of kisses had done nothing to break the desire he had for her.

CHAPTER SEVEN

June 19, 1818

CONFUSION SWIRLED THROUGH Isobel's insides as she met Fanny in the private parlor upstairs in their townhouse. Ivan trotted at her heels, for she would take him out for a walk soon, but her mind was steeped in uncertainty, and she needed to share her thoughts with someone before she burst from them.

"I apologize for my tardiness," she said while settling upon a low sofa. Ivan sat at her feet. "For whatever reason, I've been prone to woolgathering recently."

Oh, she knew exactly the reason she was having difficulties concentrating, and it all centered around a certain red-haired doctor who apparently had great skill in kissing.

"That's understandable. Life just now is blanketed by sorrow." Though Fanny smiled from where she perched on a delicate chair with her feet propped on a footstool with an embroidered cushion, she appeared wan and pale.

"Are you feeling well? You don't look quite the thing. And you missed the cadaver exam last week." The longer Isobel peered at her friend, the more she saw signs of ailing. "Please don't tell me you've contracted a wasting disease." Her chest tightened at the thought of potentially losing her friend.

I can't invite more death or illness into my life right now. What's already there is too much.

"Why are you always so dramatic?" Fanny waved a hand. She smiled, but the gesture didn't quite reach her eyes. "I'm well enough. It's just that my stomach is quite delicate and is rejecting some of the things I eat." She shrugged and laid her hands in her lap. The sapphires and diamonds of her engagement ring twinkled in the sunlight that streamed into the room from the open windows.

"I'm so sorry to hear that. William mentioned you were sick the other day; I assumed you'd have passed it by now." Isobel frowned. "Perhaps you should see an apothecary for something that might quiet your stomach."

Fanny nodded. "Perhaps I shall if it doesn't grow better. Because of it, I couldn't accompany William on his interviews today, and that makes me sad."

"I'm sure you'll be right as rain again in no time and bedeviling my brother." In many ways, Fanny was the perfect match for William. They were both intelligent and had a knack for solving crimes. The fact that Bow Street didn't mind having her along on cases spoke volumes. Perhaps someday women would be more widely accepted in every facet of society, for they had the abilities to fashion livelihoods the same as men.

"I hope you're right. It's breaking my heart." A faint smile took possession of her mouth. "We've rarely been apart since we wed."

The imminent death of their mother had delayed William and Fanny's wedding trip. But she didn't want to hear about their romance. Love and matrimony might be fine for some ladies; she didn't happen to be one of them. Now, give her a chance at scandal with a handsome man, and she would move heaven and earth to make such a thing happen.

"Perhaps the two of you can take some time for yourselves. Go down to Brighton or make use of the Derbyshire property."

"I'll talk to William about it. At present, his case load is heavy. And both destinations are far enough away that if something happened here, we couldn't immediately return to London." Fanny sighed and peered at Isobel. "Why did you wish to talk with me? You're not sick too, are you? Oh, I hope I didn't give you whatever is bothering me."

Isobel held up a hand. "Calm yourself, Fanny. I'm not ill." Perhaps chasing insanity, but it wasn't a physical malady she suffered from. "I came to ask for advice." After that kiss she'd shared with Royce two days past where he'd started tiny fires burning in her blood that smoldered still, she wished to pursue an affair with him. For, unless she'd missed her guess, he had no use for courtship or romance either.

"On what?"

She shrugged. "Men."

"Oh." Fanny's eyes rounded. Interest sprang into those light blue depths. "Have you found a suitor?"

"Hardly." Isobel snorted. She leaned down and gave Ivan's ears a scratch before settling more comfortably into the sofa's back. "Do I have your promise that what I tell you won't be shared with anyone?"

"Of course!" Fanny smiled and looked more like her old self.

"Not even William. Promise me. If he knows what I'm doing, he'll forbid it or worse."

Her friend nodded. "You have my utmost discretion." She raised her eyebrows. "Who has caught your fancy? From what I've understood, though you're an accomplished flirt, you never let men close once you win a kiss from them."

Heat went through Isobel's cheeks. She wasn't ashamed of her behavior or her flirtations, but she was annoyed she'd apparently garnered enough of a reputation that it had made the rounds in gossip. "Is it my fault that I can tell what sort of person a man is after one kiss?" The fact she didn't keep her experimentations to only members of the *ton* was perhaps telling, but she didn't care. Men were men, no matter their class, and with her aversion to titled gentlemen, she had to be creative.

Fanny shrugged. Her cheeks were stained pink. "William was

the first man to ever kiss me."

"I had no idea." Though she tried not to gawk, Isobel couldn't imagine kissing only one man. Where was the challenge in that? Where was the rush? "In any event, I've recently come across someone whose kisses have caught me off guard."

That wasn't necessarily the truth. Kissing Royce had seemingly opened the world up to her. In his arms, there was heat and excitement, but also freedom, for he wouldn't make demands of her. It wouldn't take much convincing on her part to lead him on so that he'd introduce her to the pleasures of the flesh, and if they happened to enjoy a collection of trysts between them, where was the harm?

"Who?" Fanny fairly bounced in her seat; her eyes were alight with curiosity. "Tell me. Do I know him?"

"Do you swear you'll keep this to yourself?" When her friend nodded, Isobel sighed and lowered her voice with a glance to the open doorway. "Doctor Marsden."

"What?" Again, Fanny's eyebrows lifted in surprise. "Lady Jane's brother?"

"Yes." Isobel nodded. "We've had two occasions this past week to be in each other's company, and..." A delicious shiver went down her spine. "And we've kissed twice."

"How wonderful!" Fanny clapped a hand over her mouth after the exclamation escaped. Then, lowering her voice to the barest of whispers, she asked, "How was it? Are you in love?"

By sheer willpower alone, Isobel managed to not point her gaze heavenward or response in a snippy manner. "The kisses were unlike any others I've shared with men to this point. And no, I'm not in love. That is a state not meant for me. It causes more problems than it solves." The remembrance of the arguments her parents used to have only solidified her resolve to never find herself in the wedded state. She shook her head. "I'm not in the market for marriage or romance, Fanny." Being so vulnerable in front of another person, who supposedly held one's heart in their hands, sent prickles of terror through her chest.

"I've made my peace with that."

"It's not the prison you might think." Fanny's eyes were kinds as she looked at Isobel. "With the right man—"

"Please, stop." Isobel waved a hand. "Don't give me the platitudes."

Fanny sighed. "Then what *do* you want?"

Oh, the list was quite long. Perhaps ambitious, even. "First and foremost, I want the freedom to explore. Not only a man's body in the physical sense, but to discover who I am in all this mess." She waved a hand, presumably to encompass her house, her family, her place in existence. "Beyond that, I want a man to understand me, for him to dive beneath the surface of who I am, find the tangled, messy parts, and wish to continue our association anyway." Her words trailed off into silence for the space of several heartbeats. "Above everything right now, I want to act highly improper and have an affair."

Beyond that, the yearning to fit in or belong to someone while her world constantly shifted burned strong. Over the years, she'd always been overlooked, ignored, lectured. Was there someone out there who would see her for her?

"But that means you'll forsake the most important, the most satisfying part of a relationship with a man." Fanny's eyes rounded in shock. "Why?"

Isobel snorted. "I'm willing to wager being bedded is very satisfying."

A fierce blush raged in Fanny's cheeks. "Well, I won't say that it isn't quite wonderful…"

"I want that for myself, for I feel as if my life is wasting away just as Mother's is only in a different way." The admission shocked her, but she refused to take it back. Another round of heat infused her cheeks. "Besides, Doctor Marsden is the best candidate."

"Why do you say that, and how can you know?"

Isobel leaned forward. The remembrance of his lips against her, the scent of him, the press of his body as he'd trapped her between him, and wall all worked to send languid trails of warmth through her body. But she kept those details to herself. Instead, she said, "He doesn't currently have a title, his life is his own, and he's an outsider like me."

"Has he agreed to a tryst?" Fanny's eyes remained rounded with astonishment.

"Not in so many words, but I'm confident I can bring him 'round."

Her friend frowned. "Then why do you want my advice if you already have a plan?"

"I want you to tell me this is a good step for my future." Honestly, it didn't matter, for she'd do whatever she wanted anyway.

Fanny's lower jaw dropped. "How can having an illicit affair be good for anyone's future?" Slowly, she shook her head. "If you're caught or found out, your reputation will be completely ruined. And then what will you do? Up until this point, you've hovered on the edge of scandal without much damage. But this?"

"What difference does it make? I'm a Storme, and everyone knows the Storme family is full of rumor-worthy happenings. Some days I wonder if everyone in the *ton* is watching me merely to see what scandalbroth I'll land in next." That was a sad state of affairs. Even though the Storme connection seemed larger than life, they were good people and were changing the world in their own ways.

I want that for my life.

"I understand that, but if you give them exactly what they expect, what sort of lady does that make you?" Compassion pooled in Fanny's eyes. She leaned over the side of her chair and flung out a hand, which Isobel took. "Do you feel a connection with the doctor?"

"Yes. It grows stronger each time we see each other, but beyond that, I feel he'll make a fine friend." Isobel squeezed Fanny's fingers. "He makes me feel both naughty and powerful." Briefly, she explained about dragging him to the ball. "Never once does he deny my plans, and I've not questioned him about that." She allowed a small grin. "It's a bit flattering."

"I suppose it would be, to have a man blindly follow you into anything." Fanny released her hand. "William is like that on occasion. It's adorable."

Isobel nodded. Envy speared through her tight chest. She might not want marriage and the cage therein, but she'd love to have the closeness with a man that Fanny had. "Knowing me as you do, you won't condemn me for this choice. Will you?" Why could men have all the trysts, assignations, and affairs they wanted and were often lauded for it among their circle of friends, but when a woman announced the same, she was labeled a prostitute?

"Of course not."

"I feel compelled to find entertainment before Mother dies. I don't want to arrive at the end of my life without have knowing what it feels like to lie with a man," she admitted in a whisper. "Perhaps my family will finally notice me as a person and not a Storme."

"Oh, Isobel, when will you learn that being a Storme isn't as horrible as you believe?" Then an expression of panic crossed Fanny's face and she sprang up from her chair with fingers pressed to her lips. "If this is truly what you want to do, I say enjoy it, but be as discreet as you can." A gagging noise emanated from her. "I'd hate to see you banished to Derbyshire. It's so far away..." Then with a strangled sort of cry, she ran from the room, no doubt to cast up her accounts in a nearby potted plant.

Ivan, ever sensitive to the changing moods of the family, trotted after her.

With a sigh, Isobel stood. Hoping Fanny's unsettled stomach found a cure soon, she made her way through the townhouse until she arrived at her mother's bedchamber door. For the last few days, her parent's strength had waned, and she'd been unable or unwilling to go downstairs to join the family for meals or tea.

"Mother?" In the back of her mind, she wondered why none

in the family had referred to their parents as "papa" or "mama". Perhaps they weren't as close enough for all of that. The Stormes had always hidden behind formality and had been taught to never show emotion because it was a weakness. For a long time, that had worked for her, but now? All the turmoil swirling through her chest would require an outlet, and soon.

What would happen then if she let herself break? Especially after Caroline had been sent away or Cousin Andrew had nearly ruined his life from the force of his emotions.

She came further into the room and padded over the floor toward the winged back chair where her mother said curled on with a quilt covering her lower half. William or Fanny must have situated the chair at the window so her mother could gaze up the back garden and the square beyond. "How are you feeling today?"

"Tired, but grateful to see another day." Her mother's words were soft, barely audible. She didn't turn her head from the open window. The gentle breeze ruffled tendrils of hair at her temples while the bulk of the gray-streaked brown tresses reposed in a braid over her shoulder.

Isobel came around so that she faced the chair and perched upon the edge of the shallow window seat. It hurt her heart to see her once-vibrant mother so drawn and frail. As best she could, she swallowed the lump of tears in her throat. Even more reason to enter into a wild affair with the doctor—it would help her to forget everything going on around her. "Do you want to go outside? There's a chair set up on the terrace."

"No. This is fine." She clutched a blood-stained handkerchief in her hand, which rested on her lap. "I can see the trees and the flowers from here. Sometimes a bird comes close enough to hop on the window ledge."

Isobel glanced over her shoulder. As of yet, there was no bird, but people strolled through the square, and the breeze carried the sounds of birdsong and laughter amidst the clatter of carriage wheels upon the roads. "Perhaps we should have removed to

Derbyshire. There's so much more for you to look at there."

"Nonsense." The response was little more than wisps of a voice. "I've enjoyed London and its life. Especially once your father passed. There was always something to keep me occupied." The veriest hint of a sigh escaped her.

"That's how I feel about it." Isobel ignored how tight her chest was or how much it hurt to talk with her mother now knowing she soon would be gone. "London has my heart and soul. If I were a city, it is what I'd be."

"Yes, it's as wild and untamed as you, Isobel." Finally, her mother rested her tired, faded gaze upon her face. "Though I wish you'd give a lucky young man your heart, I know why you resist."

"What?" This was a different vein of conversation than they'd last had.

"You fear your marriage will follow the course that mine did." It wasn't a question.

"I do." There was no sense in lying about it. "You and Father fought all the time. To say nothing of the fact that William argued with Father; Caroline fought with you both." She shook her head. "When I was a child, there was nothing but strife and discontent. Everyone was angry all the time. I don't want those shackles."

I only want love. Unconditional love for who I am.

"I'm sorry we failed you. That we all failed you, in a different way than we failed Caroline." Once more, her mother glanced out the window. "It was a turbulent time in both my life and your father's." She shook her head, but her eyes were far away; perhaps she'd gone back in the past. "I don't know how it happened. At one point in our marriage, we loved each other very much."

Isobel remained silent. She twisted the ruby ring around her finger. Obviously, that emotion had cooled shortly after she'd become cognizant enough to realize the world around her and feel the moods from the adults in her life. By the time her sister was sent away to the institution, Isobel had attained the age of ten. There was no hiding the truth, and her father had spent more and more time away from home.

Over the years, she'd wondered if he'd taken a mistress, but then he'd died suddenly when his heart attacked him, and there was no scandal attached to his name, so it had been but a theory only. Still, she hadn't known him well as his own person, and perhaps that was the greater crime than holding the crumbling foundation of her life against him.

Finally, she sighed. "Don't think about such things any longer, Mother. It's a waste of time." She stared at the ruby in the ring. So much like a drop of blood—anger that had torn apart the Storme family.

It's exhausting feeling that I'll explode from one reason or another all the time. Is this my legacy, then?

"Perhaps it is, and I'm glad you've realized that so early in life." Her mother glanced at her. So much sadness lurked in her eyes that Isobel's chest tightened further. "You deserve happiness, my darling daughter, and if you cannot find that within the Storme family, I pray you'll find it elsewhere." A ghost of a smile curved her lips. "No matter how it comes about."

Isobel frowned. Did that mean her mother was more or less giving her blessing on a possible tryst with Doctor Marsden? "I hope for that too," she said in a choked whisper.

"Good." Her mother lifted her face to the breeze that came into the room. "Now, why don't you lie on my bed like you did when you were small. On your belly, when you used to tell Caroline and I stories you thought up while at the Derbyshire property." Again, her eyes took on a faraway look. A series of coughs racked her body, which produced more blood on the handkerchief than ever before. "I used to adore it when you let your imagination run away with you, and for a time, those stories calmed Caroline." Her chuckle mixed with wheezing breaths. "Isn't it odd that you and Phineas have the same talent?"

"Yes, I suppose it is." Tears sprang into Isobel's eyes. Perhaps she could use that to her advantage later, after the initial wave of grief left. "I'll talk to him about what writing a book entails."

"I was always so proud to see you and your cousins turn out so strong where your parents where so weak…"

"Oh, Mother…" When moisture fell to her cheeks, she dashed them away. Walking Ivan could wait, as could the need to see Doctor Marsden. Everything would keep. This time with her mother was too precious to squander because she couldn't bear to venture into the unknown. Even though terror sat heavy on her chest and threatened to steal her breath, she crawled onto her mother's bed, made herself comfortable, and then said, "Once upon a time…"

There would be time enough to break or let the storm of her namesake have at her.

Chapter Eight

June 20, 1818

R OYCE GLANCED AGAIN at the missive that was delivered not ten minutes past from Inspector Storme.

Come at once. My wife has been ill for a week or more. Apothecary cures aren't working. I'm afraid there is something bigger at play.

Though he wasn't worried, there was a trace of concern threading down his spine. Ever since the Storme family had seen Finn thrive under his care, they wouldn't have any other doctor to attend the connection. That in and of itself was flattering, but it did present a greater issue. If something were to come up that didn't bring with it a positive prognosis, how would that affect his relationship with the family he was related to by marriage?

By the time he exited his carriage, a gentle spring rain had begun. Shoving the note into a waistcoat pocket, he adjusted his hold on the handles of his worn, black doctor's bag and glanced at his driver. "I shouldn't be longer than an hour, Jeffries. If I am, by all means pull into the mews and wait."

Rarely did he take out the carriage, for his clinic was within walking distance and the vehicle had been a gift from his father besides. He'd wished for no remembrances that he'd eventually become the earl and he certainly didn't want financial assistance from his father's estates, but the necessity of having a carriage wasn't lost on him.

Especially on days when it rained.

"Very good, Doctor Marsden."

With a nod, Royce hurried up the walkway that led to the townhouse of the Viscountess Doughton, which was also where Inspector Storme and his wife resided. To say nothing of Isobel. His heartbeat tumbled into a rapid tattoo. Would she be in attendance? He had no idea how she spent her days or what her private schedule was, and he hadn't seen her for three days due to his duties at the clinic. How had she kept herself?

And perhaps more to the point, now that she had time to think, how did she feel about that heated kiss they'd shared at the ball?

As for himself, he was slowly being driven to madness by her, for after that kiss, the desire he had for her had ramped. She constantly invaded his waking thoughts as well as his sleeping dreams. More than once, he'd woken in the night with his member hard and rampant all because he couldn't evict her from his mind. Isobel Storme was wild and without discretion. She didn't care that she was often fuel for the gossipmongers, but that made her all the more attractive. With every passing day, his interest in her grew. Oh, he was still appalled by some of the stunts she pulled, but he was hopelessly addicted to her and couldn't wait to see what she'd do next.

Realizing he stood on the stoop staring at the door for more minutes than was proper, Royce shook his head and firmly shoved all thoughts of Isobel away. He was here at the behest of William and in a doctor capacity. The logical thing to do was act like the physician he was. With no more recourse, he rapped smartly upon the door. Seconds later it swung open.

The butler—Hankins was his name, if Royce remembered correctly—admitted him at once. "Inspector Storme is waiting for you abovestairs. Follow me." Urgency rode the stately man's voice.

Royce frowned. If word of the visit had reached the servants, William must assume something was very wrong indeed with his wife. "Thank you." On his way up the staircase, he caught a glimpse of Isobel as she stood at the doorway of the drawing room. He lifted his free hand in acknowledgment. She waved back. Her lips curved in a grin that promised wicked things but there was no time to tarry. That didn't stop awareness from tingling along his nerve endings.

Oh yes, that lady would be trouble. Was he the man to stop her or encourage her?

His thoughts scattered when he reached the suite of rooms. William came forward and shook his hand. "Inspector, it's good to see you again."

"You as well, Doctor." William thanked the butler and when that man left, he drew Royce further into the sitting room. "Francesca just doesn't seem to grow better with the quick remedies we've tried. I don't mind telling you that I'm worried." Concern creased his brow and lurked at the backs of his eyes.

One of the best parts of being a physician was the ability to perform examinations that would set family members at ease with the results. "I won't tell you not to worry, for you'll do so in any event. I know how much you love your wife." He nodded to Mrs. Storme, who sat composed but pale in a chair by the window. "Good afternoon, Mrs. Storme." As he came toward her, he glanced at her. From all outward appearances, she merely looked exhausted. "Perhaps you should tell me why you believe there's something wrong. What symptoms are you experiencing?"

"For the past couple of weeks, I've been having extreme fatigue. There have been a few megrims that prevent me from concentrating on writing for the newspaper. There has been some stomach discomfort as well." She gave William a hesitant smile as he joined her and laid a hand upon her shoulder. "I'm having difficulty keeping many foods down, and sometimes, merely the scent of other foods makes me retch."

"I see." Royce glanced between them. "Has anyone else in the household or your connections been ill?"

Both of them shook their heads.

He had a good idea of what ailed the lady, but he'd keep those opinions to himself until a cursory examination had been completed. Because they were both busy with their respective careers as well as caring for the ailing viscountess, it was only natural such a thing would be the farthest assumption from their minds. "Then let us proceed with an examination. Mrs. Storme, if you'll remove to the bedchamber and ask your maid to help you into more comfortable, loose clothing? William, I shall require a few towels as well as a kettle of boiling water."

One of the inspector's dark brown eyebrows rose in surprise. "Whatever for?"

"To sterilize the few instruments I'll use in the exam." Gently but firmly, he led William to the door while Mrs. Storme disappeared into the adjoining bedchamber. "I shall need a few moments to wash my hands and prepare." He dropped his voice in the event Mrs. Storme had exceptional hearing. "You are welcome to attend your wife during the examination, of course, if that will set you both at ease. Or you could call for a midwife instead."

Shock lined his face. "A midwife. But that would indicate…"

"Indeed." He couldn't contain his grin as he nodded. "It's a presumption yet, and I won't know until I look at your wife, but some men are given to strong feelings about a man examining a woman in the places necessary."

For long moments, the inspector remained silent. Finally, he nodded. "No, we'll have you." William shook his head. "I have nothing but trust in your abilities. There is a washstand in the bedchamber. I'll ring for the requested items."

"Thank you."

Thirty minutes later, Royce came into the adjoining sitting

room. The inspector and his wife sat side by side on a low sofa, anxiety clear in both their expressions. With a grin, he placed his black bag on a rose-inlaid occasional table and then dropped into a chair near the sofa. "Your case is quite easy to solve, Mrs. Storme."

"Oh?" Her eyes were round with fright. "Have I contracted something horrid?"

"Not at all." This was one of the best parts of being a doctor. "Inspector, it is my professional opinion that your wife is increasing. At this time, she is around two, perhaps almost three months along." When they stared at him in shock, his grin grew. "Your infant should arrive at the end of December or the first of January. That's why you've been feeling those symptoms. They should pass in a couple of months."

"Oh, William!" Mrs. Storme burst into tears. "A baby."

With a look of concern mixed with astonishment, the inspector gathered her into his arms.

Royce chuckled. "I'll leave you alone. Before I go, I'll check in on your mother, Inspector, and then perhaps duck into the drawing room to speak with your sister."

"I'll catch you up there. Thank you, Doctor."

NO SOONER HAD Royce gained the drawing room with anticipation of talking with Isobel buzzing at the base of his spine than the Inspector and Mrs. Storme entered. The worry in their countenances had completely dissolved beneath joy. A stab of envy went through his chest. He didn't begrudge them this new start, but he was a tad jealous of the closeness they enjoyed together.

"Royce, er, I mean Doctor Marsden. I'd hoped you'd stop in." Isobel stood, was in the process of crossing the room to greet him, but William intercepted her, scooped her up into his arms in a hug and swung her around off her feet. "For the love of God,

Wills, have you lost your mind?" She shoved at his shoulders until he set her down while Royce watched in some bemusement while her dog pranced about them as if it were all a game.

"I have the best news, sister of mine." When William set her onto her feet, he bussed her cheek. "Well, Francesca and I do."

"Don't keep me in suspense." Isobel darted a glance between the two as William returned to his wife's side. "Is Fanny well?"

"Oh yes." Mrs. Storme's eyes twinkled. The inspector could barely contain his grin. "Can you imagine, Isobel? I'm increasing!"

"Yes," the inspector said, and he was nearly as shocked and happy as his wife. "We're to have a babe early in the new year." He beamed at Isobel. "You'll be an aunt."

At that moment, Royce happened to look at her and caught the emotions playing over her face: shock, dread, envy, and surprisingly, anger. Then she blinked and pulled a mask of blankness onto her face, but those eyes! Good God, her eyes were so haunted he thought he might have imagined it.

"How wonderful for you." Tears sprang into her eyes, temporarily obscuring those sapphire depths. "If you'll excuse me?" Without another word, she hitched up her mint green skirting and pelted from the room.

Ivan barked in happiness and ran after her.

In some confusion, William peered at his wife. He looked at Royce. "What the devil do you think is ailing her?"

"I have some inkling." With a sigh, he took up his black bag. "Again, many congratulations, Inspector, Mrs. Storme. I'm sure you'll wish to tell the viscountess the news. While you do that, I'll go after Miss Storme. Perhaps convince her to take a drive with me until her emotions are under control. Then I'll return her here."

"I'd be forever grateful." The inspector nodded. "You're a good man, Doctor."

Heat crept up the back of his neck, for that wasn't necessarily true. Once he had Isobel to himself and if she was in a proper frame of mind, he'd try to steal another kiss or two. How good was he when knowing that? "Yes, well, I should go after her before she causes too much damage."

Where would she have gone, blinded by emotions with a penchant for scandal? With nothing for it, he gained the entry hall, spoke briefly with a footman who indicated she'd rushed outside, and finally he located her at the curb. She hesitated as if not certain of her next move.

"Isobel, what's wrong?" Royce asked in a soft voice as he joined her. The rain hadn't ceased. Not heavy enough to immediately soak through clothing but just annoying enough to leave one damp. "You left the room as if you'd seen a ghost." When Ivan jumped about his legs and hers, he snapped the fingers of his free hand and pointed to the ground. No doubt there'd be muddy footprints all over his breeches. "Sit." Even to his ears, there was a note of command in his voice.

With a whine, Ivan sat on his haunches and looked at him as if for further instructions.

She shook her head. Tears wet her cheeks to mingle with rain drops. Splotchy red patches spread over her face and chest, a testament to her heightened upset. "I'm feeling out of sorts." Because she'd left the house in a fit of pique, she hadn't donned the appropriate outerwear, so every minute spent in the rain rendered her delicate muslin dress more and more transparent.

"That's understandable. Perhaps you should explain."

"There's so much pressing down on me just now." The words were forced as if she warred with herself about releasing them. "I'm happy for them, of course, but there's a part of me that's jealous, or perhaps merely envious. Not that one is better than the other." She scrubbed at the tears but refused to look at him. "I don't truly know what I feel other than this great wall of anger that fills me."

"Why? What is bringing it about?" Perhaps if he talked with her, he could better understand why she struggled. After consulting Finn and helping with his mental well-being, it had become second nature, for physical health was often closely related to the state of the mind. It wasn't classical thinking, but Royce was adamant more study was needed.

Even if it made him the butt of condescending jokes in the medical community.

Finally, she met his gaze. Tears were still pooled in those magnificent eyes, spiking her dark lashes, and spilling onto her cheeks. And the fabric of her dress clung to her delectable curves. "I don't know." She shook her head. "Everything is changing, but I'm stuck here, being left behind."

"Ah. Now I understand." Knowing what he did of the history of the Stormes, he had an inkling of her particular brand of angst. She was the youngest of the family, and she'd no doubt been neglected in the face of all the torment and animosity that had shaped the people he'd come to care about. "Come with me." Gently, he wrapped a hand about her upper arm and led her toward his waiting carriage. "You'll do well to get out of the rain." He whistled for the dog. "Come here, Ivan."

A minute later, he'd assisted the lady into the vehicle as well as the canine. Then he addressed his driver. "Please drive to Hyde Park and along Rotten Row. Despite the rain, it's a lovely day. Afterward, take a circuitous path through Mayfair before returning here."

"As you like, Doctor." Rain dripped from the brim of his hat. "I personally like the rain, so I'll enjoy the ride."

"Thank you." Royce joined Isobel in the carriage. He settled on the squabbed bench opposite her as the vehicle lurched into motion. By the time he'd rested his bag on the seat next to him, the lady had somewhat gained control of herself. "Why does the news of Mrs. Storme's pregnancy *really* send you into a brown study? I assumed you were opposed to marriage and domestication in all its forms." Hadn't she more or less told him that upon their first meeting?

"I am." Isobel wiped away the remainder of the moisture on her cheeks. She stared out the window, for the curtains had been shoved open while Ivan bounced between the benches as if he hadn't a care in the world. "This news simply means yet another of my friends is moving into aspects of life I'll not have—widening the gulf between us—and being left behind in something infinitely boring."

"That's understandable." He was still unclear of what she did indeed want for her life. "I have my brother Trey, but my other chums have dreams they chase that don't necessarily align with mine. Even your cousins have vastly different lives than they did when I met them at Christmastide last year."

She glanced at him with eyes that were still haunted. "Does it bother you, not having friends who have things in common with you?"

"Sometimes, but I'm not looking for responsibilities like they are." He shrugged. It was perhaps the most honest truth he'd shared with anyone besides Trey. "I'm content to work at the clinic and to have no claims upon my time, while men like your cousins Andrew and Finn are their happiest being wed and starting families. There is no wrong way to live one's life."

For whatever reason, Isobel snickered. "Then you're a rogue?" Interest wove through her voice. "That is something I could throw my support behind."

He snorted. Ivan barked. The dog nudged one of Royce's hands with his nose until he received the pets he wanted. "I don't know about that. I'd have to have a title and bed more women than I have currently." Admitting he wasn't a lady's man sent heat up the back of his neck. "To say nothing about the ability to court scandal. I'd be rubbish at playing the rogue. A bachelor yes, but the other, not really."

Dear God, I'm babbling! Make it stop!

A glint of *something* twinkled in her eyes. "You could, you know."

"What, be a rogue?" He shook his head. "Quite frankly, I haven't the time."

"No, court scandal." With a grin curving her kissable lips, Isobel transferred from her bench to his. Her floral scent wafted to his nose. "With me." When Ivan tried to thrust his body between them, she moved him to the narrow aisle. Deep in the depths of her eyes, sadness still lurked, but it was the deviltry dancing there that held him captive. "If you so choose."

Finally, they'd come to the fork in the road. Apprehension and anticipation twisted down his spine. Which would win? While Ivan whined from the floor and Isobel put him on the opposite bench, Royce thought about her words. "What sort of scandal? We already skirted it the other night with those kisses."

She waved a hand then let her fingers glide down his right arm. "That was naught but a baby scandal and one I've indulged in with other men before."

Something akin to jealousy lanced through Royce's chest. He didn't want to think about her kissing other men. He glanced at her, caught the golden flecks swimming through those sapphire pools of her eyes, and desire tightened his shaft. "I'm not one to blatantly wish to cause a sensation like you."

Briefly, she narrowed her gaze. "Then you're not for scandal?"

"I didn't say that." The last thing he wanted was for her to slip from his grasp.

"Good." She caressed her fingers up and down his arm. Ivan jumped to their bench and attempted to worm his body between them, but Isobel was quite skilled in moving him to her far side. "Should we let impulse guide us then? I don't enjoy making plans that might need breaking later. Especially with how precarious the situation at home is," she added, and the pain in her eyes was more pronounced.

The poor thing! In the face of her rapidly changing circumstances, she was obviously in need of distraction. Alarm bells went off in his head, but blatant need spurred him onward. "I don't see why not. As long as we try to conduct ourselves with discretion. I do have a professional image to protect as well as your reputation."

She leaned into him. "You don't believe I can be discreet?"

The smoky quality of her voice had his prick waking while the warmth of her breath skating across his neck over his cravat nearly drove him insane. All the while Ivan jumped from one bench to the other in the hopes he could gain attention.

Very much like his mistress. How exceedingly odd.

"You tell me, for already your exploits have fueled the gossipmongers." When she huffed, he rushed to continue. "However, I do have one rule."

"Oh?" She dared to trace a fingertip along his earlobe, and he nearly vaulted from the bench. "What is it?"

Acute awareness poured over him. Isobel was a storm, all right, but not the kind a man should run from. Oh no. She was the sort a man chased until he found himself caught up in the middle of it. As much as he wanted to touch her, explore her, he held back, for once he did that, he'd be lost and he wanted the terms of this agreement fixed. "While you and I are enjoying this tryst—"

"Affair," she corrected as she slipped her hand from his arm to rest it on his thigh.

He audibly gulped. "Affair, then," he conceded, for that meant more time in her company, "I want your full fidelity. I want your word I'll be the only man you grant favors to."

"Of course." She squeezed her fingers on his thigh. Need tightened his shaft to the point of pain. "I might enjoy playing men against each other for my attention, but I only give my true self to one at a time."

"Good." Royce rather doubted she'd let anyone see who she really was beneath the façade of a hoyden. "Where and how shall we begin?"

"What about now?" Before he could dissuade her, Isobel moved. She straddled his lap, resting her hands on his shoulders. The need in her eyes he understood, but the longing at the backs he did not. "Doctor Marsden, I want you to kiss me so I can decide how to create a scandal sufficient enough for hooking you."

The damp dress that clung to her frame, the way she held her mouth so that her lips were ever so slightly parted, the heat of her pressed so close to him all worked at his undoing. He rested his hands on her hips, couldn't help but trace her ribs with his fingers. Though taken aback from her daring, his engorged length quite liked this new turn of events. "What makes you assume I haven't already had my interest hooked?"

"Because you haven't kissed me yet."

"Pardon the oversight." He crushed her into his embrace, claimed her lips as he'd wanted to do since their last kiss.

Over and over, he drank from her. He bossed her lips, telling her in no uncertain terms that he wanted her, and soon. As he'd come to expect, Isobel gave as good as she got. Though she was skilled in driving a man wild with a meeting of mouths, the second he cupped her breasts, brushed the pads of his thumbs over her erect nipples, she gasped and pulled slightly away.

Had no man ever dared touch her there, or had she never granted anyone else access like she did him? For that matter, had she ever lain with a man? Surely if she had, such an intimate caress wouldn't come as such a shock.

"Oh!" She searched his eyes, questions in hers, and when she leaned into him for another kiss, Ivan chose that time to lead with his nose. He squirmed between them, his tongue lolling out, and he fairly quivered with happiness at having both of them paying attention to him. With a sigh, Isobel gave into laughter as she scratched behind the dog's ears. "Yet another interruption."

"Next time, leave the dog at home," Royce said. Need and desire graveled his voice. It would take some time for his cockstand to settle, but perhaps that was a good thing, for he could hardly have taken Isobel in the carriage with Jeffries overhearing. Still, there would have been other things to occupy their time.

"Agreed." She encouraged the dog out of the way so she could hold Royce's head between her hands, but just as her lips met his, Ivan burrowed between them once more and this time he licked Royce's cheek. "Enough. Enough. We'll pay attention to you."

Damned dog. Never had he been more jealous of a canine than he was right now as Isobel slipped from his lap to retreat to the opposite bench with the dog bouncing all around her. He cleared his throat. "When is our next meeting?"

"I shall let you know." She winked. "Anticipation makes everything that much more intense; don't you think?"

I think I'm going to embarrass the hell out of myself. Especially if she continued to look at him as if she wished to eat him up right there. "I look forward to it." He turned his attention to the window and willed his erection to settle.

Bloody, bloody hell.

CHAPTER NINE

June 25, 1818

ISOBEL WAVED TO the hired hack driver and then prowled through the shadows of Hyde Park, moving as quietly as she could. An hour ago, she'd sent Royce a sealed note asking him to meet her at half past midnight by the Serpentine when it made the bend into a more secluded section of the park.

Tonight, she wanted nothing to interrupt her time with the doctor, and if it took dallying in this place well after dark, so be it. Additionally, she would tease him until he couldn't stand it any longer, and hopefully it would gain her what she ultimately desired—him.

Her slippers made no sound on the grass, for she didn't follow the bridle path to reach her destination. If all went well, she'd arrive well before Royce, but if it didn't, there was no bother. The outcome would still be the same, but the effect would be ruined... and she did so want to cause a sensation no matter what she'd promised him.

That afternoon in the carriage when he'd tried to comfort her, discover why she'd been so upset at Fanny's pregnancy announcement bothered her more than it should. Had he been asking out of professional courtesy, or did he truly wish to learn more about her? Perhaps she didn't want to know, for that would take some of the fun from their proposed affair.

And she desperately wanted that distraction to keep from breaking.

Finally, she reached a small cluster of trees that would provide enough privacy for what she'd planned. No matter that any point in the park could produce people cutting through on the way home from *ton* functions, a mounted constabulary patrol, or men bent on nefarious violence, Isobel thought it the perfect spot for the good doctor's seduction. The threat of discovery would provide an added thrill to the tryst, and the opportunity to shock him was for her personal entertainment.

Thank goodness the night was warm enough to warrant a swim. With a grin, Isobel sneaked through the trees. All around her, the air held the scents of growing things and the mysterious smell of the river. It hadn't yet begun to stagnate with the oppressive heat of the summer.

When she found a spot she particularly liked for its privacy, she tugged a quilt from the valise she carried. Done in dark colors, it blended easily with the nighttime shadows and wouldn't immediately call attention. Then she dropped the bag, which contained a few foodstuffs she'd purloined from the kitchens as well as a bottle of brandy from her brother's study. If she were going to be truly naughty and wicked tonight, she might as well do everything she'd ever been curious about.

"This is my opening gambit, Doctor. The next move is yours," she whispered into the darkness as she removed her gown of navy satin. If someone should catch her wandering through Mayfair, she'd dressed fine enough to fabricate the lie of coming home late from a society event. Next her petticoat fell to the quilt, followed by her slipper and stockings. Once she was clad in only her fine lawn shift, Isobel emerged from the trees, gained the edge of the riverbank, and then with more haste than finesse, she slipped into the blessedly cool water. Slowly, as she gained her footing, she moved deeper into the river until the water came up to her chin.

Now, she'd wait. Meanwhile, she'd enjoy a quick swim.

It took almost ten minutes for Royce to arrive. The wheels of a carriage crunched upon the small pebbles of the road; the *clip clop* of a horse's hooves echoed in the relative silence of the night. For the space of a few heartbeats, the throb of frog song and the soft calls of night insects ceased, but once the carriage moved away, they began anew.

"Isobel?" The whispered inquiry sent tingles over her skin.

"Royce!" Her answer was as low-pitched while she swam in his direction. "You decided to show after all." She couldn't keep the delight from her voice, but it was difficult to discern him from the shadows. His dark suit blended all too perfectly with the environment. If it weren't for the white of his formal shirt, she might have missed him.

"I made a promise, did I not?" To give him credit, he glanced about the immediate area and then propped his hands on his lean hips. "Where the devil are you?"

"Taking a midnight swim." She splashed a hand in the water. "You should join me."

"Bloody hell." He advanced to the edge of the Serpentine. "You're swimming." It wasn't a question as he peered down at her location. His top hat sat at a rakish angle over his left eye. The silver buttons on his waistcoat twinkled in the light of the waning half-moon. "What the deuce for?"

She shrugged. "Why not?" Daring much, Isobel approached the shallow bank until the water barely covered her breasts. "It's a warm night. There is no one around. And I thought it might shock you."

"Oh, there's no doubt that it has." He yanked off his hat only to shove a hand through his hair, leaving it to stand in rumpled disarray. "Why do you consistently do such things?"

Isobel frowned. She hadn't anticipated a lecture. "What things?" The night wouldn't end in carnal explorations if he continued with his bad humor, so she advanced another few steps until the constantly undulating water line fell at her nipples that had hardened from the cool water.

"Things like this." He gestured at her with his free hand, but his gaze dropped to her bosom more than once.

"We had an assignation, Royce. What did you think would happen?" If there was a hint of frost in her voice, she couldn't help it. He wasn't exactly falling into her web of seduction as she'd hoped.

The doctor huffed in apparent frustration. "It never crossed my mind you'd chase scandal like this."

"How would you have me chase it, Doctor?" Isobel moved two steps closer. Her breasts were out of the water now, and with the shift plastered to her body, surely he couldn't ignore her. "After all, you knew what sort of a woman I was when we made our plans." She danced the fingers of one hand along the neckline of the shift, hoping to draw his attention more fully to her.

"Of course I was aware. It was one of the reasons I was initially drawn to you. That and I have no idea what you'll do next." He tossed his top hat away—a sure sign of agitation. "However, this sort of behavior reflects badly on your family as well as mine."

"How? There is no one here to see me." She came forward more steps. The water lapped at her hips. "I certainly won't tell if you don't."

"There is my clinic to consider. If my name is linked with yours, the gossip could harm my livelihood, Isobel. Did you ever think about that?"

"I did not." Confusion circled through her mind. Did that mean he regretted making plans with her? Was she not attractive enough? Intriguing enough?

He was at the riverbank, his eyes glittering in the darkness. "You need to be taken in hand."

She snorted. "I agree." If her chances of being with him were slipping away, she wouldn't call defeat without a fight. "Are you the man with the stones for it?" Was that truly her voice that sounded so throaty and alluring? How had she done that? To say nothing of the blatant flirting. Had it gone too far?

Royce flicked his gaze up and down her person as she came fully out of the water to stand directly in front of him. "I am not your keeper."

"That's too bad." Slight panic chased through her insides at the thought she'd lost him before she'd ever done anything naughty. She smoothed her hands down the dripping shift. "I suppose I'll continue courting scandal until you notice me then."

"Damnation, Isobel, did you truly think I haven't?" He moved, slid a hand to her nape and tugged her into his arms. "You've driven me to the brink of insanity," he said with a certain growl in his voice that heightened the awareness she already had of him. Finally, he brought his lips crashing down on hers in a kiss that left no doubts as to his intentions.

This was exactly what she'd hoped would have happened! She looped her arms about his shoulders and set out to return his kisses with all the enthusiasm she could muster. The slide of her tongue along his was one of the most erotic things she'd ever experienced; the slight taste of port came away on her palate. Perhaps he'd imbibed before heading out, but it was the strength of his arms about her, the heat of his hands as he played his fingers down her spine that sought to separate her from all common sense.

"You've teased me enough," he whispered against her lips. "It's time I returned that favor, don't you think?"

"I absolutely do." Desire tingled down her spine as she wrenched from his hold only to grab his cravat. "I've already found a fairly hidden spot in the event this meeting turned amorous."

"Where?" Quickly, he freed the length of cloth from her fingers and then tugged at the knot until it unraveled in his hand.

"Follow me."

"As if I could do anything else at this moment."

Isobel grinned. It was all too heady, this power she could wield over a man simply with a handful of words and appearing scantily clad. No wonder everyone wished to chase this sort of sensation. When she reached the cluster of trees, she ducked inside. "I brought a quilt to make things more comfortable."

"Truly, you'll be the death of me," he murmured in a barely audible voice as he swept his gaze about the small area. "I should be committed for agreeing to any of this."

Isobel rolled her eyes. "Perhaps you require liquid courage." She pulled the brandy bottle from her bag and offered it to him. "Don't think about the future or ramifications. I am fully aware of what might happen, and neither do I care."

"Dear God." Royce plucked the bottle from her hand, uncorked it, and then proceeded to take a few healthy swigs. "Please know that I'm not drinking to have the courage to do this." Once more he raked his gaze up and down her person. "You're already a handful and have caught my attention. I'm drinking because your family will call for my murder if they find out we've tarried alone together in any sort of scandal."

"They won't know." She took the brandy from him and tipped it to her lips. After a couple of gulps, she sputtered and coughed, for the spirits burned her throat and tasted vile besides. So much for enjoying *that* vice. "I'm not in the habit of lying, Royce, so when I say that I want you, it's true."

Was that too forward?

He didn't answer in words, but he removed the buttons of his jacket from their holes. Afterward, he did the same with his silver satin waistcoat. Both of those garments left his person in seconds to fall helter-skelter upon the quilt to join her clothing. "That's good to know, for I've wanted you since that evening you read the erotic poetry."

"Oh." Isobel took another healthy swig from the brandy bottle. Her eyes watered when she swallowed. If she weren't careful, she'd fall into her cups due to inexperience with drinking and from not having eaten recently. She'd been too excited to take more than a few bites of dinner.

"And now you're standing here in a transparent shift like the devil's own temptation." He yanked the cravat from his neck, let it drop. The collar and cuffs soon followed as he toed off his shoes. Had he dressed for the easy lie as well or had he come directly from an event? "If you wish to change your mind, please tell me now, for in thirty seconds, I will set out to kiss every inch of your skin and quite possibly devour you."

"Oh!" Heat blazed in her cheeks. His words and the imagery therein sent gooseflesh popping over her skin to further tighten her nipples. When her knees no longer supported her weight, she kneeled on the quilt, the bottle of brandy tilting in her hand. What did one say to a man after that? Then her customary enthusiasm for life kicked in. She recorked the bottle and set it away. "I look forward to it only if you give me the same access to your body."

When he tugged his shirt up and off his body, Isobel gawked at the naked expanse of his chest. What she wouldn't do to glide her fingers over that skin! "That can be arranged. I don't indulge in scandal often, but when I do, I make certain the deed is done properly."

Oh, dear heavens, I think I've caught a tiger by the tail. Heat twisted up her spine as he manipulated the buttons at his frontfalls. It was one thing to tease and flirt with a man while in public or even go so far as to make him kiss her. It was quite another to see one undressing in front of her while alone in a not so hidden place. Then he yanked off his trousers and there was no hiding the fact the doctor's body was pale, as well as the fact he was truly aroused.

She'd never seen a naked man before. Her mouth went dry as she stared. Even though it was dark, and shadows kept her from gawking as clearly as she'd wished, she was close enough to discern the sprinkling of red hair on his chest, follow the thin red ribbon down his lean abdomen with the slightest hint of flab, but the rampant length of him that sprang proudly from a nest of flame red curls sent delicious flutters into her lower belly.

"You are quite... something," she finally managed to whisper.

"I appreciate that." Royce dropped to his knees then easily

joined her. "Don't you think you should offer me the same?" He reached for the hem of her wet shift.

This is truly going to happen. Never had any of her previous scandals gone this far, and never had she met a man she'd let have access to her body. Apprehension chased excitement in her chest, but she nodded. After swatting away his hand, she unashamedly pulled the shift from her body and tossed it away. It wasn't as if he hadn't been able to see her form through the thin, wet fabric. Her next swallow was audible. "Well?"

"Exquisite. Delectable. Enticing." He loomed over her until she had no choice but to topple onto her back as he followed her down. "And, unless I miss my guess from previous meetings, you'll prove highly addicting."

Isobel couldn't help a tiny sigh just before he claimed her lips again. She slipped her arms about his waist, and all too soon she was lost in the wonder of the doctor's form. Oh, but he was so different from her! Hard where she was soft, strong where she was weak, and when he engulfed one of her breasts in an elegant hand, a moan shivered from her throat. "Touch me, Royce. I need to feel your hands on me."

He dragged his lips down the side of her neck. "Once we start, there's no going back," he whispered against her skin. A few nips and nibbles brought him entirely too close to the crest of her other breast. "Do you understand?"

"What exactly do you mean?"

A sigh skated over her skin. "If we do this, I want the whole affair. I want the danger of being discovered. I want you and your whole attention." He met her gaze. "Does that clarify my intent?"

Of course it did. Why did he not think she wanted that too? "Yes, but..." Her ability to form words flitted away when he closed his lips over one sensitive nipple.

"There is no other option." He blew over the wet skin he'd just suckled. The contrast in temperatures pulled another moan from her. "You either accept the consequences—good and bad—or we go no further." Around and around, he swirled his tongue, flirting with the nipple while he did the same to the other with a forefinger. "I brought a sheath, but there are still consequences."

The talk of reality while he worked to ply her with pleasure rapidly brought her out of the cloud of passion that had sunk into her brain. "I'll worry about the future when it comes." Right now, there was only *this* moment, *this* man, and how he made *her* feel. She shoved her fingers through the sparse hair on his chest and then locked her arms about his shoulders. "Show me where to touch you, or shall I go exploring?"

He laughed. The low-pitched sound of it reverberated in her chest, and the insistent hard length of him pressed into her thigh. "If you touch me, I'll be the one carried away and you won't have the scandal you've wanted since we met." The doctor claimed her mouth in a ragged, raw kiss that left her breathless and dizzy.

"So not fair." She arched her back and her thigh brushed his swollen manhood. When he sucked in a gasp, she chuckled. "So mean."

"You're the one who started us down this path, my dear." He shifted his stance, catching her wrists in one of his hands and pinning them to the quilt above her head. "To that end, it's past time to begin your seduction."

Even more unfair when she'd wished to seduce him. But she was soon lost in what Royce did to her. His hands were seemingly everywhere on her body, stroking, caressing, teasing. He had a certain knack for knowing where she liked to be touched even before she did, and perhaps that was his training as a doctor, but she was too far gone to inquire. Every time she attempted to touch him, he batted her hands away, and when he kissed and licked various parts of her body, all the thoughts were forgotten.

Down, down, down he moved, between her breasts, over her torso, kissing a path around her naval and past her mons. When she sucked in a breath, put a hand to his shoulder to perhaps dissuade him, he merely chuckled against her skin and encouraged her thighs apart. Then his mouth was on that most sensitive, private part of her no one had ever seen let alone touched, and

Isobel nearly vaulted off the quilt.

"Royce!" She furrowed the fingers of one hand through his hair, both in an effort to hold him off and keep him closer. "I can't... This isn't proper..."

His chuckle against that part of her, sent a surge of wicked sensation through her. "Of course it's not, but isn't that what you wanted?"

"But I... Ah!" Isobel bucked her hips when he used the tip of his tongue to encourage the bud at her center out of hiding. Heated pressure built and stacked within her. She clutched a handful of the quilt in her free hand while encouraging him closer with the other. This was so naughty, so beyond anything she'd ever dreamed of...

When he left off from that exquisite form of torture, the reprieve was short lived, for he surged back up her body and replaced his fingers where his mouth had been. "A woman's body is one of the most wonderful things the Creator has ever fashioned. It's an unparalleled joy to discover how to unlock those secrets."

Those words rang in her ears; she'd hoard them close them for later. Isobel's thighs quivered. Need pulsed deep in her core. She couldn't concentrate on the words he said, for foreign pleasure completely caught her up in its tide. Her hips bucked, which put her more securely into his care.

And then the most curious thing occurred that changed her life. She shattered, broke, cracked into a million pieces of light. Bliss swept in to flood her from head to toe while a scream of surprise tugged from her throat. As she came down from floating somewhere above her body, she reached for him, holding him closer. A vague sense of unfilled longing roared through her chest.

"Royce, I need... more." She popped open her eyes as confusion took hold. "I don't know how else to explain it."

"Shh, there's no need." The doctor lifted slightly off her. "Just let me retrieve—"

"No!" The sense that if he left, he wouldn't finish her took hold. She grabbed his shoulders, keeping him near. A sense of urgency rode her spine. "I'm not done with you. Don't leave me." For the first time in her life, she'd found someone who might learn to understand her, who could be convinced to accept her, flaws and all. In the darkness, she met his gaze. "Please, Royce?" She wriggled beneath him, being certain to brush his rampant length in the process. "I want you."

Briefly, he pressed his forehead to hers while encouraging her legs wider apart. "You're certain?"

"Yes." A breathless sort of waiting had stolen over her despite the knots of apprehension in her stomach. "Please." Her lips touched his with that one word. "I know my own mind."

"Botheration." He kissed her as he settled between her bent knees. The wide head of his member teased her opening. Then, with a powerful flex of his hips, he speared into her, penetrating her core. When he paused, staring into her eyes, he uttered a huff that sounded much like annoyance. "You truly hadn't lain with a man before." It wasn't a question.

"No." Experimentally, Isobel wriggled into a more comfortable position. "You are my first." Then another thought occurred. "Are you regretting this already?"

Why was she never enough?

"Of course not. It merely took me by surprise." He balanced his weight on knees and elbows. "I won't last, for it's been some time since I last did this."

She couldn't help her grin. With a nip to his chin, she bumped her hips into his. "I hope you haven't forgotten how to do it then."

"I'm not a doddering old fool just yet," he all but growled.

Isobel barely had time to grin before he pulled away from her body. When she murmured a protest, he stroked again, going deep, treating her to slow, rhythmic thrusts that gently rocked them both. Eventually, she figured out how to cant her hips and move with him. It was much like dancing but more intimate and fulfilling. Each time they came together, tendrils of pleasure streaked through her limbs igniting tiny fires in her blood.

Oh, it was such fun, this new experience! She looped her arms about his shoulders, her hands playing up and down his back, but when his pacing increased and became more frantic and faster, she wrapped her hands about his upper arms and tried to keep up the best she could.

All too soon, the familiar bands of pressure stacked inside her again. "I'm going to break," she said in a rushed whisper, unsure of what to do.

"Fall into it. Come with me." Over and over, he stroked, faster and faster he thrust.

Her body stiffened, her toes curled and pointed, and then Isobel was hurtled over the edge into a chasm of bliss greater than the first. She cried out, uttered his name as if saying a prayer, and on his next push into her spasming channel, he found his own release.

"Isobel!" His shout was soon followed by a groan of completion. As he collapsed on top of her, she wrapped her arms about him and held him close. "We probably should have been quieter," he joked with exhaustion clinging to his voice.

She giggled and this time didn't chastise herself for the silly sound. His weight pressing her into the ground was all too wonderful and a new experience for her. Her breathing was as ragged as his, and her heartbeat fluttered like mad, but still she floated on a cloud of euphoria. "That was some of the best fun I've had in years."

"I'm glad." Royce's lips brushed the side of her neck as he spoke, which set off another round of heighted awareness. "If this sort of scandal is in the offing when I'm with you, then I look forward to the next time."

"Neither can I." The moment she stirred, the doctor rolled off her. Immediately, she missed his warmth, his touch, his closeness. But he pulled her into his arms and drew her backside flush to his front. "How long do you think we have before a patrol comes 'round?"

"A quarter of an hour? Perhaps a half?" His breath warmed her ear. "Regardless, I rather doubt anyone can see us here from the path."

"That's good to know." For she was loath to give up this newfound freedom. With a sigh, she snuggled closer to his body. "It's rather lovely to be ruined."

And she hoped to repeat the experience soon.

CHAPTER TEN

ROYCE SHIVERED AS the ambient temperature in the nighttime air cooled. Not wishing to have this unexpected intimacy with Isobel end just yet, he grabbed a handful of the quilt and awkwardly wrapped it around him and the woman in his arms.

The scent of orange blossoms and spice assailed his nose while he held Isobel close, and he frowned into her damp hair that was valiantly clinging to the few pins holding it up. Only then did thoughts besiege him.

Dear God. I've taken her innocence in a fit of pique and uncontrolled desire.

What was more, he'd allowed her to tease him into doing so. Yes, he'd agreed to an affair—but they'd never specified what exactly that would entail—and now here they were, basking in post-coital lethargy.

I'm a physician and a gentleman. I knew better. Yet she'd been like a siren of old, and he couldn't resist her call. And damn if that quick coupling hadn't quelled his immediate want of her. Perhaps now his head would clear, and his concentration would return.

Except, a damned sense of honor reared its head. He couldn't escape his upbringing no matter how hard he'd tried to distance himself from it. With a sigh of regret, he stirred, loosening his hold. The conversation he'd need to have with her wouldn't go down well with her.

Or him if he were being honest with himself.

So, he did what men for centuries had done best: stalled. "We should dress." The patrols through Hyde Park were regular, but he rather doubted from this vantage point they'd be discovered. "And you're cold besides." Beneath his fingertips that he'd unconsciously drawn up and down her bare arm, the gooseflesh was evident.

"Must we?" A pout was evident in her voice. "This has been the singularly most exhilarating night of my life."

Royce couldn't hide his grin. He'd done that for her, had given her a gift that no other man had. "I'm afraid so. This is the downside of scandal. It's always conducted in clandestine locales and the consequences are rather grim."

Which brought him back to his original thoughts. *Grim and life changing for a few stolen moments of pleasure.*

"Then I'll continue to chase it, for I rather enjoy the thrill." Isobel wriggled from their temporary cocoon to rest on her knees. "I'm not of a mind to don the damp shift."

There was no maidenly decorum about this woman, for she apparently didn't care that she was still naked and her charms very much on display. The awe he already had for her edged upward as did his wariness, and damn if his prick didn't shudder to life once more. "Isobel, have a care and cover yourself," he whispered as his gaze dropped to her perfect, pert breasts that were just the right size for play.

Her low-pitched laugh caused havoc with his length. She leaned in close and brushed her lips over his. "We're already nude." One of her hands stole beneath the quilt to find his rapidly hardening equipage. "Why not have another go 'round, Doctor? I've heard enough stories from maids to wish to experiment with various positions—"

"Argh!" Never had he moved so fast or away from a lady with wicked intentions in her eyes. When he gained his footing, it was he who wrapped the quilt about his form as if he were an offended tabby at Almack's. "Devil take it, Isobel. You must practice decorum."

"Why? You enjoyed what we just did as much as I." She grabbed her gown from the grass and then stood.

"I did, of course." Royce tried to avert his gaze, he really did, but the opportunity to behold her naked form in the weak moonlight filtering between the trees was too great. Though she might act the hoyden, spend her time within clusters of males, and prefer to ride astride—dear God, had she ever worn men's breeches?—she possessed enough feminine curves that would sufficiently drive said males wild if given the chance. Isobel resembled marble states of Greek women in the British Museum—pale skin, breasts graced with hardened pink nipples, slightly rounded hips, a narrow waist. To say nothing of the thatch of dark curls at the apex of her thighs that shrouded delicate skin and the sweetest honey.

Uncertainty skated through her expression. "Did you like it enough—like *me* enough—to wish to repeat the experience?"

Well, bullocks. The lady wasn't the least bit hesitant about voicing whatever thought popped into her head. "I'd be lying if I said no." He swept his gaze up and down her person once more before she finally tugged the navy gown over her head and smoothed it over her body. With a tiny sigh, he shook his head and willed away his newest cockstand. "I want more of the same if you're willing."

I'm the biggest nodcock in England for agreeing to any of her schemes.

"I'm so glad." To see the genuine smile curving her kissable lips was worth the price he'd have to pay to remain in the scandalbroth. "I knew you'd be just the sort of friend I needed during this time of my life."

He grunted in response while anxiety knotted in his stomach. After tossing the quilt away, he made quick work of donning his clothing. "I've instructed my carriage driver to return to the spot he left me within the hour. It would behoove you to let me escort you home."

"Why?" She slipped on her petticoat beneath the gown and manipulated the ties at her waist.

"Hyde Park is no place for an unescorted lady after dark." And he'd be damned if he'd walk away and leave her to her own devices after rutting with her as if he'd had no sense in his head. The more time he spent in her company, the more questions bounced through his mind like soap bubbles. She was addicting, and he was in danger of becoming an addict. "Uh, perhaps we should have a serious talk now that things between us have… progressed."

"Why?" Her huff of frustration was all too evident. "Sexual congress doesn't necessarily need to equal in-depth conversation." Even in the darkness, he couldn't mistake the look of askance she shot him. "It was intercourse, Royce, not a binding oath."

Again, his sense of honor warred with the desire to have no commitments. "Perhaps." He did up the buttons on his waistcoat. "Why do you do this sort of thing?"

"What sort of thing?" As she reached for the bottle of brandy, she frowned. The tangled, damp mass of her dark hair swung over her shoulder and hid her face from view.

"Behave like this, as if you're daring everyone to notice you." Hadn't she said as much when she goaded him into this mess?

For long seconds, Isobel drank from the bottle. This time she didn't cough or sputter after partaking in the spirits. Not for the first time did he hope her family was abed once he returned her home, for she looked like sin and before too long, she'd be drunk besides. Finally, she sighed and shoved her free hand through her hair. "I don't know."

Now, that was an outright lie. After he donned his jacket and buttoned it, he gently removed the bottle from her hand. "What are you missing from your life that you need to find it through your irresponsible and at times questionable actions?"

For if anyone was seeking direction from being lost, it was her. Compassion tightened his chest as he stared at her, and his heart went out to her. It must have been hell on her growing up within the Storme family, and it had obviously taken a toll on her.

"Oh, Royce, it suddenly feels as if I've been tossed into an abyss roiling with confusion and fear." She plopped down on the ground to fumble with her white silk stockings. In that ordinary action and with her eyes glittering with sudden tears, she seemed vulnerable and fragile. "My father died years ago. I didn't know him all that well, for he chose to spend the bulk of his time away from his family, especially after he sent Caroline away to the institution."

"Well, damn." He took a drink from the brandy bottle. "I know how that feels. Well, the part about losing a parent. My mother died ten years ago. I was a young man sowing wild oats when I wasn't studying like mad in order to enter medical college."

"Grief doesn't truly fade. It merely sits there and simmers, waiting for me to be caught unaware." She fit the slippers to her feet. "My mother is near death. You know she is, for you looked in on her when you examined Fanny the other day."

"I won't deny your assessment, and I fear she only has weeks at this point. Consumption, in its last stages, completely ravages the lungs." He probably shouldn't have said that, for it wouldn't set her mind at ease, but he didn't believe in lying to a patient's family merely for the sake of softening a blow.

A sound suspiciously like a stifled sob echoed through the relative quiet of the night. Isobel plucked a few pins from her hair. "Now Fanny is increasing, which means my brother's fractured attention on me will become even more so. Caroline is lost to me; she refuses to see any of us even if she lives with Cousin Andrew." Her sigh was heartbreaking. "Above all, I have this anger trapped inside me, never moving but always growing."

"What are you angry about?" Now they were delving into the root of her problems. Royce hesitated to breathe for fear of breaking the spell that allowed her to speak freely.

"I'm not certain." She shrugged. Once all the pins were expelled, she twisted the dark tresses into a quick chignon at her nape and stabbed the pins into them again. "Some of it is for the childhood I never had; it was stolen with worry about my sister and my cousins. Everyone I'd ever cared for was suddenly gone from my life without explanation until I was much older."

"It was all put out into the open at Christmastide last year." That wasn't a question, for he'd witnessed the drama that only the Storme family could put on.

"Yes." Isobel nodded. "I'm still struggling to understand. And when I thought I'd rediscovered my cousins and had hoped they'd play a bigger part in my life, it was only to find they were already ensconced in their own." She sniffed and scrubbed at a trail of tears on her cheek. "Once more I've been forgotten, and that makes me angrier still."

"Not by everyone, surely." Royce put the bottle of brandy into the bag waiting nearby. Then he donned his own footwear.

"That's what it feels like, but then you came along, and I'm suddenly wanted by someone." She raised her gaze to his. It was too dark to properly read the emotions there.

"Yet you keep on seeking scandal to gain my notice."

She laughed, the tinkling sound at odds with the heavy subject matter. "Once I have it, I wish to ensure that I'll keep it."

"There is no danger of that, Isobel." He offered her a hand, and when she slipped her fingers into his palm, he hoisted her to her feet. "I'm well and truly fascinated by you." If only to see how else she'd upend his world despite the potential scandal.

"What a sweet statement, Doctor." She squeezed his hand. "Thank you." For the space of a few heartbeats, she held his gaze. "As I've mentioned before, things are rapidly changing around me, like sand is shifting beneath my feet. What will become of me once Mother passes? I'm very much afraid I'll vanish between the cracks as everyone goes about their own lives."

They were valid concerns. "I somehow doubt you'll let that happen." No one could ignore a storm like her.

"And still I'm angry. I don't want to become what Cousin

Andrew did before he found Sarah." She hung on tight to his hand as if she'd be lost if she let go. "I'm unable to release the emotions stuck inside me. There must be a way since my cousins and even William have managed it, but no one has told me the secret."

"The only secret to doing that is to make a conscious decision to no longer give it the attention it desires, else it will only grow and fester." This sort of thing was more Trey's area of expertise. "If you'd like, you can come by the clinic and talk to my brother. He knows more about the human brain than I do."

"Can he help me feel less like a powder keg, less like a storm hungry for destruction?" The words were quiet, timid, which wasn't like her at all.

"Never lose hope. It's worth a try. Until then, if you should wish to talk, I'm always here." He easily pulled her into a loose embrace. "I'm not certain if that's what an affair includes, but to my way of thinking, both participants should be able to rely on each other for things beyond the physical."

"Thank you." With a tiny sigh, she melted against him, and he held her tight.

They remained like that for long moments. Not talking but communing on a different level than intercourse had provided. Finally, he pulled away enough to peer into her face. "What now? I took your innocence, Isobel. Something must be done."

"Why must anything be done?" She retreated beyond his touch with a frown. "Can we not remain friends while enjoying the benefits of continuing our affair?"

Oh, dear Lord. The woman was a nightmare wrapped in his wildest fantasies. "You're hardly the mistress type though."

"How would you know?" One of her eyebrows arched. She popped her hands upon her hips, that only served to draw his attention down the length of her body to the delight of his hardening member. "Have you kept a mistress before?"

"Of course not."

"Then how would you know?" she repeated with an air of

expectation.

Royce sighed. "While I take no exception to continuing whatever this is," he gestured between them, "I rather think we'll have to marry if word of this tryst gets out."

"We absolutely will not." She snorted. "I'm having too much fun to find that curbed with domestication, and you've already said you're not in the market to wed either."

"Yes, but—"

"No." She waved a hand in dismissal. "You're an earl's son."

"Yet I'm not the earl yet." A thread of annoyance wove through his chest. "And the only title I ever wish to assume is that of doctor. Why shouldn't we wed?"

"You're only doing this out of a misplaced sense of honor and obligation." She yanked the bag from the ground and stuffed her shift inside. "We're not in love, and neither do I want to be. That is a useless emotion and destroys everything." For a second, she glanced at the ruby ring on her right hand. Where had she gotten it and why did it seem to mean something to her? "Why cannot you and I enjoy each other's company as well as bodies and leave it at that?"

"We can, of course."

"But?" Again, that maddening eyebrow arched, and he wanted to kiss it—kiss her—until she stopped arguing with him.

"But you'll need to promise to curb your penchant for scandal." He heaved out a breath. She left him at sixes and sevens, shook him up so much that he had no idea which way was up or out, much like he thought being caught in a whirling storm might. "Bedding you, indulging in assignations is already enough scandal, don't you think?" Except, already his mind worked to provide other locations where they could come together outside the bounds of society.

A slow grin curved her mouth, full of wicked intent that tingled through his stones. "That largely depends on the day." Then she pouted, and that proved even more erotic than the grin. "However, you're no fun, Doctor."

The worry over this first coupling didn't completely fade. "Someone must be responsible."

"Ah, then I should seek out another gentleman to fulfil my needs?" When she attempted to move past him, he sneaked an arm about her waist and dragged her to him.

"I should say not," he said around a growl as he brought her flush to his body. "For the time being, Miss Storme, you are mine." If she was hellbent on doing this, then by God, she'd do it with him or no one. "I'll decide when we're through." Then he brought his mouth crashing down on hers. By no means had his hunger for her been spent. As if he'd been wandering lost in a desert without food or water, he devoured her, explored her mouth, her lips in the hopes of memorizing her merely to analyze every second he'd already spent with her later.

With a sound that was half-moan half-sigh, Isobel flung her arms about his shoulders and met each of his kisses with enthusiasm and wild passion that threatened to carry them away.

For the first time in his life, he didn't care that his actions could put a cloud over his reputation. If he were discreet in his meetings with Isobel and if she could manage not to brag about her conquest, there was no reason why the rumor mills of London should get wind of their activities, and it was the best of both worlds. He needn't marry or attend to responsibilities past what he'd incurred at the clinic, and he could enjoy the company of an attractive, addictive lady in the process. Additionally, the affair would give her the freedom—the security—she so sorely desired, for he suspected that's what she was after with her behavior.

And with each subsequent meeting, he would seek to understand her better, for there was no doubt in his mind that she was hurting deep within her soul.

Struggling for breath, Royce wrenched away. Oh, she was trouble in a big way, and he was well and truly snagged. Like an addict in an opium den, he wanted more and more. "Come." He tugged on her hand. Urgency and need throbbed through his length. "My carriage should arrive soon. We'll continue this there."

She practically purred in response. "I rather like this side of you, Doctor. You're quite commanding when you want to be."

Heat went up the back of his neck. Being in control was what he'd learned from his father when they'd spoken of him assuming the title one day. It was who he was beneath the man he preferred to be, but for the moment, he ignored the foreboding that circled with cold precision through his gut. All he wanted was her body wrapped around his. "Perhaps I'll show you just how much... if you'll stop trying to take the lead."

The woman was a challenge but one he was more than willing to undertake while there was nothing else pressing upon his time.

And God help him keep everything secret from her family...

CHAPTER ELEVEN

June 29, 1818

ROYCE'S LIFE HAD been turned upside down and inside out with the advent of Isobel and their unapologetically torrid affair. Ever since that night at the Serpentine, it had been as if a match was dropped onto dry tinder, and he couldn't have enough of being with her.

For the last week and a half, he'd worked at his clinic like he always did, but the nights belonged to them, and he'd met Isobel in the most clandestine places about London. At one point, they'd even conducted a quick coupling in a wine cellar during a society event because they simply couldn't wait.

Being with her made him feel vital and alive. Her enthusiasm had given him a hunger for life, and the fact they'd managed to be discreet about their relationship always felt like the best joke he'd ever played. Isobel was exactly what he'd needed to find a new appreciation in his existence, and like the strongest opiate, he craved being with her. He'd been touched by a Storme and now finally understood how difficult it was to ignore them.

"Hey." The sound of Trey's voice as well as the triangle of toast smacking him in the head yanked Royce from his musings. "What the devil is wrong with you this morning?"

He blinked, brushed the crumbs from his clothing, and then

focused on his brother. "Nothing that I can see. Why?"

"You've been woolgathering more than at any other time I've ever known you."

"I don't think that's true." He glanced at his breakfast plate and realizing that he hadn't much touched his hamsteak or eggs, he speared a mound of the golden eggs with his fork. "I'm merely thinking about things."

Trey grunted. "Do you have a woman? It would signify since you've been curiously absent from home lately and I rarely see you."

Heat crept up the back of his neck. A woman, a lioness, a lover, an addiction… But to his brother, he said, "My social life is uncommonly busy at present, but no, there's nothing to concern yourself over." He glanced at the carriage-style clock that sat on the mantle. Quarter past nine in the morning. Too many hours to wait until he saw Isobel again.

Another triangle of toast sailed across the breakfast table to bounce off his left temple. "You're sinking into musings again. If I didn't know better, I'd say you're going tip over tail for someone, but since I've not seen you squire a woman about Town, it must be something else."

With a huff of annoyance, Royce brushed crumbs from his person again. Then he threw his napkin onto the tabletop. Clearly, he wouldn't finish his breakfast so why even try? "Would you please leave off?" He narrowed his eyes on Trey, who sat there with questions in his expression and speculation in his eyes. "There is nothing in my life that is cause for alarm. I have much on my mind right now but will work through it."

The least of which was how to grab a cat nap during the days at the clinic to make up for the lack of sleep he was receiving due to bedding Isobel every night as if he were a green boy just out of university.

"I rather doubt that." Trey crossed his arms at his chest. "I know you better than you know yourself at times. To that end, you're lying, and because you haven't told me about it, that means it's something big. Perhaps scandalous."

"Such gammon." Above all, he had to protect Isobel's reputation. As a lady of the *ton*, she was in danger of becoming gossip fodder merely due to the fact she was a woman. Men could have affairs, and no one would bat an eye, but those same tabbies would gleefully tear down the character of a woman for the same sin.

"I don't know *why* you're lying, but I will discover why."

Royce wasn't given the opportunity to reply, for his sister Jane came pelting into the room, abject distress lining her face. He shot to his feet, as did Trey. "What's wrong? Is it Finn?"

"No." Jane's complexion was uncommonly pale. Moisture lingered on her cheeks as a testament to crying. "Finn and I were informed not forty minutes prior. Hadleigh was there when it happened, for he was quite on Papa's side of that same bill. He stayed to try and render what assistance he could…"

She made absolutely no sense. As worry circled through his insides, Royce crossed the room, slipped an arm about Jane's shoulders, and led her to one of the empty chairs at the table while the butler hovered in alarm. "What is amiss? You're quite upset."

"Oh, Royce, it's horrible!" Another round of tears took possession of her, and she gratefully accepted the handkerchief Trey offered. "Papa's heart attacked him last night while he was on the floor of the House of Lords giving one last argument for the law he backed." She mopped at her face. "You know there is heavy infighting in Parliament and he wished to make his party's voice heard."

"What?" His knees were suspiciously wobbly, and he promptly fell into the chair beside her. "Where is he? Why wasn't I called for at once?" He shot to his feet again as the urge to render medical assistance burned strong. "I need to attend to him."

Jane shook her head. She clutched at his hand with her free one. "I'm afraid he expired on the floor. According to Hadleigh, it was all quite sudden. Nothing he or anyone did could revive

Papa." His sister shook her head as tears pooled in her green eyes. "He passed on just after three this morning. But take heart, he was doing what he loved and believed in."

"I can't believe this." Acute pain went through his chest, and he once more sank into the chair he'd just vacated.

Trey came around and kneeled at Jane's side. He laid his hand upon her knee. "Where did they take his body?"

"Hadleigh said he directed the coroner to bring him home." She cried all the harder. "But there's no one there at present and he'll be all alone. Oh, it's horrible!"

"Shh. It will come out all right." Trey patted her knee while shooting an aggrieved glance at Royce. "Good God, but our lives will change."

"Yes, and I'm not ready," he managed in a choked whisper as the enormity of his father's death pressed in on him. Once they laid his father to rest and Parliament approved the legalities, the title of earl would be given to him. Icy fear twisted down his spine. He bounced his gaze between his siblings. His chest was so tight he could hardly breathe. "I thought I had more time."

The whole of his life was shattering around him. What would happen to the clinic he'd worked so hard to build with his brother? How the devil was he to follow in his father's footsteps and do right by the Worchester title? Hot bile rose up his throat. And most importantly, now that he'd be the earl and a titled peer, he would need to cease his affair with Isobel. Suddenly, she was a liability to living a respectful, proper life. Additionally, her behavior was acutely and potentially damaging when that the eyes of the *ton* would be focused upon him.

Dear God. How am I to survive?

But he kept those thoughts to himself. No one would need know. He looked at his siblings. Their faces reflected the same shock and sorrow that churned through his gut. "I hadn't spoken to him for a few weeks; I was too busy at the clinic and with other... matters."

Trey snorted, but then remorse skated through his expression. "Your social calendar aside, I hadn't seen him for just as long. There have been a couple of interesting speakers that have theories regarding how the human brain works, and I've buried myself in reading their papers during my free evenings…"

"Boys, don't lose yourself in guilt." Jane squeezed Trey's fingers and dabbed at her streaming eyes. "How do you think I feel? I've been so wrapped up in my husband and learning how to navigate that new life and all that it entails, as well as my charity, that I've only popped in on Papa here and there." Then she shot him a watery glance. "Oh, Royce, you'll be the earl."

"I'm not ready." Royce could barely speak above a whisper for a wad of tears clogged his throat. "Perhaps I'll never be ready; it's too soon. Too much to ask of me." He rubbed a hand along the side of his face. Worry tightened his chest. "I don't want to do this. What will become of the clinic or my call to heal?" How could he leave that behind to attend to the responsibilities that would come with the title?

"You shouldn't worry about all that right now." Jane leaned forward and grasped his hand. "I don't think any of us was ever ready for anything that's happened to us thus far."

"Indeed." Trey rose to his feet. He laid his hand on Royce's shoulder. "Give it time, Brother. We're here to help in every way we can. Until you're ready, we shall concentrate on living one day and then the other. This is the way of things."

"Yes." Still mired by shock and doubt as well as the inexplicable feeling that nothing would ever be the same, Royce nodded. "There are plans to make, but just now, I'm glad the two of you are here."

July 8, 1818

ROYCE FROWNED AT the rain that dotted the drawing room windows as he stared down at the Mayfair streets. His father had been laid to rest in the churchyard he'd indicated within his will. It was in London, for when they'd buried the countess, his father had wished her close so he could visit her grave often. Now he would spend his eternal rest beside Royce's mother. May they both find peace. Shortly afterward, Royce had moved his belongings into the Marsden townhouse in Berkley Square, for it was only befitting the newest Earl of Worchester would reside there instead of sharing a bachelor house with his brother in the Marylebone neighborhood.

Yet he hated every second of it, for nothing was familiar, and every corner and nook reminded him of his father as well as the grief found therein.

The clearing of a masculine throat at the doorway interrupted his maudlin thoughts. "Your Lordship, there is an Inspector Storme here to see you as well as his sister, Miss Storme."

At the mention of Isobel's name, his heart seized, and his pulse quickened. Squaring his shoulders, Royce turned about. "Very well, Boswell. Show them in here and you might as well bring tea. It's a miserable afternoon, and a trifle chilly with the rain."

"Very good, my lord." Then the butler left, and Royce was alone once more.

He cringed at the change in address. Gone were the days when his father's butler called him Doctor Marsden no matter how many times he'd instructed that good man to do so in the last week since he'd been in residence. But how could he be the doctor when he'd only been to his clinic a couple of times since it was discovered that his father had died?

I'm doing a piss-poor job at tying both threads of my life together.

By the time his visitors entered the drawing room, he'd tamped most of his rising emotions... until he laid eyes on Isobel. *Dear God*, she was gorgeous in jonquil silk, looking as brilliant as the sun itself. How did he ever think he could ignore her?

"Good afternoon, Miss Storme. Inspector."

"You have my condolences, Worchester," the inspector said

with a countenance that conveyed his grief. "Your father was a good, fair man."

"Thank you." His chest tightened, for it was entirely too soon to talk about his father.

Isobel extended a hand as she crossed the room. "I'm sorry for your loss, Your Lordship."

As he took her hand and brought the gloved fingers to his lips, heat careened down his spine, for he wanted her regardless of his personal crisis. Yet when he peered into her eyes, saw the sorrow and disappointment there, he *knew* their status had changed, and it wasn't merely due to him refusing to see her while his immediate life had been in upheaval. He held a title now, and that was something she could never forgive. "Thank you, Miss Storme. Your words are appreciated." Then he kissed her middle knuckle, lingering over her hand a fraction too long before releasing her.

"How have you kept yourself since it happened?" There was a certain hunger in her eyes as she raked her gaze up and down his person, and it fired his own.

"Well enough." He gestured to a grouping of low sofas and delicate chairs. "Please, sit, and for God's sake, leave off with the titles. I am too tired and at enough sixes and sevens to have my friends use them."

"I can't say as I blame you, Doctor." The inspector dropped heavily onto one of the sofas. Isobel perched on the daintily on the edge next to him, but while her brother was relaxed and unconcerned, she fairly vibrated on her cushion. "I imagine your time hasn't been your own of late."

"No, it has not." Tears and emotion crowded his throat. When all he wished to do was whisk Isobel upstairs to his rooms and have his wicked way with her merely to escape his new reality, none of that was possible. Not even if she'd come alone. "I fear for the future of my clinic. It would break my heart if I was forced to close it, but since I'm the attending physician and I'm not there…" He let his words trail off as an ache set up around his heart. "Well, that's neither here nor there and certainly not your concern."

Boswell returned with a tea service. Once he left, Isobel busied herself in pouring out.

Odd, that. Seeing her do something so domestic without complaint bothered Royce more than he would like. She wasn't one to let the dictates of society tame her, and he rather missed the wild and free woman he'd come to know over the last few weeks. When she spilled a few drops, he couldn't contain his grin. Ah, there she was. His hoyden.

"Of course it's our concern, Doctor." The sound of the inspector's voice yanked Royce's attention from the contemplation of Isobel. "You are our friend, and you're related by marriage. You are family, and Finn reminds us all time out of hand that you are an honorary Storme."

"Yes, perhaps I am." He accepted a cup from Isobel. When their fingers brushed, heat rushed to his elbow. She met his gaze. Such want was reflected there that he nearly gawked, but he couldn't betray their secret. "In any event, I don't wish to put my troubles on anyone else's shoulders. It's early days yet. If possible, I shall find a way to sort everything."

Isobel gave her brother a cup as well. When she took up her own, she looked at Royce from over the rim. "What will you do?"

"To be honest, I have no idea." He took refuge in sipping his tea. Thank goodness it was strongly brewed and not softened with sugar. "At the moment, the family is in deep mourning. I miss my brother and the clinic." In a softer voice, and holding her gaze, he added, "There are many things I miss."

Would she know that he meant seeing her?

She nodded. "No doubt there is. In the coming days, you'll need to discover those interests you value most over others."

"Indeed." Royce quickly drained his cup. He set it on the low table in front of him and could barely sit still with having her so close to him yet so far away. "For the moment, and out of respect for my father, I'll not take his seat in the House of Lords until next session, so that is a great burden taken from my shoulders." As he shook his head, he rubbed his eyes with the heels of his hands. "Just now, there is an intensification of party conflict, as the Whig opposition, having gained a few seats in the general election has installed George Tierney as their Commons leader. From what I understand, they've made a strong initial muster and wish to mount a motion of censure against the Liverpool ministry." He heaved a sigh. "It is quite a headache."

The inspector nodded. "Politics is certainly not for the faint of heart."

"Yes, so I'm beginning to realize."

"You don't wish to become involved." The other man's words were not a question.

"I do not, for I am a healer, not a fighter, and I don't enjoy arguing." Again, his attention jogged to Isobel. God, what he wouldn't do to spirit her away and lose himself in her welcoming warm heat. Like an addict dependent on opium, he yearned to touch her, taste her, just one more time before he quit her for good.

"Understandable." William narrowed his eyes. "You don't wish to be an earl either." Again, it wasn't an inquiry.

"Correct." He looked between the siblings. Where they were accustomed to living through upheavals in life, Royce was not. It was taxing upon his spirit to know both sides of himself were at war. "But there is no escaping it. I'm compelled to do my duty to the title. What else can I do? Yet I'm still deeply involved in my calling to remain a physician."

"Why can you not do both?" Isobel narrowed her eyes. Ah, there was a shade of the woman he'd come to know, the lady who challenged every society norm. "There is nothing written in laws or rules that an earl cannot have a livelihood beyond the title." She shrugged. "Why, there are a handful of peers who've gone on to work their trades while holding titles."

"Perhaps, but my father never had extra time, and he was quite adamant that being the earl came first." Another round of sorrow poured over him the longer he talked. Where did that leave him? Somewhere trapped in the middle? To say nothing of the yawning responsibilities which came along with being the Earl of Worchester. Already he was nearing forty quite quickly. Soon the pressures to marry well and set up his nursery, beget an heir, would press upon him. And that would take up even more time away from the project of his heart—his clinic.

"There are times in a man's life when he must decide for himself what he'll be known for, and whether or not he'll be the one to buck tradition." Slight panic lined her face while disappointment threaded through her voice. Abruptly, she stood and shook out her skirts. "We should go, William. I'm sure His Lordship has much on his schedule for this day."

Bloody hell, but she'd made no secret of emphasizing his formal address.

Royce rose to his feet the same time the inspector did. "My calendar is rather bleak at the moment, Miss Storme, for mourning has seen to that."

"Ah, well then perhaps you'll call upon your family if you should need to talk or seek other... comfort," she said as she swept across the room and then into the corridor beyond.

"What sort of bee does she have in her bonnet now?" the inspector wondered aloud while he stared after her.

"Who can say?" he answered vaguely, for he knew exactly why she was cross. Those needs and longings were the same that currently battered him. It hadn't been fair of him to cut off their affair at the legs without explanation and let her form her own conclusions, but everything had happened so quickly, he didn't know how to soften the blow.

But damn he missed her.

The inspector held out a hand. "Truly, I'm sorry for your loss. I am facing the same myself imminently."

Royce shook the man's hand. "Indeed, you are, and for that you have my condolences as well, Inspector."

"William, please." He nodded. "Isobel is right, though. If you should feel the need for family around you, call on either us or Finn. We all understand."

Would he offer such a boon if he knew that Royce had not only stolen Isobel's innocence but had gleefully and without remorse engaged in a heated affair with her? An affair that he sorely wanted to continue?

"Thank you. I'll bear that in mind."

But he knew, deep down in his heart, everything had changed. He couldn't risk having Isobel back in his life in any capacity beyond acquaintances, for she was far too scandalous by nature, and now he had a title to protect.

For the first time he understood all too well what Isobel was feeling with the numerous changes to her life.

Damn it all to hell.

CHAPTER TWELVE

July 11, 1818

I SOBEL LAID IN her bed, staring up at the ceiling, as the long-case clock in the downstairs hall chimed half past the midnight hour. The full moon outside sent shadows skittering over the walls and floor, for she hadn't bothered to close the drapes at the window.

What was the point of anything now that Royce kept himself aloof and withdrawn?

She'd been all too shaken when she and William had called on the new earl. Granted, his life had been thrown into shock, chaos, and grief, but the fact he hadn't even tried to arrange an assignation with her made her nearly sick to her stomach. Was she once again considered not good enough? Since he was a titled peer, did he have no more use for her?

With a huff of annoyance, Isobel flopped onto her side and punched her pillow for good measure. Yes, she still detested any man who held a title within the *ton*, but she'd hoped the doctor would prove different. Sadly, that wasn't the case, for with his absence and silence, he was quickly making himself into the very thing he'd never wished to be.

So she assumed, for when it came down to brass tacks, she didn't know him well at all aside from the delights she'd gained from exploring his body and bedding him in the most unusual and risqué of places.

That thought brought about a grin and a delicious heat moving through her veins. As a lover he'd been incredible, but over the course of being with him, laughing with him, she'd come to rely on him as a friend, and though they hadn't discussed deeply personal things, gut instinct told her he could become a close confidant with very little provocation.

And right now, she sorely needed to talk with someone, for her world was shattering piece by piece about her proverbial feet. It was only a matter of days before her mother would leave this mortal coil, and Isobel could scarcely breathe from the fright that it brought. For the last few days, Wills and Fanny had been keeping constant vigil at her bedside. Isobel attended to her mother when she could but being that close to imminent death only brought about more anger and a sense of hopelessness she couldn't escape.

This is ridiculous.

Lying in bed thinking about a man was beneath her, yet here she was, wondering where he was and what he was doing. It was unbecoming and unproductive, especially when they could be together for a quick tryst. She needed to know if he'd been deliberately avoiding her or if life's circumstances had merely taken his time. Either way, it was all part of the trap of changes that currently shaped her life, and she didn't like it one bit. Isobel flung back the bedclothes. She swung her legs over the side of the bed.

I need answers.

THIRTY MINUTES LATER, she marveled that the Marsden clinic in the Marylebone neighborhood was still open. Granted, it probably wasn't, for there weren't candles or gaslights giving off illumination, but knowing Royce like she did, this was where he'd be.

Moonlight left silver pools over the tidy hardwood floor as she waited on the perimeter of the large, open room that contained perhaps eight cots, all containing tidy stacks of bedclothes and a pillow. The slight medicinal aroma mixed with the more astringent scents of soap and cleanser tickled her nose. It didn't feel as deserted; someone must be in residence, and she hoped to God it was Royce. Otherwise, scandal would once more be her lot, and this time not of her making.

"Doctor Marsden? Are you here?" Her inquiry sounded overly loud in the silence. The rustle of fabric alluded to the fact she wasn't alone. "It's Isobel. I... I thought you might wish for company."

Among other things.

Shadows moved in a doorway at the opposite end of the room. Fear leapt into throat while her pulse ricocheted through her veins, but when the form of the doctor separated from the clinging darkness, she uttered a sigh of relief and relaxed.

"Isobel." He stared with the expanse of the room separating them, and even from that distance it was evident he'd passed more than a few fitful nights. "I fear my mind is tired for it's as if I conjured you here from my thoughts."

"Well, that is a step in the right direction." Quickly, she turned the lock on the door before prowling over the floor toward him. "Uh, I hope you don't mind that I've sought you out." What would she do if he didn't wish to see her in any capacity?

"At this point, I could use the company." He shoved a hand through his hair, leaving it in rows of red disarray. Clad in his waistcoat, shirt with no collar or cuffs or even a cravat and rolled to the elbows like he'd been that evening of the cadaver exam, dark gray breeches and scuffed boots, he resembled a pirate of old, especially with the faint shadow of stubble clinging to his jaw and cheeks. And he was irresistible. A shiver of need careened down her spine. "Yet this is highly irregular."

"As if what we've done to this point has been staid and proper?" she couldn't help but tease as she closed the distance.

"True." His laugh sounded forced, and when she peered upward into his face, the grief and longing that mixed in his hazel eyes tugged at her chest, for it mirrored some of her own struggles. Like he couldn't help himself from touching her, he rested a hand upon her shoulder and drew it down her arm leaving heated tingles in its wake. "Why are you really here?"

It was both troubling and flattering that he knew her so well, and that made some of the bars about her heart rust away and bend. Suddenly, she didn't want to go about presenting a strong front where emotion was frowned upon. Her chest tightened, and once more drawing breath hurt. To her horror, quick tears sprang to her eyes. "Quite honestly, I want to be held, comforted even, and I didn't know where else to go," she admitted in a choked whisper.

"Ah, Isobel." He took her hand and led her into the dark corridor beyond where he'd first appeared. "We can be companions in misery, but I warn you, I've already made inroads into feeling sorry for myself."

"It matters not." The touch of his hand holding hers was enough to make her tremble. For far too many days she'd missed that. When he guided her into a small room at the end of the hall, she frowned. Equally dark and with moonlight filtering through a half-shaded but open window, it contained a desk that was littered with papers and journals and thick books. There was a cupboard under the window, and a narrow bunk on the opposite wall with disheveled bedclothes, as well as a washstand. "Do you spend many nights here?" Clearly, it was an office of sorts.

"It depends upon how busy the clinic was from day to day." He guided her to the bed and gently pushed her onto it. An empty bottle of brandy spun when the toe of her slipper bumped it. Beside it, an open bottle of whisky waited.

"You've been drinking." It wasn't a question, and the fact that he'd turned to spirits stood as a testament to the state of his mind.

"I have. All day, in fact, and pacing myself." Royce sat beside her and reached for the bottle. "Not yet in my cups but close enough that my feelings are beginning to numb." He took a swig, his swallow audible, then he offered it to her. "It'll help, at least temporarily."

She took a few sips and gasped when the liquid burned her throat, but it tasted different than the brandy and provided a smoother finish. "Not bad." The feeling of vulnerability she remembered from childhood came over her, but the difference was that she had Royce... at least for now. "I despise that life is changing on all fronts and I can do nothing except watch."

"I'll drink to that." He took the bottle from her and downed another swallow. "What has happened at home to bring you to my doorstep, such as it is?"

She inhaled, and the crisp, clean scent of him spun through her senses, left her nearly wanting to beg him to make the pain, the sadness go away. "My mother is fading and so very frail." Her words sounded small in the pressing darkness. If not for the warmth of Royce at her side, she would give into the tears that grew in her throat. "I fear it won't be long before she leaves me." A few tears spilled onto her cheeks despite every effort to keep them at bay. "I both want to be at her side but want to run far from there, so I don't need to bear witness to death."

"That's understandable. There is no joy in it, and it only makes a person's life more complicated." He took another drink then placed the bottle on the floor. When she dashed at the persistent tears, he stretched out upon the bed and encouraged her to do the same. With her back flush to his front, he wrapped his arms around her. "Stay with me awhile."

She didn't want him to see her in such a vulnerable state. It didn't go well with the image of the devil-may-care lady she'd carefully cultivated. "But I—"

"Shh." His breath warmed the shell of her ear. "Let me hold you, Isobel. Borrow my strength and let me do the same from you."

There was a certain comfort in that. By increments she relaxed into his embrace and let the heat of his body seep into hers. "I'm so afraid, Royce." Her tears came fast and furious, but she let them fall, for perhaps that was what she needed. "Once Mother dies, I'll be alone. I don't know how to acclimate to that."

He stroked a hand along her torso, up and down, the gentle motion soothing. "You have the whole of the Storme connection around you. That's the wonderful thing about a large, extended family."

"I suppose." Isobel ran her fingers down his arm. "They're your family too." And frankly, they'd rally behind him more than they would her. That made her tears continue. "Caroline is out of reach. She rarely visits, and I rather doubt even Mother's passing will change her mind. William is married and has started his own family. His time is already split. To say nothing of my cousins and their busy lives." A shuddering sigh escaped her. "But I've told you all of this before. Nothing has changed, and I largely feel as if I don't matter. Exactly like I felt during my childhood."

"I'm sorry." He didn't offer empty platitudes or advice; he merely held her and caressed his hand up and down her body. Was he even aware he did it?

"Once Mother leaves me, I'll have no one left to talk with. She was a good listener." Isobel wiped at her tears. The ruby ring twinkled in the moonlight, yet another reminder that a life of domesticity wasn't for her. Perhaps the other Stormes were made for it, but she wasn't. "I rarely took her advice, but she always listened."

His chuckle reverberated in her chest and set off frissons of need throughout her body. "Somehow I believe you don't take advice from anyone." He moved his hand to her right breast, cupping it through the muslin of her dress.

"Of course not," and the words came out as a breathless whisper. "I know myself better than most, so I'll do what I see fit."

"Even if those things rarely bring about the satisfaction or security you unconsciously seek?" he asked in a soft voice. His whisky-scented breath skated across her cheek. "You forget that I know you fairly well too."

That he did. She ignored it and concentrated on how he felt layered against her back. There was a certain part of his anatomy that was *quite* interested as it pressed insistently into her bottom. Imagining that hardness pushing into her core left her heated and needy, but she didn't try to initiate intercourse. For this night, she was all too vulnerable and wished to let him make the first inroads if that's where this interlude would go.

"It's neither here nor there. I'm not a lady in the usual style."

"Ah, my dear, that is the understatement of the year." With a couple of insistent tugs to the loose-fitting bodice—she'd chosen a dress she could manipulate herself without a maid for the stays—he bared that breast. Soon enough, he brushed his wandering fingers around and around that mound of flesh, bringing the nipple to erect attention.

A tiny whimper left her throat. Desperate for either his approval or attention, she blurted, "Over the past handful of days, I've tried to act the proper *ton* lady."

His hand stilled on her breast, and she nearly begged him to continue, but she bit her bottom lip. Well-bred women didn't give into their lustful urges. "Why the devil would you wish to do that?"

"As you mentioned, I've yet to find satisfaction or security, and since the woman I am hasn't brought about those things, I thought perhaps being someone else might." Oh, how she hated herself for both the admission and the wish to mold herself into the same sort of people she despised. *How weak can I be?* Yet it was a trying time.

"Then the world will suffer for the loss of the individual you've become." Once more, he stroked his long, elegant fingers over her breast, and this time, when he trailed the pads of those fingers over her nipple, her poorly stifled moan echoed in the silence.

That little bit of praise temporarily buoyed her spirits. "I failed. Quite miserably in fact." Pleasure rippled over her body at his continued play. "My embroidery thread kept knotting. My attempts at doing watercolors resulted in my paints running into each other. Ivan deserted me when I tried to play the pianoforte. He, in fact, howled his displeasure. And it's become painfully obvious that I do not know how to make a perfect pot of tea." To any other woman, that list of failures would result in self-recriminations, but to Isobel, she shrugged it off. Those skills simply weren't what defined her.

Yet, what did?

"You have much more to give the world than those mundane things." Why did his voice sound strained and tinged with disappointment? "However, it would behoove you to find your purpose in this life. Discover what sets your soul on fire and follow it with fierce determination."

"Like you have with being a physician?" She gasped when he lightly pinched that aching bud. Oh, what she wouldn't give to feel his naked body against hers! During the course of their apparent ill-fated affair, she'd become all too accustomed to sharing carnal relations with him.

"Yes." That one-word answer was graveled with emotions she couldn't identify. "No one should ever feel useless in this world; there is something special and unique waiting for each of us." For long moments, silence reigned in the cozy room while he kneaded and caressed her breast. "I've had years at following my heart. Now I must shift my focus to the title."

With every pass of his fingers, she yearned for more, but talking with him so candidly took some of the edge off her longing too. How curious. "What if I'm unable to find my calling?" Clearly, there was nothing she excelled at except flirting, for it there had been, wouldn't she have found it by now?

"It will come, but you must be open to it, and it might prove painful in the beginning." Royce left off from playing with her breast to draw up her skirting. Once the fabric bunched at her hip, he put a knee between her thighs and encouraged her to rest a leg over his, leaving her body open. "Above all, never let it go once you do find it." He slid his fingers through the feminine curls shrouding her sex, and when he used those talented digits to coax her swelling pearl out of hiding, a strangled sort of moan escaped her. She laid her hand atop his, guiding him to exactly where she needed him to be.

"Royce..." When he took the hint, she sighed. Isobel lifted her arm and wrapped her hand about his nape. She wanted to feel his lips on hers, know that he still desired her even though a gulf of distinction had formed between them. Now they moved in opposite directions and there was naught she could do about it, but here, tonight, in the dark with a relatively cool summer breeze coming in from the window and the moon's light frosting everything in silver, she could pretend nothing had changed.

"Shh." Around and around that button his finger went, and with every pass pressure built and stacked in her lower belly. "That fact of the matter is that you and I can only be who we are, no matter if we've found our purpose." He nuzzled the crook of her shoulder, and the scrape of his stubble over her skin gave a new awareness to their play, a wicked edge she desperately wanted to explore. "There is no escape from that. I suppose there never has been, and I've fooled myself too well over the years."

Her heart ached for him and the desolation that threaded through his voice. Perhaps he was as trapped and as hopeless as she was only in different ways. Though her body grew more and more wanton the longer he rubbed his fingers over that nubbin, she said, "What if that's not good enough?" For while she was quite good at finding scandal, none of that would elevate her in his eyes. Not now that he was an earl, and she was merely the forgotten youngest child of a troubled and volatile viscount.

"We have to hope there's a way to square with that." As he increased the friction and left her panting, he turned her head toward him and kissed her lips.

What if I don't want to?

A release caught Isobel by surprise, but it stole her breath from its intensity. Heat prickled her skin while pleasure tingled through each nerve ending. She moaned into his mouth and curled her fingers into the hair at his nape. Longing still circled deep in her core. Did he feel the same?

"Devil take me for a fool, but I want you. Crave you like the most potent of opiates," he whispered against her lips. Seconds later, Royce shifted on the narrow bed and scooted her body beneath his. "I've missed you like this," he murmured as he fumbled at the buttons of his frontfalls. He nipped at her lips. "Hell's bells, I missed *you*."

"There's nothing stopping you." She wrapped her legs about his, folding them until he was nestled comfortably between her bent knees. Seconds later, the wide head of his member glanced along her sensitive folds to kiss her opening. She held his head between her palms, so he had no choice but to meet her gaze. Questions and sadness glimmered in those hazel depths, now more green than brown. "Don't hold back, for I've missed you too."

It was the closest she'd come to begging, and for once in her life she let someone else take the helm.

"Dear God, do you even realize how wonderful you truly are?" The barely audible words danced through her ears like the most heavenly music moments before he thrust into her body with such authority that he didn't stop until he was fully seated.

She fell down, down, down, splashed into those comforting pools, let the feel of him envelop her in a cloud of bliss and comfort while she surrendered everything to a man for the first time in her life.

Again and again, Royce kissed her. Then he moved, stroking into her with long, tender pushes that gently rocked their bodies together. When he dragged his lips down her cheek, along the column of her throat to play with her exposed nipple, teasing it with his tongue and teeth, contractions in her core began once more.

And still he penetrated her. Over and over, he claimed her body in a dance as old as time itself with such care that tears stung the backs of her eyelids. She smoothed her palms along his shoulders. The quiet strength of him as he held her within the cage of his arms brought her closer to the security she'd longed for her whole life. Isobel clutched him close, fairly clinging to him in an effort to become one, loathe to let him go, for he'd become the one constant she could count on in recent weeks.

What seemed like endless seconds passed as they communed without words. Their bodies glided together. Her shift lay plastered to her back from the sweat of her exertions. She kissed his mouth, licked a path on his neck, and as her lips encountered the skin where his stubble began, the contrast between smooth skin and that erotic roughness sent her into a whole new level of delight.

Royce halted his movements. She popped open her eyes, fully intent on questioning him, but the look on his face stole her words and her breath. The emotions there were too shadowed for her to fully identify, but the longer she held his gaze, the farther she fell down a slippery slope she'd never come close to before.

In the space of a few heartbeats, they floated in a realm that no longer included the moon-frosted clinic. Instead, Isobel felt much like flying, but in a different way than intercourse could ever do. She lost a couple of pieces of her soul to him in that moment, and in return, she received matching bits of his. In that perfect second of time, she belonged exclusively to someone and if was as if she'd waited for this to happen since the day she was born. And what was more, she'd found someone who would understand her, who would accept her despite her flaws.

"Royce..." The sound of his name in her voice broke the magical spell.

"Right." He resumed his quest to send her into madness, for his thrusts grew more frantic as if he remembered what he'd been doing. Harder, deeper, faster he drove, and it was all Isobel could do to match his rhythm. In the end, she didn't even try. With her earlier surrender, she merely wished him to take care of her needs. Higher and higher she floated as the terrible pressure and need built inside of her.

"Almost." She touched her nipple, rolled the bud, and the additional stimulation was exactly what she required to dive over the edge of the precipice into bliss. "Royce!" A white void sucked her under, full of pinpoints of rainbow-hued light as she broke into a million pieces to join with it.

He grunted, thrust as deep as he could go one last time, then the doctor followed her into the valley of pleasure. While he ground his pelvis into hers, his member jerked and pulsed. The warm jet of his seed filled her, and she reveled in it. "This… You…" He claimed her lips, treated her to long, drugging kisses that had her body shaking in renewed hunger and joy. Finally, he rolled onto his side and took her with him. He held her so close, their heartbeats jumbled together, and his labored breathing rasped in her ear. "Bloody hell, Isobel."

"I know." She wrapped her arms about his middle and rested her head on his shoulder. For a long time, and certainly until well after her breathing returned to normal did she remain in his embrace. But there will questions she had to ask. "What now?" Her voice sounded small and slightly muffled against his shirt. "Will you continue to work in the clinic?"

He hesitated, so slightly most would miss it, but not her. "I'm not certain yet." That gave her pause, but before she could say anything, he continued. "What will you do once your mother passes? Will you stay in Town?"

Was that a wistful note in his tone or her imagination? She curled a hand into the fine lawn of his shirt. "I don't know. I was young when my father died so don't remember much of that time. Now, I suppose I shall have to be a part of it." The urge to cry rose up in her throat. Isobel swallowed a few times to stave it off. "I detest that death changes everything."

"You and me both," he said in a barely audible voice. His

arms tightened around her, but she didn't mind. It made her feel safe and wanted. "Perhaps it means you'll receive a distinct lack of attention." Though there was obvious teasing in his tones, she still teared up.

"Yes, exactly." A few of them escaped to her cheeks, and she let them fall. Perhaps emotions weren't all that bad after all. "Being grown is more difficult than I'd anticipated."

"It usually is." His chuckle washed over her and brought her unexpected comfort. "But this too shall pass."

"I know, and where will that leave us?" There was no answer, of course, and she snuggled more fully into his body.

For a long time, they lay entwined together as the night feel deeper around them. There was no heat or passion exchanged between them now, only mutual support given and received. In that small handful of moments, there were no demons to vanquish or decisions to make.

There was only peace and rest. As Isobel's eyes fluttered closed, she sighed. *I could become all too used to this...*

Chapter Thirteen

July 15, 1818

Royce frowned as he was shown to the Earl of Hadleigh's table in a private room at White's in St. James Street. Never once had he set foot inside the lauded gentleman's club. Once he'd made a name for himself as a physician, if he frequented a club, it was usually Boodle's or occasionally Brook's across the street from the other establishment. But those nights were few and far between. His clinic and ongoing study claimed his attention, more often than not.

And recently, there had been Isobel…

But when a missive from the earl had been sent over with a time and location for an impromptu meeting, he'd been intrigued enough to attend. Except, the timing was atrocious, for when the earl's note arrived, it had come with a short scribble from Isobel asking him to meet her tonight at Viscount Radford's ball, for socializing and other more… interesting endeavors.

Now that was delayed, he wasn't best pleased with the prospect.

"Good evening, Hadleigh," he greeted the earl, and then nodded at William as well as Finn. "This is a surprise. I was given to understand you rarely attended a club," he said in a blanket statement to include the two men as he took the remaining chair opposite the earl's position at a highly polished cherrywood table.

They both shrugged. Finn glanced at him with a somewhat annoyed gleam in his eye. "We don't. However, we were summoned."

"Ah, so then I'm not the only one." That only gave him a modicum of comfort. Once more, he glanced at the earl. The man didn't appear to be in a temper, nor did he seem overly distressed, though the signs of fatigue were evident on his family. And well they should be. His infant girl was nearly three months old. "What has occurred to bring you to this pass?"

"All in good time, Doctor."

A waiter came over to their table. He deposited a carafe of brandy as well as a couple of bottles of wine and a collection of crystal glasses. With a nod to the earl, he departed on silent feet. The low hum of conversation as well as a smattering of masculine laughter wafted into the room from the bowels of the club.

Royce raised an eyebrow. This certainly didn't bode well. "You must feel bothered about something if we've all been ordered here instead of having such a conversation in your drawing room." He poured out a measure of port into the appropriate glass and drew it toward himself. "Why not just come out and say it? We are all busy men."

Both William and Finn nodded their agreement.

"Indeed, Cousin. There are other ways I could choose to spend my time," William said as a slight flush rose over his cravat.

Finn snorted. "We all know what that means." He shifted in his Bath chair and wheeled the contraption closer to the table. "You're still much a newlywed, Inspector."

Good natured laughter went around the table.

"Yes, well. There is that." William cleared his throat. "To say nothing of my mother's health. Her time is near, I'm afraid, and I'd rather not spend too much time away from home."

That reminder put a sober pall over the proceedings.

"I understand." The earl poured out a measure of brandy into a snifter. His eyes reflected grief. "You have my condolences during this difficult time."

"Thank you. Francesca is sitting with her during my absence."

Royce couldn't help himself. "And your sister? Is she taking turns relieving your vigil?" How desperate was he that he craved merely hearing her name spoken aloud?

"Isobel tries, of course, but she's more sensitive about these things than the rest of us, so she'll pop in and sit with Mother for about twenty minutes before she flees." William shrugged. "I can't say that I blame her, for she was young when our father died, or even when Hadleigh's father gave up the ghost."

Finn nodded. "Death, for her, is a relatively new experience."

"Yes, and in recent days, her attendance on any of us has been anemic. I fear once Mother expires it will make her even more open to scandal. Grief often makes people do things they normally wouldn't, and she's always been more headstrong than I would like."

Royce tamped the urge to grin. Headstrong? Isobel was more aptly described as a storm that blew in and shook everything up, leaving men in disarray once she left.

"Yes, and that is one of the reasons I've called you all here." The earl rapped his knuckles upon the highly polished tabletop. When he had everyone's attention, he sighed. "I have reason to suspect Isobel is sneaking out to meet a man for scandalous intent."

Apparently, this wasn't much of a revelation, for none of the men's faces reflected shock or even surprise. Royce, to his credit, merely raised an eyebrow despite the fact that his pulse had accelerated. "Why do you assume this is true?" And if did think exactly that, why had the earl summoned *him* here?

Good God! Does he suspect I'm the man she's meeting?

"There have been a few rumors circulating through the gossip mills that her attendance at various events has been abbreviated."

"Meaning?" Royce asked in what he hoped was an even

voice. He willed his fingers not to tighten overly much on his glass.

"Meaning that she'll arrive and perhaps spend a half hour before she vanishes. Unfortunately, the gossipmongers haven't been as forthcoming in the identity of the man—or men—she's chosen to accompany, if that's even what she's doing."

"So you've chosen to malign her reputation within our family based on hearsay?" Finn snorted. "Since when do you put much stock in what comes from the gossips?"

"When the Storme name is continuously bandied about," Andrew said with narrowed eyes. "I've worked too hard to keep our family in respectability, and I'd assumed the danger had passed once William married." He leveled a look on the inspector. "However, Isobel is proving that not only have I been wrong, but that she'll soon bring scandal right to my doorstep."

"Drew is correct. I've also been concerned about Isobel's comings and goings." William nodded as he poured out a measure of brandy into his own snifter. "Or at least I was a few weeks ago. I'd even seen her sneaking out of the house well after dark. She doesn't return until the wee small hours of the night, always disheveled."

Bloody hell. Royce took a rather large gulp of his port. Would their indiscretions soon be discovered?

"Indeed. I've heard the same." Slowly, the earl nodded. "However, I'd hoped she'd finally come to her senses, for the gossip had died down in recent days, and from everything I've seen, she's stuck close to home." He shrugged. "You've even confirmed that, William."

"I have." The inspector drained his brandy in two large gulps. "She'd been quite sad for a long stretch of days, as if her best friend had died, but since Isobel doesn't have many close friends, I doubted that was the cause." He heaved a sigh as he set his snifter on the table. "Then last night when I came to relieve Francesca at my mother's bedside, I witnessed my sister sneaking down the corridor. She was dressed in dark clothes no doubt clearly chosen to help her blend in easily with the shadows."

Finn fought off the grin that tugged at the corners of his lips. "Perhaps her clandestine behavior was for something else entirely. There's no evidence she was going to meet a man for a tryst. There is every possibility she wished to attend a secret meeting for the advancement of women's rights or some other such business."

Andrew scoffed. "Except our cousin hasn't shown a proclivity since we've known her."

Out of necessity, Royce took another gulp of his port. Last night with Isobel had drawn him closer to her than ever before. It hadn't been his intention to have relations with her, but once the discussion was underway and she'd let him see her vulnerability when she'd never done so prior in their relationship, it had seemed the next natural step. And during that intimacy, he'd felt as if he'd given pieces of himself to her, that they might have come to a mutual understanding. So much so that they'd lain together in the empty clinic for a couple of hours following coitus. There had been no commitments, no decisions, no realizations that they were probably not well-suited. He'd simply held her, and it had been the most glorious night he'd ever spent with a woman.

Something he refused to share and would guard possessively.

"This is rather a sensitive subject and one that should be discussed among family," he said with a healthy dose of wariness. "So why am *I* here?"

All three men focused on him. So much so that he had to quell the urge to tug at his suddenly too tight cravat. It was the earl who broke the silence.

"You are an honorary Storme and a doctor besides. I thought you might bring a different insight to this discussion."

"On whether or not Miss Storme has taken a lover? Sometimes there are no obvious signs." At least he hoped not, but then he hadn't exactly seen Isobel outside of their clandestine meetings…

William rolled his eyes. "My sister has always been a bit on the wild side. She hasn't appeared changed, this is true, and she remains the same tart-mouthed sibling she's been in recent months." He shrugged. "Perhaps she hasn't found a lover, but I don't like the idea she's sneaking out of the house."

"I rather think Cousin Isobel is more intelligent than to stumble back home looking like she's been thoroughly bedded," Finn added in such a droll tone that Royce couldn't tell if he was joking or not. "And if that's the case, then the man she's taken as a lover must be quite clever as well." For a fraction of a second, the man glanced at him with speculation in his gaze before sweeping his regard to his brother. "Regardless, if this is what she wishes, it's her life and her decision. We have no part in it."

"Poppycock!" The earl's exclamation made Royce flinch in his seat. His face reddened, but then he took a few deep breaths and eventually he calmed. "I am the head of the Storme connection now. The lives of my brothers and cousins are my responsibility." Again, he drew another deep breath and let it ease out as he looked at all of them around the table. "Even when you're married and settled, I will still worry over you."

William snorted. "Don't you have your hands full with a new baby?"

"Don't you with an increasing wife and a newlywed at that?" the earl shot back, but both men wore cocksure grins that alluded to a life Royce was quite left out of. "It's because of your distraction that Isobel is in this mess."

It was Finn's turn to laugh. "Knowing our cousin as we do, I'm rather certain she'd find and coax trouble even if none of us were married. I knew it as soon as she read those pieces of erotic poetry last month."

Both Royce and William exchanged amused glances. Oh, if only these men knew that evening had been the jumping off point to scandal he continued to chase with Isobel.

"Undoubtedly, that is true." Andrew sobered. He took a sip of brandy. "However, if she lands in more disgrace than she's currently courting, it will reflect poorly on all of us, and now we have another generation to worry over. The children don't need any sort of taint on their names."

Knots of anxiety pulled in Royce's belly. That was something he hadn't considered. To say nothing of the fact that he and Isobel hadn't been as careful as they should have each time they'd indulged in intercourse. If something occurred, it would change both of their lives forever... and she would hate him for just as long. "Surely it's not as bad as that."

"Perhaps not just yet. What she needs is to be matched." The earl glanced about the table. "Does anyone have a qualified candidate that has the nerve and drive enough to tame her?"

Royce frowned. "Why would you want Miss Storme tamed? Yes, her personality is a touch more wild than other women, and yes she's a bit more unstable than others, but if you match her with a man who'll take that from her, will she be the same woman?" His chest tightened with annoyance, for he didn't like the thought of any other man being in her company.

"Interesting theory, Doctor." For long seconds, Finn rested his gaze on Royce's face. Could he tell just by looking that he'd been lying? That it was he who'd willfully engaged in illicit activities with the major's cousin? "And one we should all consider, for when we married our wives, we certainly wouldn't have if they hadn't met us toe-to-toe in all matters."

"Hmm." The earl sat back in his chair. "Meanwhile, ponder your connections. The trick is to see her hooked before she realizes she's caught."

Sitting there casually discussing Isobel's potential future brought back the urge to retch. She was not an obligation to drop if one was tired of her, nor was she a piece of meat dangled to the nearest lion. Quickly, before he could voice unwelcome outrage, Royce took another sip of his port. "Where is Miss Storme tonight?"

William sighed. "She mentioned going to Radford's ball but that if it proved dull, she'd come home early."

"Ah." Here was the opportunity he needed. "As a matter of course, I've been invited to the same event and am late. I could watch over her tonight and escort her home if you'd like."

Dear God, would these men see through the thinness of his excuse? He hated to keep putting the wool over the eyes of his friends, but seeing Isobel again won out over caution.

"Excellent idea." The earl nodded with enthusiasm. "Best you do the pretty whenever you can since you'll come into a title of your own once the powers-that-be give you the nod of approval." He chuckled. "A man's whole life changes once he's handed a title."

"Don't remind me." The feeling of wanting to retch climbed Royce's throat. He swallowed a few times in succession to keep it at bay. The facts stared at him with unrelenting accuracy. He needed to let Isobel go and focus on courting a woman much better suited to being a future countess, a woman without scandal and rumors attached to her name. He owed that to the title and his father's memory. "I should go." As he rose to his feet, Andrew lifted a hand.

"Of course, of course, and let me say how much having a man of your sterling reputation looking out for my cousin eases my mind."

Bloody, bloody hell. Hot guilt poured through Royce's chest. None of the Stormes deserved his current deceit. They'd been nothing but kind to him.

"However, I do have one last item of interest to impart."

"Oh?" Please don't say someone in the *ton* had seen him together with Isobel in a compromising position.

"I had a letter from Brand yesterday." Everyone looked at him with interest. "His wife has been safely delivered of a son at the end of June." The earl beamed, as if that was the best of good news, and Royce gawked. Truly, the man was changing for the better. "My mother and Lady Jane are even now planning to visit them in Ipswich."

Quickly, Royce took up his glass. "To the new parents. May

they know nothing except happiness and hope."

"Here, here!" Finn said, but there were haunted shadows in his eyes as he lifted the port bottle.

Poor Finn. Royce's heart went out to him. As of yet, he and Lady Jane hadn't been able to conceive, yet he was forced to watch while his immediate family expanded in ways he couldn't help. Then dread mixed within his chest to tamp the anticipation at seeing Isobel again. "May we all be fortunate enough to find happiness on whatever paths we trod," he added in a soft voice, for whatever he decided, someone would be hurt.

IT TOOK ROYCE the better part of an hour to locate Isobel at the viscount's home. There was quite a crush inside, and since it was a fair enough night and hot besides, guests had spilled out onto a back terrace that looked out onto the tranquil green space of Hanover Square. She was there, standing at the stone railing, peering unfocused into the gardens below.

"Miss Storme," he said softly as he joined her, his shoulder barely brushing hers. "I apologize for my tardiness. Hadleigh summoned me for a meeting that I couldn't refuse."

"Already making excuses, Doctor?" she said in quiet tones but didn't look at him. "You're well on your way to acting like a titled gentleman, aren't you?" In the illumination from the drawing room, she fairly glowed with her own light in a gown of silver satin, the same one she'd worn for the masquerade ball they'd crashed. An overskirt of some sort of fine mesh sparkled with her every movement. It was if she'd fallen from the star-strewn sky merely to tarry with him.

And I'm about to play the cad.

Icy fingers traced down his spine. Once more the ugly specter of change loomed between them. Despite the other couples mingling on the terrace, he briefly touched a gloved a hand to hers. When she met his gaze and he spied the annoyance glinting in those blue pools, his unease only increased. "It has nothing to do with the title." If his words were sharper than he'd intended, he had good reason. Did she not understand the strain he was under?

"I wanted you to meet me here tonight for food and dancing. That we might have met in the shadows of the garden for a bit of heat and friction. You need it—*I* need it—especially after what we shared last night." The tiny waver in her voice spoke of her high emotions, and it tugged at his chest. "Yet with your actions you've shown that such things aren't important." She lowered her voice so much that he had to lean toward her to hear the rest. "That *I'm* no longer important."

Damn. She was falling back into old patterns, thinking he, too, would leave her life. He kept his voice just as low. "While it's true that I'll be an earl as soon as the legalities of it go through, none of that negates our friendship, our relationship." Would she see the lies of that in his eyes? He would leave her, of course, because his life demanded it. "I cannot flaunt the rules of the *ton* any longer. Please say you understand?" A part of him acknowledged he'd come to the ball tonight to put an end to their affair before it became evident to society, but a part of him rebelled against the idea. Yet the Storme family shouldn't have to have the imminent discovery of this affair looming over their heads.

What was everything so suddenly confusing?

"Bah!" She waved a hand in dismissal and put a few inches of space between them. "I understand you are losing your identity, the very things that made you... you when I first became acquainted with you last Christmastide." Unnamed emotion gave her tone a smoky quality that went straight to his prick. "That's a crime, and it's not fair to you."

He reeled from her words, for she was right. Then he shook his head. "It's always been my fate. If not now, then years from now." Though he'd been adept at ignoring it, he was the firstborn son. It was always evident he'd eventually become the earl.

"No." Isobel shook her head. Infinite sadness reflected in her eyes. "The title is who you are known for at present, but you will always be a doctor." Her sigh ruffled a few escaped dark curls on her forehead. "Don't abandon that. If you do, you're not the man I thought you were."

His heartbeat quickened. "Why do you care?" Was it possible she'd developed romantic feelings for him?

She darted her gaze to something over his left shoulder. "I'm not certain."

Ah, that was a lie. "Well, you aren't after my title." His laughter was a tad forced.

So was hers. "No, I'm not." When her chin quivered, he nearly threw himself on his knees at her feet to beg forgiveness. "I never wanted any man's title, and the fact that you have one frightens me, for I will lose you in a different and more wretched way than I've lost others in my life."

The divide between them grew. "How so?"

"You won't have died, which means I'll be forced to see you move within society knowing I'll never again have you."

His throat tightened. *Devil take this life!* Both sides of him warred, to say nothing of his own budding feelings for the woman before him. Royce shoved all of those thoughts to the back of his mind as the string quartet struck up a few preliminary chords of a waltz. Some of the couples on the terrace moved back into the drawing room. Slight panic welled in his chest, for his time with Isobel was extremely limited. "Please indulge me in a waltz."

"I don't feel like it." She took another step away.

"Isobel, please?" He dared to take her hand. The other couples who'd decided to linger had returned inside. "We needn't go inside to enjoy a dance." When she still hesitated, he tugged her away from the open French-paned doors, down the flight of stairs, and then led her into the garden until trees and shrubbery hid them partially from the windows. "Don't think beyond tonight. Let us both enjoy ourselves as you intended. The future can worry about itself when it comes."

You're naught but a fool, Marsden. A fool who's well on his way to becoming a lovesick puppy.

Perhaps that was true, but how could he deny it when Isobel smiled at him and that adorable, wicked gleam returned to her eyes? It would seem his addiction hadn't quite been conquered, and for the moment he didn't care.

"I would like that very much."

"As would I." Though Royce cursed himself for a bacon-brained idiot twelve times over as he took her into his arms, he ignored the warnings screaming through his head. There would be other days to disappoint her and tonight would only postpone the inevitable, but he cared not. For the moment, she was still his.

When the first notes of the waltz reached their location, he started them off. Due to the close confines of the garden, he was obliged to adjust his steps, but the dance was no less magical. Her skirting swirled about his legs; her breasts brushed his chest, for he held her closer here in their shelter than he ever could inside that drawing room.

"You are beautiful tonight," he murmured with his lip near the delicate shell of her ear. "It's inconceivable to think you haven't managed to charm some poor gentleman inside." The floral scent of her combined with the heat of her as they moved in ever tightening circles sent him closer to the edge of reason.

Isobel's smile could light up the night, but instead, she gave it only to him. "I'm glad you noticed."

"How could I not? You've made certain of it from the first." And fool that he was, he continued to follow her when she led him a merry chase, for he craved her company.

She drew her hands up his arms, slid them along his shoulders, and pressed herself closer, forcing them to a halt. "Would that nothing had to change. I've fully enjoyed this affair." The warmth of her breath skated over his neck just above his collar, and his control faltered.

"So have I, which is odd because I never knew just how much I look forward to each one of our meetings." How could he give her up in the face of his title? For that matter, how could one woman be so good for him yet so bad? He refused to be the first Earl of Worchester who set fire to the title due to scandal and gossip no matter how utterly captivated he was with Isobel.

"Then we should continue on as we have." With a few insistent pushes, she urged him deeper into the shrubbery and foliage. The pungent scents of evergreens and other green fauna assaulted his nose, but he hauled her hard against him. "I want you."

"I've never known a woman quite as voracious as you." Regardless of how hard his length had grown or how great the urge to claim her body was, he tamped on those feelings. The risk of discovery was much too high, and soon he'd be thrust into society in a different vein than he'd been before. Proper etiquette had to be observed, and soon.

"Perhaps I merely needed the right man to bring it to the forefront." Isobel lifted up onto her toes and pressed her lips to his. With her eyes wide open, she watched him, waiting, but for what he couldn't say. When she applied the slightest pressure at his nape, he was lost.

"What am I to do with you?" he murmured. Seconds later he crushed her into his embrace as well as the greenery and set out to kiss her senseless. There was still plenty of time to play the cad and call an end to what they shared.

While heat and passion clouded his brain and he explored every centimeter of her sweet mouth, Royce finally acknowledged what he'd been denying for a few days now. He was in danger of falling in love with Isobel... if he hadn't already started.

Bloody, bloody hell.

Chapter Fourteen

July 14, 1818

"Isobel!" Urgency rang in the whisper. A jostling to her shoulder followed. "Isobel, please wake up."

With sleep still clinging to her brain, she came to consciousness and blinked her eyes open to find Fanny leaning over her. Worry and sorrow filled her expression in dawn sunlight that flooded the room. Had her friend thrown open the curtains or had a maid? And why the devil was she being so violently encouraged to awake so early?

"What's wrong?" Isobel levered up on an elbow. It couldn't be good if Fanny was here.

A few tears slipped down her friend's cheeks. "Perhaps it's better if you come to your mother's room."

Immediately, her heartbeat quickened. "Is Mother...?" She couldn't bring herself to utter those words that would make the inevitable final.

"Please come." Fanny dabbed at her eyes with a crumpled handkerchief.

Without hesitation, Isobel flung back the bedclothes, swung her legs over the edge of the bed, and then vaulted to the floor. She grabbed the dressing gown of Chinese silk from off the back of a nearby chair, and as she followed her friend down the corridor, she donned the garment, but the cool silk didn't bring her comfort or confidence in this moment.

At the door to her mother's bedchamber, Fanny paused. "She passed from this world sometime in her sleep. Quietly. Peacefully. William was with her," she explained in soft tones. "I'll leave you alone with him so you can grieve together."

Even though the news wasn't unexpected, Isobel's heart broke and the pieces crashed to the floor. With knots of worry and regret pulling in her belly, she entered the room where she'd spent many hours talking to her mother about whatever had come into her mind. "Wills?" Her brother sat on a wooden chair at the bedside where her mother's body lay peacefully, his head resting on his folded arms. "When did she go? Why didn't you come for me?"

He lifted his head as she moved to his side. "It happened so quickly, I wasn't certain that's what was occurring." Her brother stood and offered her the chair. "Dawn broke. Mother stirred. She briefly woke, looked at me, patted my hand." Exhaustion lined his face, but grief shadowed his eyes as he took her hand. "She told me to look after you and Caroline, told me to tell Caroline once more that she was sorry. Said she hoped the man you were seeing would be everything you'd hoped he would, and then she trained her gaze to the window, smiled, and said Father was waiting for her." He shoved his free hand through his hair. "She left this world with a smile. I'd like to think she's finally out of pain and that she's free from guilt and regret."

"Oh, poor thing." She'd told her mother everything that had currently bothered her, including the fact she'd willfully entered into an affair with someone. Thank goodness the name wasn't betrayed at the last. "We said our goodbyes yesterday, but I'll never forgive myself for not being here when she went."

"You couldn't be here every second." William enfolded her into a hug. He let her cry into his cravat before he set her away. "I'd only just relieved Francesca."

Isobel nodded. Panic quickly climbed her throat as she gazed down at her mother's still form. A slight smile played about her faded lips. Peace made her pale face beautiful again. *What will happen to me now?* Grief battled with anger in her chest. Life was so unfair to take her one remaining parent from her when she needed her the most. Tears welled in her eyes, and she took shallow breaths to stave off the need to rail at someone or something. "What do we do?"

"There are plans to be made." He put an arm about her shoulders, but at the moment she didn't wish for comfort and pushed him away.

"Will we bury her in London?" From the depths of her memories, she recalled that her father had found his eternal resting place in a vault on the Derbyshire property, surrounded by generations of other Stormes.

"No. She'd indicated that she wanted to lay beside Father." Emotion graveled William's voice. He frowned as Isobel slowly retreated toward the door. "I'll make the arrangements. We'll leave for Derbyshire within the week. I expect you to attend the services. No more of your inability to give serious matters your full notice." A hint of censure rang in his tones.

Another load of guilt piled upon her shoulders. Her whole body shook from the force of the emotions she'd kept back over the years. She would break from them and soon, and she'd rather not do that in front of her family. "I rather think it's no one's business how I conduct my affairs or how I keep my emotional state." Her throat was tight, her words stilted. She balled a fist in the voluminous folds of her night gown.

"You're going, Isobel. On this I'll have no argument." He pinned her with a hard glance. "You owe it to Mother's memory to behave just this once."

A couple of tears escaped to her cheeks. *Oh, God*, her heart felt as if it would twist right out of her chest. The shock of everything came hurtling into her at once, and she gasped from the force of the blows. "Someone will need to inform Caroline." It was all too much to contemplate just now. She pressed a hand to her throat. "Will this affect her negatively, send her further into herself and away from the family?"

"I don't know." William shook his head. "Francesca is sending over a missive to Cousin Andrew. Perhaps he'll have advice… or you could tell her. It might go over better coming from a woman."

"I couldn't!" Isobel gasped. Her world was collapsing around her feet. The last thing she wanted to take up was doing the same for her poor, lost sister. "It might remove the small progress she's made since coming to live with Andrew."

Her mother's death, couple with Royce taking up the mantle of the Earl of Worchester made her reel from the weight of expectations and the enormity of the changes she faced. Though she'd seen him two nights ago at that ball, it hadn't ended with the torrid love making she'd hoped. No, it was further testament that his new life was pulling him in that direction, disrupting their affair and leaving her behind to clutch at the unraveling threads of her mental wellbeing. To say nothing of the budding feelings she was beginning to have for him as a man.

It was all too much, all too confusing, all too fast.

"I have to go."

"Where?" William frowned as he followed her over the floor.

"I don't know, but I cannot be here. Not right now when so many things are threatening to pull me apart. When *everything* is changing and there's naught I can do nothing to stop it!"

He caught her up at in the corridor beyond the door with a hand on her wrist. "What is the name of the man you're seeing?"

Isobel fought to breathe as her chest tightened. What was she to do with her future? She wrenched away from hold. "It matters not."

"I only wish you happy, Isobel." The lines on his face softened into affection. "In many ways, I think of you as the strongest of us all; you deserve to find a place in life that makes your soul feel at home."

I don't feel very strong at the moment. If a gentle breeze blew into her on the street, she would shatter into a million pieces. "William, please…"

"But you can't continue to run from what is uncomfortable or frightening." Again, he took her hand. "Facing the problems is the only way you'll find peace, and I hope you do that long before you end up like Mother."

When had he become so wise? Their mother had agonized for many years over the mistakes and foibles her life had included, and she'd only found a surcease in death. For a fraction of a second, Isobel considered diving into her brother's arms and letting him counsel her, but how could she explain to him what was happening in her life since she didn't fully understand it herself?

"Oh, Wills, somehow I don't think even you would understand," she said in a choked voice as her heart continued to ache. Slipping from his hold, she turned tail and ran down the corridor until she locked herself in her room. "I have to remove myself from this house of death and dying dreams." With every rush of her pulse, sorrow and uncertainty whispered to her, reminded her that she'd not achieved anything worthwhile in her life and now she was left with nothing except shifting sand.

<hr />

JUST AFTER NOON, Isobel alighted from William's carriage in front of the Marsden Clinic in Marylebone. It was the logical place to find Royce at this time of the day, and deep down in her soul she felt he'd be the only one to bring order to her jumbled thoughts.

Yet as soon as she stepped into the familiar room that contained cots and now a few patients, emptiness and hopelessness once more took control. She must have looked a fright, for Royce's brother Trey glanced up from talking with a man on one of the cots and immediately rushed to her side.

"Miss Storme. What brings you here?"

What indeed? "I... I'd like to speak with Doctor Marsden."

"Royce is out making calls on some of his patients that are unable to come to the clinic. He left no word on a possible return." He peered at her with speculation. Concern wrinkled his brow. "Uh, but Lady Jane is scheduled to be in around three, if you'd rather come back then?"

"I... I don't..." The emotional storm brewing inside her chest wouldn't wait that long. She pressed a hand to her heart and then laid it against her cheek. Heat seeped through the thin kid of her glove. Everything felt magnified, somehow, as if the feelings she'd always held back were now giant caricatures of themselves. Tears sprang to her eyes. *Merciful heavens, I'm going to break in front of strangers!* Her breath came in quick pants. She clutched at the strings of her reticule as if it alone would keep her grounded into the present. "I think I'm going to faint," she finished in a choppy whisper. Never in her life had she experienced such lightheadedness as she did now. How could she be the strongest member of the Storme family as William had said if a tiny thing as Royce being gone from the clinic would send her into unconsciousness?

Perhaps I've failed in that too.

"Come with me." Trey wrapped his hand around her upper arm and quickly led her from the large room, with a few words of instruction to one of the nurses as he went. All too soon he guided her into the room that served as Royce's office where she'd spent that lovely night with him. Gently but firmly, he encouraged her to sit upon the bed. "You look at sixes and sevens. What has occurred?"

"My mother died this morning." When the admission did nothing to alleviate the tightness and horrible morass of emotions churning within her, Isobel stared at him. She surprised both herself and him when she uttered a heart-wrenching scream and then burst into tears. "My mother is dead, and my life is a tragic mess."

The sound of running footsteps in the corridor outside betrayed the arrival of a nurse, who stood in the frame. "Do you require assistance, Mr. Marsden?"

"No, no. Miss Storme is quite upset after a death in her family. I think it's best she lets the emotional torrent have at her."

"Please call for me if you should want assistance." Then the nurse left, and once more Isobel was alone with the former solider.

"As much as I'm a proponent of releasing tension, your reaction is rather a shocking manifestation, but I understand." Trey pushed a handkerchief into her hand. When she tried to stem the tide of her tears, the scent on the fabric square wasn't as comforting as Royce's clean, crisp smell, and that made her tears fall all the harder. "I've worked with many patients over the years to help sort the issues in their minds. This isn't about your mother's death." It wasn't a question. "However, I'm heartily sorry just the same. It's never easy to lose a parent."

The fact he offered her words of comfort so close after he'd lost his father intensified the onslaught of her upset. For long moments she sobbed into the borrowed handkerchief. "No, losing Mother wasn't what has caused me to break." In many ways, she was grieving the loss of many things, least of all hopes and silly dreams she'd had no idea she even wanted. "I don't feel myself just now."

Had she ever? Who exactly was she, both within the Storme family and outside of it?

"That's understandable." Instead of being the typical male who'd pat her shoulder and utter empty, useless words, the younger Mr. Marsden pulled over the only chair in the room and sat upon it, his knees nearly touching hers. "If you'd like to unburden your soul, you have my complete discretion."

He was so much like his brother that she cried all the harder. "Everything is convoluted. I don't know how to move forward; each step I take feels wrong."

"That's due to you knowing in your heart what is right for you, so when you act in the opposite way of that, then your mind is blanketed by confusion."

She huffed. "I beg your pardon, but *every* decision I'm facing just now will either bring heartbreak or more confusion. There is no silver lining."

"Perhaps you should tell me why." The soothing sound of his voice urged her to let loose all her secrets.

Bit by bit, Isobel told him about her relationship with her mother and family, about how she'd always been overlooked throughout her life due to the break between both factions of Stormes, of her inability to fit in with the image society was forever touting, of feeling acutely lonely even when surrounded by her loved ones.

Throughout it all, he merely nodded and remained silent, apparently content to let her vent her spleen. That was more appreciated than anything else.

Finally, when the bulk of her tears were spent, he met her gaze. "Tell me about your tempestuous relationship with Royce."

Was he fishing for information, or did he truly suspect the affair? In the end, she was too exhausted to deny it. Besides, it might clear her mind to talk openly about it with someone who understood the doctor. Isobel sighed and mopped at her damp cheeks. "I've seen your brother sporadically over the last couple of weeks."

Trey snorted. "He's a doctor with a full roster of patients. However, there was a time shortly before our father died that he was never home in the evenings. I assume that was due to seeing you?" When heat infused her cheeks, he nodded. "There was the assumption he had a lady bird; I just never thought it would be you."

She narrowed her eyes. "Why, because I'm not his societal equal?"

"What has that to do with anything? I never thought he'd chase after a woman who had no wish to keep gossip to a minimum."

That wasn't far from the truth. "When we first came together, neither of us had concerns or responsibilities. It was heady and wicked, and the affair carried us away. He actually paid attention to me when no one else would." She twisted the handkerchief in her fingers. "Now, he's rather unavailable to me; he's changing. I... I'm finding that difficult to acclimate to."

"We all change, Miss Storme. It's called maturity." When she kept silent, he continued. "Besides, from what little he's managed to share, you haven't given him a reason to call on you that doesn't smack of clandestine scandal."

Oh, those were harsh words indeed! She stared at him, this man who was so much like Royce it hurt her heart to talk candidly with him. "I have been... confused in recent days. And now he's an earl."

Trey frowned. "Why does that matter? Don't most women aspire to snare a man with a title?"

"Don't be more of an idiot than you can help," she shot off with a hint of annoyance snapping in her tones. "I'm not that sort of woman. And I certainly don't want a titled gentleman for any purpose."

"Why?"

"The *ton* put too much pressure upon my family's shoulders with its insistence on proper deportment, among other things. Being a part of the *beau monde* has doomed my family and brought on the premature deaths of my father and uncle. Their expectations had much to do with splitting the Stormes asunder. I will not invite that into my personal life."

"Royce is hardly like other titled men."

"I cannot take that risk," she admitted in a soft voice and hoped he'd offer some sort of comfort to ease the still-swirling emotions in her chest.

"Yet you came here to the clinic today to see him, seek comfort from him." Trey lifted a red eyebrow in question. "You must feel something for my brother, have a connection with him that lead you here... for him."

Heat slapped at her cheeks. Was she so easy to read, then? How much had Royce shared with his brother? "How could I not,

Trey? Despite everything, I… I care for him. I think."

"Ah." He sat back on the chair and rested an ankle upon a knee. "Perhaps we've arrived at the crux of your mental anguish."

Talking with him made her stretch her brain, dig deep to analyze what exactly the battering emotions meant, and that terrified more than everything else. "It was only natural a certain… fondness would occur after spending so much time with him."

"The attraction or connection between you two has grown, changed though. Yes?"

She nodded. "It's frightening, especially in light of his holding a title."

"Again, I ask why it matters?"

"Because I'm afraid I'll fail him at every level. I've failed at being a proper lady of the *ton*, regardless of practicing on and off for the last few weeks." Isobel heaved a sigh and focused her gaze on her lap. "I've made no secret of the fact I'd rather chase scandal than respectability. If Royce was intelligent, he'd see that sooner rather than later."

"Yet, from your own admission, you don't want him now that he's an earl."

"I know I said that!" She blew out a breath. "It's why I'm at sixes and sevens around him. A person can't want one thing and then want the exact opposite, can they?"

A grin tugged at the corners of Trey's lips. "That depends on what the end goal is." When she didn't answer, he asked a different question. "Why do you feel you need to suddenly begin deporting yourself in a proper manner? You're a woman grown, Miss Storme. Your irreverent personality is one of the things that makes you unique."

Another round of heat went through her cheeks, from her thoughts or his slight praise, she didn't know. "I assumed Royce would want that in whomever he will chose as his countess. We both know these new responsibilities that come with the title cannot be ignored, and he's too much an upstanding gentleman to ignore them."

"True." Surprise sprang into Trey's hazel eyes. "You know him well."

"I'm not a prostitute, Mr. Marsden. I do have the capacity for becoming emotionally involved with a man regardless of how wickedly we come together."

It was his turn to blush, and the mottled redness crept over his collar and into his cheeks. "Except you don't want Royce due to his holding a title. While I understand that you perhaps don't wish for domestication, I didn't think you'd be so heartless as to play with his affections in such a manner."

Was that what she was doing? Only wanting him in the physical sense, and would push him away merely due to him coming into a title? But the alternative was terrifying. She simply didn't have it in her to aspire to the title of countess and would doom him besides. Everyone in London knew what sort of woman she was and that she'd long washed her hands of the *ton* or their ridiculous dictates. Then Trey's words sank into her brain. She gasped. "Does he have feelings for me?"

"Who can say. Perhaps you should ask him that."

"Even if he does, he's a noble sort and would push them aside because the title would demand it."

"Then you're giving up just when the need to fight has reached its peak." He clicked his tongue against the roof of his mouth. "That's not the sort of woman I thought you were."

Anger slashed through her chest. "Then we've apparently both been wrong about me." Isobel waved a hand as the heat of embarrassment renewed itself in her cheeks and confusion once more took hold of her mind. "Leave me alone, Trey. I've grown weary of examining the contents of my brain when there is nothing worth considering there."

Yet his questions and words continued to ring in the silence.

"Very well." He stood and then dropped his hand on her shoulder, squeezing in comfort. Compassion filled his eyes as he looked at her. "If I may offer a suggestion? The answer is relatively simple once you get out of your own way, Miss Storme."

"I've stood there for longer than I care to admit, Mr. Marsden. Any sort of change is difficult for me. I *am* a Storme, after all, and perhaps in that I'm cursed."

Nothing in the family line was easy.

"Isobel?"

She came awake to the doctor's hand on her shoulder and his voice, filled with concern, ringing in her ear. "Royce!" The light in the room had shifted to the other side in an indication that it was late afternoon, and the rumbling in her belly proclaimed it teatime. "I'm glad to see you." Heat went through her cheeks as she struggled into a sitting position on the bed. "I must have cried myself to sleep." It was embarrassing to admit, but he'd see that evident on her face regardless.

"I'm sorry I wasn't here when you needed me." He took her hand and once he'd pulled her to her feet, he took her into his arms and held her tightly. "You have my condolences on your mother's passing."

"You're here now." His clothing muffled her words. She let herself fall into his quiet strength. "I'm so lost, Royce." The tears began anew, for talking with Trey had slightly clarified her confusion. It had happened so slowly she hadn't been aware, but she was falling in love with the doctor, a man she had no business attaching herself to, for her very presence in his life would damage his chances in every aspect. "So lost." What would she do if he left too?

But how could he not if he had any sense?

"Thing will grow better. Not with time, but you'll learn to live with the grief, make room for it, if you will."

"It seems I'm grieving for many things just now," she whispered and pulled back enough that she could peer into his face despite her tears. "So many decisions to make." Not only concerning her mother's last wishes.

"How well I understand that struggle." Did he refer to their complicated relationship? She lacked the courage to ask. Instead of offering words of comfort, he moved a hand to cup her cheek and then claimed her lips in such a tender kiss that her tears fell all the harder. When the embrace ended, he set her at arm's length. "I noticed your carriage outside. Let's get you home. You need your family around you at this time."

I need you, Royce.

But she didn't say it aloud, and he didn't suggest he'd stand by her during the bereavement period or that she had a place next to him beyond that... even if she'd want him now that he was an earl. An ache set up around her heart, squeezing until it stole her ability to breathe. For the first time she regretted her penchant for chasing scandal, yet if she hadn't, she would never have known Royce like she did.

With a sigh she followed him out of the office. She'd give anything to stop time at that one perfect night she'd spent with him in that very room, when life's responsibilities had no bearing.

What am I to do now?

Chapter Fifteen

July 19, 1818

ROYCE RUBBED A hand along the side of his face as he prowled through the empty townhouse that had once belonged to his father. Though filled with furniture, décor, and other trappings of wealth in accordance with an earl, there was no life there, no gaiety, nothing to look forward to or bring him comfort.

Twilight had given way to a lovely, clear evening, and as he allowed his valet to put the final touches on his toilette, he finally allowed the thoughts he'd denied to bubble to the surface of his mind. "I'm a damned fool, Vincent."

"I wouldn't know about that, Your Lordship," the valet responded. He was a man of indeterminate age and had followed Royce over to the new townhouse.

Years ago, he'd been a patient at the clinic, a former solider, and when he'd healed, he'd found employment as a valet in a Mayfair household. But when that baron had died, Vincent was once more in need of a position. Royce snatched him up, and they'd been fast friends ever since.

"Well, I am." He drew on a pair of fine kid gloves as he crossed the room. Isobel had sent a note 'round asking him to meet her at the Duke of Sussex's annual summer ball. Even though she was in mourning as well as he, she'd said she needed stimulation and to remind herself that there was still life and happiness in the world. And, nodcock that he was, he'd agreed to the scheme, for he'd wanted one last night in her company. "I fear I'm about to make a rather large mistake."

Not only did he wish to see her again, but he intended to break off their affair. He couldn't continue to take the risk and put his new title in the offing for the gossips.

"If you already know it's a mistake, then logic would tell you not to make it in the first place." One of the valet's black eyebrows rose in question. "Wouldn't you say?"

Heat crept up the back of his neck. "There are so many reasons I have to do this." The last of which was that if he didn't put a stop to his relationship with Isobel, he'd find himself too far gone over her and then where would he be? In a proper mess, that's where. His father had been above reproach as the Earl of Worchester. How could he—Royce—be any less?

"Yet, does the one reason not to supersede all the rest? When he didn't answer, Vincent moved across the room, his limp impeding his speed only slightly. "May I make the assumption that your current mental muddle centers around a woman?"

"You may." Was he that easy to read, then, or did everyone think that when a man's mind was in conflict, there was always a woman at the center?

"Perhaps you should sort your feelings for said woman away from your feelings regarding whatever might be keeping you back from making the correct decision."

"That's exactly the problem, Vincent. One decision will cause scandal and disgrace, and that same decision might bring with it the possibility of being happy for the remainder of my days *if* I could convince the lady in question to do it up properly." And that was a huge complication on its own, for Isobel had stated more than one time that she'd never marry a man with a title. "While the other decision will protect the man I've had no choice to become, it will cause grief and anger for all parties."

For long moments, the valet regarded him with speculation in his eyes. "And there is no hope of being happy or content if you might blend both choices?"

"I can't see one at the moment, for the lady in question is quite adamant that she wants nothing to do with men high on the instep."

"That is a rather big obstruction."

"Yes, and a month ago, it was never there. Life was simple." When he would have shoved a hand through his hair, the narrowed eyes of his valet kept his hand still. "I'm an earl, Vincent. That's what society will know me as now instead of a doctor." His chest tightened, for he couldn't give up his chosen profession, but how to keep both? "The title demands respect and an adherence to the *ton's* rules, no matter how strict or ridiculous, correct?"

Dear God, I miss you, Father. Would that you are here to give me counsel. Though his father had often and early trained him to take up the reins of the title in his stead when it was Royce's turn, he'd made certain his children also had other interests in the world that didn't revolve around position. Yes, it had been one of his father's fondest wishes that his children marry well and find matches suitable to their stations, he hadn't been so overbearing that he couldn't compromise. Didn't he eventually come around and see that Jane's choice of marrying Finn was the best one for her?

Vincent snorted. "Those rules aren't likely to grow lax any time soon."

"No, I suppose they won't." In the back of his mind, he heard his father grousing about the number of men and women within the *beau monde* who had no respect for decorum or social standing, for the very traditions the whole of society had been built upon. "Father always told me to marry someone worthy of the title. I'm honor bound to find a lady who is above reproach, who won't continually set tongues wagging from her improper behavior."

"While I'm sure that is so, I wonder if your mother would have agreed. From snatches of stories I've heard, the countess had a mischievous streak."

Royce nodded. "At times, I suppose, and she did chafe against the conventions upon occasion, yet she was everything proper."

The valet chuckled. "I'll wager my back teeth that wasn't the reason your father married her." He handed Royce a top hat. "Of course, there are loads of proper women throughout society. A man can't throw a teacup without hitting one, but that doesn't mean any of them provoke excitement or a zest for life. And isn't that what a man truly wants when he takes one to wife? Otherwise, your existence would be quite long and dull."

"Hmm." Was that the reason his father delighted in stirring up trouble on the floor of the House of Lords, because there was no excitement in his marriage? That certainly put a different perspective on things. "That only adds to my confusion."

"Then think harder, Your Lordship."

An annoying ache had set up around his heart. Inconvenient to be sure, and perhaps it signified nothing. Royce shrugged. "I'm wondering if my first assessment was even correct. Perhaps I'm *not* in danger of falling in love with the lady. Indeed, it could quite possibly be that I became enamored with the idea of being with her throughout the course of our affair." The more he thought about it, the more he warmed to the idea. "Attraction and desire are often mistaken for love, so when I end this relationship, there should be no feelings of ill-will. We've enjoyed each other quite splendidly, but deep down we both knew this wasn't a lasting commitment."

Devil take it, man, you're doing nothing except fooling yourself.

Both of Vincent's eyebrows soared into his hairline. "If that's what you need to tell yourself to gather courage, then by all means run with it. However, might I remind you that men are very often wrong in these situations? Denial will gain you nothing, and heartbreak will meet you all the same."

"I can't think about that now." He'd have this one last night with Isobel and then turn her loose. Because she'd never wished for marriage, she should understand the reasons for the termination of the affair. Yet, did he? With a sigh that seemed to come from his toes, Royce wrenched open the door to the dressing room. "I've tarried here long enough. Perhaps the right decision will come to me in the carriage ride over."

And damn my eyes if it doesn't.

IF HE HADN'T danced a waltz with Isobel, he would have been fine, but as Royce guided her through the last circuit about the floor, he knew beyond every doubt that he was the biggest bacon-brained idiot to ever have existed in London. By rights neither of them should be out in society, and to be truthful, this was the only dance they'd each indulged in, but there was a certain headiness in escorting her about the floor for all and sundry to see.

To be sure, this was the last time such a thing would occur, and for the moment she felt all too right in his arms. He didn't know how she did it but the gown of dyed-black silk with tiny jet beads lining the scandalously low neckline suited her pale complexion. The only splash of color she'd allowed this night was a teardrop-shaped ruby on a silver chain, and with each dip and turn, the gemstone bounced at the hollow between her collarbones. It matched the ruby ring she'd taken to wearing since they'd begun their affair nearly a month ago.

"I don't believe I've ever seen you wear jewelry." His own clothing was black by the requisite dress code, but his waistcoat was a dark charcoal hue, and he wore a black cravat to better signify his mourning status. "Do you have an aversion to it the same as you have for title men of the *ton*?"

Damn, he hadn't meant to mention that this evening, but it had slipped out anyway.

Amusement twinkled in her sapphire eyes. "I do, actually. In many ways, I believe that displaying one's wealth is abhorrent and unneeded. Society has become convoluted in many ways. People should let their good acts and leadership speak for them instead of riches."

Every time he was in her company, he learned something new about her. For all Isobel's penchants for creating scandal and sensation, she was remarkably down to earth. "Unfortunately, coin is what makes much of the world we know work."

"Bah." She shook her head. Jet-encrusted combs sparkled in her dark brown hair. "There are many aspects of the *ton* I despise simply because they're not fair, and the wealth divisions within England are appalling when one thinks about them. Yet men at the helm in Parliament do nothing except argue against the men trying to make a difference."

The steps of the waltz brought them close to the terrace doors that had been thrown open to encourage the cool night air into the overly crowded room. "Why do you care so much about that? You were hardly raised in poverty, nor are you facing such extreme circumstances." With the touch of his fingers on the small of her back, he swept her through the doors and into the midnight-shrouded terrace.

"Surely you've seen for yourself the disparity of our world when you treat patients at your clinic." When he nodded and pulled her into the shadows, she sighed. "All of the recent upheaval in my life and family has shown me that I have an overwhelming responsibility to do something with the privileges I've been born with." Her eyes twinkled in the dim illumination. "For the first time I feel like I have a purpose instead of merely waiting for the next scandal."

His respect for her soared. "That's a wonderful sentiment. What will you do?"

"I don't know yet." She shook her head. "I haven't had much time to think about it since this notion just came to me in the last few days." Her laughter sounded a trifle forced. "Having one's stomach revolt lends one time to ruminate on many things."

Royce frowned, immediately alert. "Are you ill? Trey told me you'd nearly fainted at the clinic the day your mother died."

Grief shadowed her eyes, covering the previous liveliness. "I think everything going on has taken a toll. Exhaustion is catching up with me. As for the illness, perhaps I ate something that didn't agree with me." She shrugged, and once more his gaze dropped to her décolletage. What he wouldn't give to take full advantage and taste that silky skin, enjoy those perfect breasts. "I hardly believe it's cause for worry."

He knew an acute urge and longing to delve into the reason she wasn't feeling quite the thing. After all, he was a doctor and healing people was what he'd been called to do. How could he give that up merely to do his duty to the title? Icy fingers of fear played down his spine. How the devil could he balance the two while keeping Isobel in the mix?

The bald truth was that he couldn't. Something had to give, and unfortunately, it was his relationship with her. "Perhaps." The longer he delayed his original intentions for this evening, the more difficult it would be the make the break from her. So why, damn it all, didn't he say the words?

She took hold of his cravat and tugged him deeper into the shadows until they were out of sight from the doors of the ballroom. "I wouldn't say no to a thorough examination from you, Doctor." The heat of her breath skated along his cheek and chin as she pressed her body against his. "I'm quite certain you can easily summon your carriage…"

Oh, she was a tempting baggage indeed, and one he'd so easily become addicted to. Cold regret slid through his gut like the most unwanted of serpents. "Isobel." He took hold of her hands to prevent further exploration that would land them both into trouble. "There is something I must say to you that I cannot put off."

"All right." She edged backward until she hovered on the edge of the golden pool of light made by the open ballroom doors. Like a lamb to the slaughter, Royce followed. "What is it?"

The longing that filled her expression set fire to his own desire that all he wished to do in this moment was spirit her away and take his fill of her body until they were both too sated to do anything else. But that madness had to stop lest he'd never climb out of the miasma of confusion he'd fallen into. "Circumstances between us have changed since we began this affair. I think you can agree about that."

"I do, for course, but that doesn't mean we must let them affect our enjoyment."

"Oh, but it does, for a myriad of reasons." This would prove more difficult than he'd anticipated. "I have a title now, Isobel. I'm an earl of some standing. That means something and demands that I appear above reproach within society, that I keep scandal and the potential for it far from my door." He hated himself for every word he said, but it couldn't be helped. "Like you, I've been thinking upon the purpose of my life. I have reach and power that I've not had before, and I need to decide how to use that."

"Gammon." She huffed and it ruffled a few curls on her forehead. "You never wanted to be the earl. Now suddenly you're acting as if you're the authority on it?"

"No, of course not, but I can't ignore my responsibilities." Damn but he was mucking this up. When he went to take her hand, she snatched it away.

"What *exactly* are you trying to say, Doctor?"

God, but he despised everything about this night. "We must end our affair. It's too risky to continue."

Shock moved over her face quickly followed by grief that went deeper than merely losing her mother. In fact, if he peered more closely, the grief bordered on devastating. "Then don't call what we have that. You can't toss our relationship away as if it means nothing." She snapped her fingers and dropped her voice. "Make me your mistress, I don't care, but please don't shut me out of your life."

"You're not cut of the same cloth as women who occupy that

moniker."

She snorted. "Isn't that what I was before you had a title? Neither of us were squeamish about it three days ago. Why is us continuing on in the same vein so abhorrent? Many titled men in the *ton* conduct affairs."

Was she aware that her argument contradicted things she'd said to him before? When the urge to grin took hold, he tamped it down. "I'll need to marry, find a countess who is proper and not a proponent of chasing scandal as you are."

Tears sprang to her eyes, making them luminous and more gem-like in the dim light. "If that's the reason you're doing this, you needn't marry right away. Find your identity within the title, and we can still continue to each enjoy other."

"You know why we can't." When one of those crystalline tears fell to her cheek, hot panic rose within his chest. "Unless you suddenly wish to wed an earl?" Dear God, why had he said *that*? Is that what he secretly wished to do, and with her? A scandalous affair was one thing, but having a scandalous wife was quite another. "Er, I mean—"

Isobel held up a hand. "Relax, Royce. My sentiment on titled men still stands. I want nothing to do with them… or you, I suppose, since you're adamant on crashing down this arrogant, priggish path. And being wed to anyone at this moment in my life isn't something I want. There's a certain freedom in being my own woman without needing to answer to anyone."

"But I… You must take your family's wishes into account."

"No. Not any longer." Slowly, she shook her head and dropped her hand. "I won't lie and say I'll not mourn your loss, for you provided a safe haven, a reprieve from the storms that are battering me. However, I know you better than you think. As a doctor, you were fearless, considered your calling an adventure, a bid to continue to learn. But now you're afraid."

He gasped as the magnitude of the statement came over him. "Absolutely not." Not knowing what to do with his hands, he crossed his arms at his chest. "I saw fighting in the war. Came back and healed men who had wounds inflicted upon them by other men. You have no idea the horrors I've been subjected to, so your statement is quite false. I am afraid of nothing."

Except losing you.

"No." Isobel closed the distance, laid a hand on his arms until he let them relax. "Being the earl terrifies you in ways you've never dreamed of before."

"How is it possible you can guess that when we've not shared anything deeply personal?"

A ghost of a smile curved her kissable lips, but those damned sorrow-filled shadows in her eyes would haunt him for the rest of his life. "Perhaps you and I didn't need much talking. At times two people just connect on a level that doesn't require conversation."

Which made this all the more difficult. His chest tightened to the point of pain. Finally, he nodded. "I'll admit, the title, the life it will exact from me, *is* terrifying." Especially if she wasn't with him, prodding him to grow, to come up to the mark, to hold his ground. But how could there be anything between them now that his reality had shifted?

"I'm disappointed you're considering giving up your clinic, your whole identity, the man I knew you as in the face of holding a title that relies more on tradition than the advancement of knowledge that you adore so much."

It was as if she'd stabbed him through the heart. Royce pressed a hand to that organ. It ached so fiercely that he forgot the music and revelry occurring behind him in the ballroom. For the first time in his life, he was without direction. A chill went down his spine as he found her gaze. "I don't know what to do, Isobel. I can't see who I am any longer, and it's going to tear me apart."

Please help me find the way back.

She wiped at her tears with her gloved fingertips and laid her other hand on his chest. "You are Doctor Royce Marsden. The man who lives for the advancement of medicine, the man who believes wounded, forgotten soldiers are still worthy of finding a place in society." Questions flitted through her eyes to mix with the sadness. "I suspect you've never wavered from wanting to become a physician even from childhood, yet here you are willing to toss that life's work into the bin through a set of adverse circumstances." She sighed. "Who you are beyond that is solely up to you."

Anger speared through his chest to pierce the sense of doom that had come over him ever since he'd told her they needed to quit the affair. "Those are brave words from a woman who has made it a point to run from everything that smacks of change in her life." When she gasped at his effrontery, he plunged onward. "Do you even know who *you* are, Isobel, or are you patronizing me?" The more he hurt her as he was, the easier it would be to break away.

Wouldn't it?

"No." Her admission surprised him. She shook her head and took a step away from him. "I am still discovering that, bit by bit, day after day, especially when I separate myself from my family's wishes." For long moments, she remained quiet. "Some of what I'm finding out is surprising and some is disturbing. I fear I'm too much a messy storm most times, but if that's my truth, there is naught I can do but accept it."

"What if you can't?" Could he accept who he was and dare that answer to be different than who he was expected to be?

"Then unhappiness will be my lot." She held his gaze and lifted her chin at the stubborn angle he'd come to know and love about her. A hint of frost lingered in her stare. "If the people around me refuse to accept me for who I truly am, that is their loss, and I'll wish them well."

Oh, God. She referred to him and how he didn't want her due to her personality and reputation. *I'm the lowest of the low.* He rubbed his fingers over his painful, cracking heart. "I'm not certain I can do what's expected of me, Isobel, for everyone on either side of the issue will come out disappointed and angry."

Her expression softened. She grabbed onto his fingers. "Then do what you believe is right. I imagine you did the same when you embarked on the study of medicine."

"Yes. My father objected strenuously." He'd somehow forgotten that.

"But you believed in that and in your abilities to heal." With a squeeze of his fingers, she imparted a bit of strength. Isobel looked at him with such hope, such feeling in her eyes that he trembled, swayed at the edge of a precipice. Was she aware of those emotions? And what should he do about them? "Do what your heart tells you."

For the space of a few heartbeats, it was on the tip of his tongue to properly ask her to be with him in whatever capacity she could manage, that they'd stumble their way through no matter what, but the future was too new, too overwhelming and littered with too many expectations, and he suspected that if he somehow managed to marry her, it would put her into a gilded cage that would ultimately clip her wings.

I don't want to tame her, but how can I encourage her to keep on as she is without finding myself in those same flames?

The remainder of his heart broke into a million pieces as he pulled from her grasp. "I am the ninth Earl of Worchester." That had always been his destiny, damn it all to hell.

"Oh, Royce." Her sob nearly sent him to his knees to ask for her forgiveness. "But your life's work... the man you were meant to be the moment you took up your first scalpel..."

"Will have to fade away into obscurity," he said, and he hated the bitter taste of each one of those words. Just like he would once this night was over. He forced a hard swallow into his suddenly tight throat. "I'm so sorry, Isobel."

"So am I." Another few tears dropped to her cheeks. "I hope you find happiness." When she turned to leave, he caught her hand.

"Please don't think less of me." He was a fool and an idiot. "I have to do what's right."

"Well, you're doing a piss-poor job of it." She shook her head. "How can I not think less when you're giving up in the face of tradition, or responsibility, of fear of being true to yourself?"

"I don't know." Quite possibly, he was the biggest dunce in all of England. Not having the words to explain what he felt, Royce yanked her against him. He kissed her hard and deeply, never caring for who might see from the ballroom doors. A pox on society right now when it was ruining his life. With Isobel in his embrace, the future didn't seem so frightening, which was odd since she was her own storm. So why was he throwing it all away?

Isobel shoved out of his arms. Anger flashed in her eyes while her posture reflected the height of annoyance. "How dare you!" When she lifted her right hand, he didn't have the wherewithal to move, so when she slapped his cheek, the echo of flesh hitting flesh resounded loud in the sudden silence. "You can't have me if you want the title, Doctor Marsden, and I certainly don't want an earl. My mind is quite firm in that regard."

Then she fled the terrace to dart into the ballroom, where she soon melted into the crowds. "Bloody hell." Royce stood there with a hand to his stinging hot cheek. He feared he'd just lost the only thing of value he'd ever managed to find in the whole of his life.

Dear God, what have I done?

CHAPTER SIXTEEN

July 26, 1818

IT HAD BEEN a week since she'd seen Royce and he'd unequivocally put a halt to their affair that had begun a handful of weeks ago. Not to mention that he'd cut her out of his life. She'd spent those days in a fog, alternately crying and nursing her still-rebelling stomach, as a handful of those words ran around and around her mind like ponies on a loop.

I'll need to marry, find a countess who is proper and not a proponent of chasing scandal as you are.

As much as she'd hoped to steel herself against the inevitable, those words had cut her to the quick. Her heart still ached from them, for once more she hadn't been enough for someone, and to know Royce wouldn't accept her as she was had left her gasping and in pain as if he'd flayed her open for all to see.

"I thought he was different," she whispered to the window as she peered out at the Mayfair streets. A gentle rain was falling, making the streets a touch muddy and the closed carriages that passed below shiny with the moisture. "I thought I'd found in him a man who might understand what it is to be not in the usual style."

Even if she didn't wish for marriage with a man who held a title.

That was perhaps the most unfair and ironic part of it all. If circumstances had been different, she could let the feelings she held for him progress and grow from respect and affection into love. None of that was possible now that he was an earl. Such a life wasn't for her, and it was never what she'd wanted.

That didn't soothe the broken heart she currently nursed. And that in itself was dreadfully wretched, for if she didn't feel anything beyond fondness for Royce, why the devil did it hurt so badly that he'd rejected her?

The longer she stared out the window, the more lost she became. Hard on the heels of losing her mother, the loss of the one person who'd been able to anchor her battered soul had turned his back on her because she wasn't good enough to fit in with his new world. Hot anger speared through her chest and brought with it quick tears. All of those emotions mixed with her until she shook from the confusion they made.

They swirled and swelled until she curled her hands into fists and the only thing she wished to do in that moment was scream at the unfairness of it all or perhaps smash several objects throughout the room against the wall.

"I'm a Storme for good reason." Now she finally understood great depths of passion and despair the men in her family had gone through and how wrong she'd been to make jest of them. Apparently, members of her family didn't feel things on a normal level like everyone else. Tomorrow, a large contingent of them would leave for the Derbyshire property in order to bury her mother. Cousin Andrew had made the arrangements and he'd already made his displeasure known when she'd asked to stay behind. "Why can they not see I know what's best for my own life?" Then she frowned at a man riding along the street. He was familiar. When she pushed open her window and leaned out to better assess the situation, she allowed a tiny grin. "Lord Alder!"

The young peer had been a particularly devoted acolyte of hers before she'd become involved with Royce. He hadn't been that skilled in kissing but his enthusiasm for everything had fed her own energy, and he was easy on the eyes with his blond hair and tall form. When he jerked his head about and led his horse closer to her townhouse, he lifted a hand in greeting and touched the brim of his top hat. "Miss Storme! How nice to see you again."

Isobel waved. "Agreed!"

"You'd vanished from society for so long I feared you'd already left for the country."

"Tomorrow, I will." But not for the summer holiday. Mourning would follow, and that was just so dreary and dull. "What are your plans for the day?" She didn't care if someone within the house heard her exchange; she was beyond caring about many things. Royce's defection had put cracks in her heart, and she had no idea how to recover from that. What she needed in this moment was to make a large sensation so the people around her would have no choice but to notice her, to see her pain, to offer support.

Lord Alder shrugged while his bay mare danced beneath him. "Some of my friends and I were hoping to take my new charger out in Hyde Park and put him through his paces."

"How exciting!" Excitement fluttered at the base of her spine. "What say you to a friendly race? My brother has a fast Arabian thoroughbred I'd like to match against your charger." That's originally how she'd met the young lord, for she'd seen him riding through Hyde Park a few months prior. William had acquired the piece of horseflesh as a gift of appreciation from a titled peer whose case he'd solved some months ago.

"Sounds like a bang-up time. Where and when, Miss Storme?"

The need to find something to return her lost confidence and self-worth grew strong. Besides, she desperately wished to escape the silent house of mourning. She wanted life and excitement and color around her, if only to delay acknowledging the emotions building through her chest that would cause her to break soon.

To distract her from thinking.

I will not cry over a man, especially a titled one.

"Four o'clock today. At Cumberland Gate on St. George's Row. We'll race past the guardhouse at Kensington Gardens then over the Serpentine, ending at the Kensington Gardens gate. Rain or shine." There were multiple paths they could take to reach the guardhouse and it would depend on how much foot traffic there was in the park, but the added unknown upped the excitement.

"A fine course!" He nodded. "What are the stakes?"

By this time, a few interested passersby were staring at them as they conducted the not-so-private conversation. No doubt a crowd would assemble in the park merely for the curiosity of watching the race. Would it be enough to draw Royce to her side, for him to see that she was better and more vital than a society heiress or vapid young woman who only wanted to marry a title? Let him eat his heart out for tossing her aside.

If he couldn't be true to himself, she didn't need him.

Well, all the better for a crowd. The more witnesses, the better the scandal. It mattered not to her any longer on keeping her reputation somewhat untarnished. Royce didn't want her at her best so she might as well appear at her worst. "If you win, I'll let you kiss me in front of everyone this evening on Rotten Row. If I win, well I'll have the accolades of beating you and the horse you're so proud of."

Really, she wanted nothing except the gossip… and perhaps the destruction therein. Let the tattlemongers have at her. Let them tear the remainder of her reputation to shreds, for she'd never be good enough. If Cousin Andrew demanded she live in Derbyshire for the remainder of the year, she could mourn in peace for many things, and if she were far removed from London, the likelihood of seeing Royce would lessen. Only then would this unrelenting pain in her heart cease, a pain for something she'd been adamant she hadn't wanted a week ago, but now that she couldn't have it, the anger at losing it had multiplied tenfold.

"I'll take that wager. See you this afternoon, Miss Storme!" Then he once more touched his top hat and then trotted away with a wide grin.

Isobel came back into her room. A shuddering sigh escaped her. The ache in her heart intensified. Truly, the last thing she wished to do was kiss someone who wasn't Royce. *I'm rather tired of having things end in disaster.* She glanced at her mother's ruby ring and shook her head. Love was for women who didn't know themselves and who weren't strong enough to go through life without a man. What she needed now was an outfit worthy of the crime, something that would make her smile even through the lectures she could almost feel were coming after this stunt.

BY THE TIME she'd reached Hyde Park sitting properly astride her thoroughbred, Aisha—which meant alive and well in Arabic—instead of in a sidesaddle, her heartbeat raced from excitement. She'd also chosen not to appear in public in the trappings of feminine mourning. Instead, she'd delved into William's closet. That foray had led to her donning an old pair of his breeches from some years back in a tan color as well as a loose-fitting lawn shirt. Paired with well-scuffed boots she'd borrowed from one of the stable lads, there was no doubt in her mind that she'd create the scandal of the year.

Her lips curved with a wicked grin. Oh, this was just the sort of fun she'd lacked over the weeks! She'd managed to sneak out of the house on the pretense of taking a walk while the rest of the household attended to the last of the packing. William had indicated that he would imminently visit with Cousin Andrew to discuss the possibility of taking Caroline with them.

All the better. With the men occupied and quite possibly arguing over her adamantly stubborn sister's immediate future, Isobel could do what she pleased without having her disgrace discovered prematurely.

I don't care what anyone says. I'll live how I wish or die trying. If she wasn't good enough for the people around her, she'd at least come up to her own marks and be proud. *This is who I am. A pox on everyone else.*

She led Aisha along the road. As she crept closer to the start of the racecourse, a small knot of people had formed on either side of the gate. Isobel grinned. This was what she loved, the thrill of indulging in scandal to the entertainment of others. How did she think she could have given such a thing up for a man?

"Miss Storme!" Lord Alder's grin was wide when he caught sight of her. There was no doubt in her mind that the black charger he sat atop held banked strength. Hyde Park wasn't the sort of place where such a horse could be given his head, and he was a massive equine besides. But she had faith in William's thoroughbred. Though what her brother needed such a horse for, she couldn't say. "I didn't know if you truly meant to show up this afternoon." Appreciation lit his gaze as he drew it up and down her frame. "And in such dress."

"Of course I did." She glanced down at herself and her dark brown hair in a thick braid fell over her left shoulder. "This is vastly more comfortable than navigating a horse in skirts."

"I should have argued for higher stakes in this wager," he said in a lowered voice. "Perhaps the chance to pay court to you."

Heat went through her cheeks. "We can talk about that once the race is over." Though it was quite flattering to have a man show interest in her, it rang entirely too false. Lord Alder didn't possess magnificent, fiery hair like a certain doctor, nor did he have the sort of anchoring spirit she needed to stay grounded.

Then she pushed all thoughts of Royce from her mind. He'd made his choice. So had she. It was time to move into the future without him.

"Are you ready to begin, Miss Storme?"

"Oh, absolutely." For too long she'd waited for her life to start, for her to take up a new adventure and find a new way forward. Isobel leaned down and stroked her horse's neck. "I know you can do this, girl."

The horse flicked her ears in reply and danced impatiently beneath her.

Isobel frowned. Knots of concern pulled in her belly. She'd only ridden Aisha a couple of times since the horse had come into William's possession. The true personality of the animal hadn't come to light yet. Would that prove a folly during the race? Then she glanced at Lord Alder and smiled. "The question really is: are *you* ready?"

"I am." He nodded and gathered his reins more tightly in his hand as his black horse danced. "I've long awaited the day you'd take notice of me."

Perhaps we're all wishing someone of consequence will pay us attention because our lives are lacking something vital.

And wasn't that a sad commentary on life?

"Then I hope you'll impress me, Lord Alder." She guided her horse forward through the gate and to the point where they would begin. As the peer drew his mount alongside hers, she gazed over some of the assembled crowds. When she spied bright red hair beneath a top hat, her heart squeezed and excitement tumbled down her spine, but upon further inspection, it wasn't Royce. It was, however, his brother Trey. He shot her a fierce scowl, but she gave him a merry wave. Let him go find his brother and tell him that she was doing just fine without him.

"So do I," her racing partner said, and the sound of his voice pulled her wandering thoughts back to the task at hand. "You're rather a paragon, Miss Storme. An unachievable goal, a rare and unconventional diamond many men would die to possess."

She rolled her eyes, but her cheeks warmed at his praise. Why couldn't Royce see the situation like that? "How sweet of you to say, Lord Alder, but perhaps we should concentrate on the race?"

"Of course." He nudged his mount a few inches closer to hers. "On my mark." When she nodded, he said, "Three, two, one. Go!"

Isobel dug her bootheels into Aisha sides. "Come on, girl!" She leaned forward over the horse's neck and held the reins tight as her heartbeat surged.

For a few minutes, her horse and Lord Alder's remained neck and neck. He tossed her a victorious grin, but that only motivated her to encourage her to try all the harder to gain the lead.

Then, on a bend as they raced along a portion of the Serpentine, Lord Alder took the lead. He laughed with good-natured glee, which earned him a scowl from Isobel.

"Give me all you have, girl," she whispered to her horse and leaned even further over the equine's neck, rising in her stirrups as she did so. She was a lighter rider and her horse not as heavy as her opponent; surely that would give her the advantage.

They swept down the bridle path at reckless speeds, scattering unwary riders and pedestrians in their wake. A few men followed after them on horseback or with curricles, for no doubt this scheme had wagers hanging on it.

Isobel blocked out everything from her mind as she put the whole of her attention onto beating Lord Alder. The rhythmic pound of hooves thundered in her ears. Sweat plastered the shirt to her back despite the camisole she wore beneath it. Her heartbeat swished through her veins with every curve and straightaway in their path.

All too soon they made the transfer to the last stretch of the race. The light, annoying rain that had seen them off at the beginning of the race changed into more steady precipitation. The bridle path, already pock-marked with hoof prints and ruts, gave up the ghost into mud and puddles, but still they raced.

Water ran into Isobel's face and soaked her braid. It made the back of the reddish-brown thoroughbred slick and smooth. The pungent scents of sweat and horseflesh and mud wafted to her nose. With her chest tight with anticipation and exhilaration she once more stood in the stirrups. The goal was nearly in sight.

I'm going to win!

But she couldn't resister one last taunt to her opponent. "Is that all you've got to show for yourself, Lord Alder?"

"Hardly, but if it's a fair race you're after..." He dug in his heels to his horse's side and then shot ahead by a length.

"Well, damn." Isobel smothered a curse beneath her breath. She slapped the reins against her horse's sides. "Just a little bit longer, girl."

The exuberant barking of a dog penetrated the concentration in her brain, and she frowned. When the noise became more annoying and louder, she glanced to one side of the path. A white and brown beagle had broken away from its owner. It bolted like blur toward the rushing horses, trailing its lead behind. Isobel sat down hard in the saddle and tugged on the reins in an effort to halt the inevitable collision. And still the dog barked, in excitement or warning she couldn't say.

"Watch out, you fluff for brains nodcock," she called to the dog, but neither he nor her opponent paid her any mind.

Then he was on the path, barking at them both. Her horse neighed and reared up on her hind legs, pawing the air with her forelegs. The whites of her eyes were clearly visible, for she'd been startled by the sudden appearance and noise of the dog.

"Easy, girl. It's all right." Isobel tried to soothe the equine as best she could while Lord Alder rocketed ahead of her on the path. Gasps and cries from the gathering crowds on the sides of the path further worked to disorient her horse, but she finally gained control. Aisha resettled all for legs on the ground, but the damned dog decided to apparently challenge the horse. The beagle barked and growled, darting at the horse's hooves, nipping and dancing.

Aisha was having none of it, and her patience had clearly evaporated. She bucked while Isobel held onto her mount's neck as best she could while trying to keep her seat. Just when she thought the horse had settled, Aisha darted to one side to avoid the dog. By increments, Isobel relaxed, thinking the worse was over.

Lord Alder had turned about to return and render aid, presumably, but the beagle rushed at his horse. Her mount had no doubt tired of the whole proceeding. She bucked again and this time succeeded in unseating Isobel.

"Aaaargh!" She was ejected from the saddle and for the space of a couple of heartbeats, she was airborne, flying. Then a stand of stout oak trees rushed into her view. Her head smacked against one of the gnarled trunks. Pain exploded through her brain and her vision went fuzzy. As a moan escaped her, she hit the ground, landing on her side, with her heart in her throat and her stomach wishing to expel what little she'd managed to eat at luncheon.

"Miss Storme!" Vaguely, and from what sounded like a long distance, she heard Lord Alder call her name.

Isobel tried to maneuver into a sitting position, but she retched and didn't turn her head fast enough. Vomit splattered on her arm and legs. The pain in her head increased. When she looked in Lord Alder's direction, he appeared quite fuzzy.

"Isobel!" The voice held the same tenor as Royce's. It was followed by the sound of running footsteps.

She squinted, but the images were now doubled. A man with red hair shot toward her, and her heart fluttered as she sank to the ground and rested her cheek on the muddy grass. "Royce..." *Drat. Why was he here?* He'd be so angry at what she'd done...

"Damn it, Isobel, don't move." The man with red hair threw himself to his knees at her side. His gloved hand went to her forehead, preventing movement, while he peered into her face. "I'm going to take you home and then summon my brother."

The words echoed weirdly in her head, and the pain shook them all together until they didn't make sense. "I don't think you should tell him... about the race," she finally managed to whisper. The more she tried to focus on the man's face, the dizzier she felt. Her stomach muscles bunched in preparation of retching. "Oh, no."

"Please, don't move. You're bleeding and your head's been given a right proper smack."

"Royce will be angry. This wasn't proper..." Then the pain came up and sucked her under. Around and around, she went into a spiral that was both black but filled with spinning lights.

There was no chance the doctor would forgive her now. Tears welled in her eyes and fell to her cheeks. Every heartbeat was tinged with hurt. "He's beyond my reach." But then, there wasn't any chance she'd ever be with him because he didn't want her anymore.

And she didn't want a title…

Her chest tightened while her heart broke all over again. That pain blended with the one in her head, and she couldn't form further thoughts because the words kept becoming jumbled and jarred.

"It's all mucked up." With a tiny sigh, she let the deafening silence have at her.

CHAPTER SEVENTEEN

"DEAR GOD!" ROYCE read the short missive, done in his brother's rushed handwriting, again to make certain he'd seen it correctly the first time.

Come at once to Inspector Storme's residence. Isobel has been in an accident. She's unconscious and bleeding from the head. Uncertain of prognosis.

"What is it?" Jane's tone practically demanded that he tell her everything as she snatched the note from his lax fingers.

"I have to go." It had been hell being away from Isobel or anywhere that reminded him of her, so he'd kept close to the house. His sister and Finn had come over for a few of those days to help refresh the furnishings and décor. Thank goodness she was here now because his chest was so tight, he couldn't breathe. "I have to go," he repeated, telling his feet to move, but they remained as if stuck to the floor.

"Of course you should." She prodded his shoulder. The note fluttered unheeded to the floor. "The woman you love is in peril and you're a first-rate physician." Again, she shoved at his shoulder.

Royce stared at her with a frown. "I don't love her. She's a… Well, she and I were… That is to say we aren't—"

"Stop." Jane took his hand and pulled him from the drawing

room. A pleased grin curved her lips. "You're tip over tail for the woman, and if you'd stop being so stubborn or giving yourself a hundred excuses of why you can't be together, you could see that."

"No, that's not true." He shook his head and yanked his hand from hers. "There's a certain level of respect and concern related to being an earl and I—"

"Don't be a bigger nodcock than you can help."

Icy fingers of fear played his spine. "How did you figure it out? We'd kept our relationship secret."

"You might be my oldest brother, but you're not as sophisticated as you wish to believe." She prodded him toward the stairs in the direction of the entry hall. "Finn was the first to suspect it. He told me, and then I saw the two of you together at the duke's summer ball before she stormed from the ballroom. There was much magic between you."

His hand shook as he raked his fingers through his hair. "Magic fades in the face of reality." He'd let Isobel go a week ago. Had told himself a thousand times he was better off without her and her habit of chasing scandal. Had nearly convinced himself that he didn't need her in his life... and now this.

"And you're still showing me you haven't learned anything from her." Jane shook her head. Affection and exasperation warred for dominance in her eyes. With one hand on Royce's arm, moving him along the corridor, she yelled for her husband. "Finn! We have to leave immediately. It's an emergency with your cousin!"

"What happened?" Finn rolled his Bath chair out of the library. A book rested in his lap.

"I don't know." Royce shrugged. He moved past the butler and out the door without a thought to hat or gloves. "Trey sent 'round a hastily scrawled note. I'm going over to William's house." Then he stopped. "I need my doctor bag."

Jane snorted. "And also the carriage." She glanced at the butler. "Please have the open carriage brought out, and a footman to assist with the major."

"Of course, Lady Jane."

Urgency smacked into worry as Royce returned up the corridor. He looked at Finn, who met his gaze with equal concern. "Oh, God. What if she's—"

Finn held up a hand. "None of that until we assess the situation, but time *is* of the essence."

EVERY THRUM OF the blood through Royce's veins echoed with Isobel's name. As soon as his carriage arrived at her home, he vaulted from the vehicle before it had come to a complete stop. Bag in hand, he jumped over the gate, rushed up the short walkway, and then let himself into the house without knocking or waiting on the butler to admit him.

"Where is Miss Storme?" he barked while the affronted servant trailed after him.

"In her bedchamber. However, Lord Hadleigh and Inspector Storme wish to see you in the drawing room before that," the butler informed him as Royce took the stairs two treads at a time.

Both men pelted out of said room as soon as Royce gained the landing, followed by Trey. "Thank you for arriving so quickly," the earl said as he approached the staircase.

Royce paused. As much as he wished to go to Isobel's bedside, he did need to know how the accident had happened. "Tell me all that you know so I can make a proper assessment."

"I was there." Trey pushed him way between the two Storme men. Worry creased his brow, but it was the shadows in his eyes that sent foreboding deep into his gut. "In Hyde Park. Miss Storme was out riding. Racing, really. Tried to best a Lord Alder through the park and on Inspector Storme's untried Arabian."

"What the devil was she doing racing horses?" He glanced up the staircase as if he could see her from his location.

"Honestly, I couldn't begin to tell you." The inspector's dark brown hair stood on edge as if he'd shoved his hands through it multiple times. "According to your brother, there was a rumor of a wager between Isobel and this lord. And now this scandalbroth is brewing..."

Royce held up a hand. "That can wait. I need to know about her injuries." He glanced at his brother. "Explain. I assume you were instrumental in bringing her here?"

"I was." Trey nodded. On the floor below, the sound of Jane's and Finn's voice carried upward. "Lord Alder was kind enough to render assistance and someone else offered a carriage." He sighed and rubbed his hand over his pale face. "She hit her head against a tree when the horse bucked her off. From what I could see, there's bruising on her left side. Additionally, she cast up her accounts at the scene. No doubt due to the head taking a jostling. She lost consciousness shortly after."

"Cousin Isobel hasn't awakened since." The earl cleared his throat. Annoyance flashed over his face. "William told me she has been ill on and off for a good week or so with no definitive cause. And she's slept quite a bit when she's not causing havoc." He shrugged and shared a glance with the inspector. "We all assumed her mother's death took much out of her."

Well, buggar. "I assume Fanny is with her now?" The inspector's wife was the closest thing Isobel had to a confidante outside of himself. Perhaps he could ask for more personal information from her, for exhaustion and suffering from stomach upset were generally signs of other, more troubling and permanent things than mourning or eating unsavory foods.

William nodded. "Yes. Francesca hasn't left Isobel's side since she arrived. Has sobbed for the duration."

At times, too many Stormes were, well, too many Stormes. "It's not good for your wife to be overwrought in her condition, nor does Isobel need hysterics when she's trying to heal." He put a foot on the next stair tread. "Someone fetch my sister for me. She can assist."

Trey nodded. "I'll go down and ask her."

"Thank you." Then he focused his gaze on the earl. "You'll wish for me to do a full exam on your cousin? As well as to check for any internal injuries I can assess?" Everything that he was strained to go to her immediately. "And perhaps ascertain the cause of her stomach issues?" Apprehension gripped his chest so tightly he could hardly move. He was always studying medical journals and would always push for greater advancement in the field, as well as technique with examinations for both men and women.

All those times he and Isobel had come together without the use of the protection available to him to prevent pregnancy… There were a few things he could do to perhaps guess at whether or not a woman was with child, but nothing would be absolute until a few months or so had passed.

Dear God, if what I suspect is true, I'm going to have to face a tribunal of angry Stormes.

Hadleigh nodded. He narrowed his eyes. "If you deem it necessary."

William chimed in. "We trust you."

By that time, Jane had come upstairs while Finn waited on the lower level. She glanced at Royce. "We'd best get to it straightaway. Time is of the essence, especially with injuries to the head."

"I know." He nodded. A certain numbness had fallen over him. Everything was changing, and the temporary level ground he'd found by breaking his connection with Isobel had suddenly shifted quite violently. "I'll send Mrs. Storme down to you in the drawing room. If you'll wait there for word of Isobel's condition?" When the men nodded, he looked at his sister. Though her smile was encouraging, it was small and tight. "I'll need my instruments sterilized," he began as they climbed the stairs together. "I'll also need a clean wash basin and towels."

"I know, Royce. I do the same every day I'm in the clinic." She touched his arm. "I'm sure it's not as bad as you think."

Oh, if only he could tell her what he was thinking!

As soon as he stepped into her bedchamber, his heart lurched the second he rested his gaze upon her. She was so pale. Vomit stained the fine lawn of the man's shirt she'd worn, and despite his position there as a physician, he couldn't help his attention jogging to her legs clad in male breeches. Yes, obviously she'd been riding, and not in a lady's sidesaddle. Damn it all to hell! If only he could ring a peal over her head, but she was so still, unconscious, and unmoving. At least Trey had had the presence of mind not to prop her head upon pillows.

He shot a glance to Jane. "Please remove Mrs. Storme."

"No! Please let me stay!" The woman was near inconsolable as Jane half dragged half pushed the woman from the room. "But she's my friend and she needs me."

"She'll still need you when she wakes." The soothing sound of Jane's words drifted to him from the corridor. "Save your own strength, Fanny. Depending on the doctor's diagnosis, there might be a long recovery period."

"But—"

"Come. Perhaps you can help by answering a few rather personal questions regarding Isobel..."

It was so refreshing to work with his sister and know that she had things well in hand so that he could do what he needed to do.

However, before he could act like a doctor, he was a former lover first, and right now, the fact that Isobel was lying there as pale and still as death left him frozen and shaking with fear. After placing his bag on the bedside table, Royce paused at her side, staring down at her. "If you were trying again to gain my notice, sweeting, you have it," he murmured as he brushed at the damp curls plastered to her forehead. Damn, but she needed out of those rain-wet clothes. Blood stained the bedclothes upon which she rested. Gingerly he turned her head and visually inspected the wound. There was a sizable lump on her skull from the force of impact, but perhaps the blood had come from the gash in the skin, buried in her hair, and not something more serious. "How did I ever think I could forget you?" A shaft of pain went through his heart. "I can't live with myself if you did this because of me."

Then Jane returned to the room bearing a stack of neatly folded towels and a steaming teapot in the other hand. "Will you be able to do this, Royce?"

"It matters not if I can't; this is what I *will* do. For her." He glanced at his sister. "For the Stormes because I can do nothing less... after everything."

"That's what makes you a good doctor." She shot him a soft smile. "Try not to worry until we know more."

"Easier said than done." Especially when the patient wasn't merely a wounded soldier or a man he was related to by marriage who needed greater understanding than what other, older doctors could give. Screwing his courage to the sticking place, Royce crossed the room and gently closed the door. "Let me wash my hands and we'll begin."

Half an hour later, the examination was completed. "At least there is nothing horrifically wrong with her." He stared at Jane as mild shock rolled over him. His mouth moved but no sound came out. After clearing his throat, he tried again. "But bloody hell."

His sister snickered as she wiped her hands upon one of the thin towels. "I rather think our findings deserve a healthier oath than that." Though there was teasing in her voice, shadows of grief and perhaps envy pooled in her eyes. Such an event hadn't yet happened for her and Finn, and now this had occurred when her own nodcock brother hadn't even thought it possible even if he was a physician. "And be warned. You are under obligation to tell Andrew and William. To say nothing of Finn. He's a bit protective of his younger cousin since she's shown an affinity for writing."

Oh, dear God. How was he supposed to tackle any of this? However, one thing had been made abundantly clear while he'd conducted the study of Isobel's wounds and an examination of her stomach and abdomen by touch and feel. There was absolutely no way that he could give up being a doctor or working in his clinic. Too many people needed him and what he did, and he adored helping others who had no place else to turn.

The question was, could the doctor part of him live alongside the earl part of him?

He didn't know, but he did know that he needed advice, and not from his sister.

With a shuddering sigh, he rubbed a hand over his face. "I'd best go down and face the lions."

"And hope they're not hungry, because they *will* eat you alive." She crossed the room and laid a hand on his shoulder. "I'll clean up here and dress Isobel into something comfortable and dry. After that, I'll find Fanny and talk to her." Compassion lined her face. "You have much to think about."

"Yes, and for the moment, I'm flummoxed at how to proceed."

"You'll do it with integrity and courage. Just like you've done everything else in your life." She offered a small smile. "Go face the men. I'll be down as soon as I'm done here."

"But the Stormes are—"

"Loud and big and scary at times, just like their namesakes. However," her eyes twinkled, "they're the most supportive people you'll ever find once they're on your side."

"Yes, but how long does that take?"

All the way down the stairs and along the corridor, Royce's insides knotted themselves and then knotted again. Worry held him captive; honor demanded he completely change his life to accommodate this shift. Yet at the back of his mind, he wondered what Isobel would do. This was yet another change she would need to square with.

Would she even want him in her life after this?

He gained the drawing room with a sense of doom hanging over his head, yet there was a sliver of excitement that kept breaking through that he couldn't quite keep buried. Trey sat in a chair a bit removed, reading a book. The three Storme men were all in a heated discussion upon a subject Royce didn't care about, so he cleared his throat. "I have some answers and some news."

Both William and Hadleigh stood while Finn adjusted his Bath chair so he could look at Royce. Varying expressions of concern crossed their faces, and seeing them all together like that, the Storme line was evident in them.

"Will Isobel come out right?" William wanted to know. "I already have one sister whose mind is decidedly not normal. Will I have another?"

Trey rose to his feet. He tossed the book aside. "I'm not convinced the elder Miss Storme's brain is damaged. It might be that she simply thinks differently than others. Until we find out how it works and how to communicate more effectively with her, she'll always be thought of as odd."

How much did he admire his brother? And why the hell did he think he could walk away from the clinic and all the strides he and Trey had made in the medical field since they'd opened it? Royce's chest tightened further. He cleared his throat. "Caroline's treatment can wait. Right now, I need to speak about Isobel."

All eyes turned toward him, and he resisted the urge to tug on his suddenly too restrictive cravat. "Isobel remains unconscious. However, I don't believe it's a permanent state. She briefly came back while Jane and I were conducting the exam, but fainted again. There is some swelling on her head at the point of impact. She'll undoubtedly have a concussion, which means she'll suffer a headache when she does waken and will need to be watched for signs of lethargy, blurry vision, speech impediment, at the least." He pressed his lips together. This next bit would land him in the middle of the storm. "Aside from a few lacerations and contusions consistent with being thrown from a horse, she's suffered no broken bones."

Relief flitted over William's face. "That's good to hear."

"Indeed." The Earl of Hadleigh narrowed his eyes. "There's more though." It wasn't a question.

"Yes, there is." Royce cleared his throat and wished he were anywhere but in that drawing room facing these men. When he glanced at Trey, his brother raised an eyebrow in challenge and gave a tiny shrug as if to say, *best have it over with*. With nothing for it, Royce shoved a hand through his hair. "During the course of the full examination, I have found evidence that Isobel might be increasing. That state would certainly explain the other symptoms she's been exhibiting. However, more time is needed to be absolutely certain. Tests that fishwives have touted simply aren't accurate and they *are* rather unpleasant."

The silence after that statement was absolute and deafening.

"You're certain?" The earl crossed his arms at his chest. "There is no other explanation for her recent bout of stomach distress?"

"I am. It's only a guess at this point by putting together other information we've accumulated, but there's the possibility she's nearly six weeks along." Heat crept up the back of his neck, and the longer he stood there in front of these larger-than-life men, the more his courage shrank.

"Oh, dear God," William breathed. His face paled as he glanced helplessly at his cousins. "How the deuce did this happen?"

Finn, always the irreverent one in the group, snickered. "I would imagine in the usual ways, Cousin."

Then Andrew became the roaring storm he'd been known for a year ago. Mottled red rose up his neck into his face. His chest strained. He clenched his fists. Just when Royce assumed he would explode, he took a few deep breaths and regulated his breathing. Eventually, he calmed, and it was a true testament of how far he'd come under his wife's care. "Do we know who Isobel has been clandestinely seeing for the past month or so?"

Though William shook his head, both Finn and Trey stared at Royce with expressions of expectation and speculation.

Bloody hell.

This time, Royce *did* tug at the knot of his cravat. "Uh, *I'm* the man Isobel has been trysting with. It's been a tempestuous and torrid affair, which I broke off a week ago."

The men erupted into exclamations and accusations at once.

"You dastard." William lunged at him, but the earl restrained him and held him back. "You compromised my sister. Now what's left of her reputation will be in shreds once her condition becomes obvious."

Guilt and excitement twisted down Royce's spine as he skirted around Finn's Bath chair to keep the older Stormes at bay. "If you'll but listen—"

"By Jove, Marsden, I'll have your head for this." Andrew popped his hands on his hips and glared. "What possessed you to do such a thing?"

"Honestly, Drew, we all know how Cousin Isobel acts around men, and she's always courted scandal," Finn interrupted with a mischievous grin flirting about his mouth. "Can we all agree, though, that it's good she's settled on one man and that she hasn't left him cowering in a corner somewhere?"

"Do shut up, Finn." The earl glared at his brother. "Now is not the time for humor."

"I'll argue that it is. Until we hear what the doctor has to say, anger is unproductive." He slid a glance to Royce. "Did she lead you a merry chase or did you encourage her?"

Again, the room exploded into accusations and threats that grew progressively louder. Trey joined the fray to defend him while Finn was apparently bent on playing the devil's advocate, which only incited further annoyance into the group.

Royce put space between the seething men. When he gained the middle of the room, a swath of peace came over him, and suddenly, he came into own as the Earl of Worchester. "Enough!" Authority rang in his voice, enough to quiet the din. As everyone looked at him with disapproval and speculation, he put up a hand. "That will be enough." One by one, he met each man's gaze. "Yes, we are facing an acutely embarrassing situation, and it can't be dealt with until Isobel heals from her injuries." His voice was level and steady. He lifted his chin a notch as a feeling of power surged through him. This must have been what his father felt at times. "Whatever happens from here on out is my decision and hers alone. Do you understand?"

Andrew bristled. "But, I am—"

"No." Royce held his gaze, dared him to object. "It's a private matter and does *not* concern you, Hadleigh."

"Are you threatening me, Doctor?"

"I am not, and since you've forced my hand, if you can't be civil, you should refer to me as Worchester. I will only respond to 'doctor' from my contemporaries and friends." Though his stomach was tied in knots, a certain thrill of victory shot down his spine.

"Fine, but that doesn't excuse your part in this."

"Oh, I quite agree, and I take full responsibility, but you must let me talk with Isobel. She needs copious amounts of coaxing to come around." He sighed, and some of his newfound confidence wavered. "I've come to know the woman she is better over the time we've spent together, and she needs a delicate touch."

A gasp issued from William. "Dear God. Isobel will flat-out refuse your suit since you hold a title now."

Yes, the odds were well and truly stacked against him. "I'm well aware of her aversion, but I am a patient man, Inspector. Give me a chance."

Finn wheeled over and paused beside Royce. "You've heard his stance on the matter. I suggest we all take some time to digest the events of the day and come back together later to discuss them properly over tea."

The Storme men exchanged irritated glances. Trey said nothing, but he had a smirk on his face as he quit the room ahead of the others. Andrew nodded. "We are not done, Worchester."

"No, we are not. There is much to decide, but it needs to come from a place of compassion and understanding. Not intimidation and anger." When the men left, he looked at Finn and his shoulders sagged. "Will you lecture me too?"

"Of course not. Certain things in life happen. They probably seemed like good ideas in the moment, but now, when the consequences come calling, it's a rather harsh reality to swallow." For long moments, the major regarded him as if he were searching for the right words. "I'm speaking to you as a friend."

"I appreciate that." As the strength left him, Royce sank into a nearby chair while Finn turned his to face him. "It's still a shock."

"I'll wager it is." Grief flickered through Finn's eyes but was gone just as quickly. "How do you feel about Isobel?" When Royce didn't answer, the major continued. "Women have the tendency to throw us into a whirlwind. They'll tear out our hearts and make us chase them, drive us to things we probably wouldn't otherwise, but in the end, they're essential to our very existence beyond desire."

"Yes." Royce nodded. He planted an elbow on the armrest and then dropped his face into his hand. "What's between me and Isobel is complicated."

Finn snorted. "Have you ever known a woman who wasn't?"

"Isobel is the most stubborn one of the lot." With a sigh, he lifted his head and met Finn's gaze. Sympathy and amusement swirled together, damn him. "I'm supposed to be in mourning, Finn. So is she. Neither of those deaths is a month old. Nothing can be done due to society's laws, yet she's increasing." He groaned, for it was a sticky wicket indeed. "We can't put off a marriage. Imagine *that* scandal. Alternately, I can send her away to my father's—mine I suppose—country estate, for there will still be the babe if she refuses my suit."

"Oh, she'll refuse. You know that already."

"I do, but…"

"Listen." Finn leaned forward and jostled Royce's knee. "Have you learned nothing from her?"

"What do you mean?"

"Isobel is a Storme. That means she feels things deeply and is intense." He pressed his lips together. "She is like water, which in essence means she's powerful enough to drown you."

"This is true. I often feel like that in her presence, for I'll never know what she'll do next."

Finn nodded. "But she's soft enough to cleanse you and runs deep enough to save you." He patted Royce's knee before leaning back in his chair. "Society and its rules—guidelines, really, if you want my opinion—can go hang at times."

"But I'm an earl and I must abide by those rules. Shouldn't I?" Why was everything so buried in confusion?

"You are overthinking the problem, my friend. The answer is quite simple."

"Oh?"

"Do you love Isobel?"

Those four little words sent both terror into his heart and budding joy. Life had certainly lost its color without her in it, and now there was the possibility of a child. An infant they'd both made together… a family. It had been a dream, of course, and one for years into the future. He heaved a sigh. "I suspect that I do. She's both amazing and terrifying, and I nearly lost my mind when Trey summoned me here after her accident."

"Because you thought you'd lose her." It wasn't a question.

"Yes." Royce nodded. "It will break me if she dies."

"Then you have your answer. Once you're caught up in a storm, the only way out is through." He chuckled. "Now I know how Jane must have felt just before we were engaged." Mirth danced in his eyes as he met Royce's gaze. "I should apologize to her." Then he sobered. "Marry Isobel discreetly and quietly."

"If she'll have me, but I'm sure that will be a fight in and of itself."

"Oh, indubitably." Finn snickered. "Our families will be the only people who know. After six months or so, you can announce it formally to a few select members of the *ton*." He shrugged. "Let society talk. Isobel doesn't let that trouble her. She never has, and who cares if they talk? They'll move on to something else as quickly as they'll gossip about this. In the end, you'll have her to wife, and isn't that all that matters?"

Spending a lifetime at Isobel's side as her husband sounded

too good to be true. "Andrew and William want her tamed by marriage."

"But what do *you* think?"

Royce allowed a grin. "I thought I wanted a proper, scandal-free wife to be my countess. But now I see I would never be happy without attempting to take on a wild and independent Storme. With her, the title will be strengthened and perhaps refined. I can't help but think that might be a good thing." Why had he never looked at it that way before? He felt like a fool as he peered at Finn, who grinned back like the same kind of idiot.

"I look forward to hearing the tale of how you finally managed to land my cousin."

"Your brother and hers will object."

"How can they? You're an earl. It's a good match. They'll come around after they blow themselves out." Finn wheeled close enough to clasp a hand on Royce's shoulder. "I wish you good fortune for when that time comes."

"Thank you. I'll need it." Now, to plan the words that would win her heart while he kept vigil at her bedside.

CHAPTER EIGHTEEN

July 27, 1818

WHEN ISOBEL CAME awake, she was met with a raging ache thudding through her head. At first, she didn't remember where she was, but slowly she began to recognize the familiar furniture and décor of her bedroom at home. Darkness had engulfed the space, broken only by the flickering flame of a single candle that rested in a brass holder on the far bedside table.

"Welcome back."

Oh, that delicious, masculine voice! It sent tiny flutters down her spine. Slowly, carefully, she turned her head to the opposite side of where the candle sputtered. "Royce." Then the happiness she'd had upon seeing him evaporated. Why was he here? Hadn't he told her he didn't want her any longer?

But his grin was soft and there was a glimmer in his hazel eyes she didn't quite trust. Why would he look that way if he wished to leave her? "What are you doing here?" Her throat was scratchy and dry, and when she raised a hand to her head, her fingers encountered a length of cloth wrapped about her head. "What happened?" When she tried to push herself into a sitting position, his hands were on her shoulders holding her in place.

"Easy. It's best not to move suddenly." Once he regained his seat on the straight-backed wooden chair at her bedside, he spoke again. "You were thrown from a horse yesterday afternoon. When your head hit a tree, you were rendered unconscious. Do you remember that?"

"No." Why the devil had she been on horseback? "Is that why my head aches so fiercely?"

"Yes. You have a mild concussion and a rather large bump on the back of your head, but everything will be right as rain in a few days." His eyes were filled with such tenderness, she didn't know how to interpret that emotion. "Do you hurt anywhere else? Though Jane and I did a cursory examination on you shortly after the accident occurred, it's most helpful if the patient can catalogue other injuries themselves."

Isobel frowned. She wore a thin lawn shift. Here and there, bruises dotted her arms. When she experimentally moved her legs and then her hips, she let loose a faint moan. "I feel quite battered but otherwise, my insides don't hurt, if that's what you mean." Why was he here, acting in a doctor's capacity, if he'd turned his back on the profession in favor of his title?

"That's good to hear." Then he took her hand. The warmth of his fingers on hers sent tendrils of peace to soothe the worry that built in her belly. "You don't remember the accident nor of riding into Hyde Park to meet a Lord Alder?" The softness of his tones lulled her into a relaxed state. Truly, he was a good physician. It was a crime for him to give it up.

She scrunched up her nose. "I remember Lord Alder from a society event weeks ago." A frown tugged at the corners of her lips as she found Royce's gaze. "Why was I with him yesterday?"

The way he rubbed the pad of his thumb across her knuckles made her breath catch. "You and he apparently got up a wager to race through Hyde Park, and you entered with William's Arabian thoroughbred."

"Why, though? I'd not ridden that horse much."

"It seems your short-term memory is lost."

"Is that a bad thing?" She didn't want to move lest he release her hand.

"Not overly much. It might return; it might not. As long as you're still able to speak and think, you'll be fine." For long moments, he remained quiet, apparently content to look at her with a faint grin before it vanished under an expression of concern. "In any event, the race you entered went awry when your horse spooked and ended up throwing you against a tree. Trey happened to be in the vicinity and witnessed the accident. He and others got you into a carriage. Then he sent notes to me and your cousin Andrew."

That made no sense. Why would she even wish to race through Hyde Park? "How long was I unconscious?"

"About a day and a half. It's now nine in the evening. Your accident was yesterday." He cleared his throat. "There are other things I need to inform you about, but would you rather have your brother in? Or perhaps the earl? Or Fanny?"

Why was he suddenly uncomfortable? Did he remember that he was now a prized bachelor who could be trapped into marriage if he was alone in an unmarried woman's room? Hot panic rose in her chest. She certainly didn't want that. Once more, she attempted to struggle into a sitting position, and this time she succeeded. "I'd rather not see anyone." The movement broke the connection of their hands, and she mourned the loss of that warmth. "Does this have something to do with my health?"

"Yes, as well as your future."

There was no glint of amusement in his eyes, no teasing in his voice. Instead, he was as somber as she'd ever seen him, and good heavens he was so handsome in the candlelight! That little shock of hair that fell over his brow gleamed like molten copper in the dim illumination, and his eyes were now more green than brown. The only other time they'd done that was when he and she had had that tryst in his clinic. Things between them had shifted and they'd grown closer...

Isobel's heartbeat accelerated. "Tell me." Was he here for more than the role of her doctor?

"You were bleeding profusely; head wounds usually do. Both

your brother and the earl indicated that you'd been ill for a week or more. They urged me to conduct a more thorough exam on you than I would have done originally." His Adam's apple bobbed above the knot of his black cravat, and belatedly she remembered he was in mourning. So was she. "My sister Jane assisted."

"And?" Why wouldn't get tell her straightaway? Would she die?

"The few tests I performed by touch indicate that you're increasing, Isobel. Six weeks or so along." He cleared his throat as her lower jaw dropped and astonishment swept through her person. "I have to know if you laid with another man in the time you and I were together."

"I… I…" Is *that* what he thought about her? Is *that* what her reputation suggested? Heat of both embarrassment and fury slapped at her cheeks. "No." She shook her head. "There's only been you." Merciful heavens, but that would explain why she'd been sick at her stomach lately, as well as the dizzy spells. "Only you." The first man she'd trysted with sent her into this state. Shock gripped her insides. It was all too much. As her breath came in tiny pants, tears welled quickly to her eyes and spilled frantically over onto her cheeks. "Surely you're wrong."

"I could, indeed, be incorrect. Only time will tell. However, there are certain signs a physician or midwife look for in the early stages, and you have them all." Compassion lined his face. "Is your upset happy or sad?"

"I don't know." The words came out on a wail.

"Here." Royce thrust his handkerchief into her hand. "You'll feel better if you talk to me. And trust me, I was just as shocked as you."

"Yet you'll suffer no consequences, nor will you be shunned by society for this indiscretion." She snuffled into the linen square, and when the crisp, clean scent of him hit her nose, her tears fell even harder. "Oh, this is impossible," she whispered, refusing to look at him. "I don't know what to think, and now I know why you're really here." Another wail erupted from her, and she pressed the handkerchief to her cheeks. She knew what would come next, and she didn't want it.

"It's a pregnancy, Isobel, not a death sentence." Once more he took possession of her hand. When she tried to pull it away, he tightened his hold. "If you're afraid, please talk to me. Perhaps I can set your mind at ease."

"This changes *everything*." She dabbed at the moisture on her face. "I don't like change." That brought another round of heavy tears. "And I don't like that you're here because of *this*."

"I've been here since you were brought home. Haven't left your bedside, in fact."

Now that she looked closer at him, she discerned the shadow of stubble clinging to his jaws and chin, noted how rumpled his clothing looked, as well as the loosened way his cravat fit. How dreadfully unfair was it that he looked like sin and scandal, while she was in a bandage and bed, being told she'd soon grow wide as a barge with a babe in her belly?

"Oh. You can go, then. As you can see, I'm well enough."

"I'm not leaving you." Though the words sent more flutters down her spine, she sniffed. "Tell me why this news upsets you as much as my presence."

Drowning in emotions she couldn't sort nor control, she blurted, "Because you'll want to marry me out of obligation, and I don't want a man like that." Isobel paused to wipe at an influx of new tears. "I'll be a burden and you'll come to hate me."

"I wouldn't." His thumb slid over her knuckles, soothing, quieting... exciting.

"You would. You'd resent that you were forced into a marriage to a woman who would continue to bring nothing but shame and scandal to your name." She shook her head. The braid on her shoulder stank of mud, sweet, and vomit. Her stomach dry-heaved as she threw the hair over to her back. "You'd always wonder if you could have done better had you not trysted with me." Her voice broke on the last word along with another torrent of tears.

"That's not true."

She huffed and wiped her streaming nose. "You put an end to our affair because I wasn't good enough for you and your lofty new status."

His eyes narrowed. "I seem to recall you saying that you'd never marry a man with a title the first time we walked in Hyde Park. We both have a few issues to work out."

"I haven't changed my mind about that." She looked at her right hand where her mother's ruby ring still rested. "If I became your wife, and you only ask me due to this child, once you beget your heir and a spare, we'll drift even further apart. It's the way of marriages in the *beau monde*."

"My parents weren't like that. Their union was held together by love for the entirety, and as far as I know, my father never strayed." He tightened his hold on her left hand. "You only need to look about and find the good ones instead of concentrating on the bad ones."

Oh, she refused to let him rout her with logic. Isobel shook her head. For the moment, her tears had stemmed. "Beyond that, there are other worries."

"Such as?"

Another wave of panic welled in her chest. "I'm afraid I'll be a terrible mother. Just look at the horror my family is." The urge to cry returned. "My father sent Caroline away due to his and Mother's inability to understand her. Cousin Andrew's father and mine fought so much about what the Storme family should do that it tore a huge rift between them. And they're only now learning how to live with their emotions. I don't want to add my mess to the melee."

"Ah, Isobel, don't you know that you already have?" Royce's laugh both comforted her and set her teeth on edge with aggravation.

"Do shut up." She hurled a pillow at him, and then bit back a groan when the bruises on her arm ached.

He easily caught the pillow and tossed it to the foot of her bed. "Sweeting, look closer at the Stormes. Every one of them—excepting Caroline of course—have managed to make their lives work and succeed despite the obstacles and terrible beginnings." He smiled at her in that certain way he had that sent tiny fires into her blood. "That speaks volumes to the people they've put into their lives, as well as the wives they've chosen."

"Perhaps." She wasn't ready to concede defeat. One truth shimmered more brightly than all others. "I never wished to marry, Royce. You know that."

"Actually, you said you never wanted to marry a man with a title."

"Yes, because I'll fail miserably at being a countess." Her hands shook from fear, so she quickly clasped them in her lap. "The thought of it takes my breath away, and I don't like that feeling."

A teasing grin flirted with his sensual lips. Her gaze dropped to his mouth for half a second. Oh, why couldn't he just kiss her and forget about all this serious talk? "You're awfully certain I *want* to marry you." He shrugged. "Maybe I don't.

"What?" Shock speared through her chest as she stared at him. "You'd let me flounder in scandal as my belly swells and the whole of society casts me out?"

"I'm sure your cousin would send you to Derbyshire. How bad could it be?"

"Quite." The prospect of having to raise an infant alone felt like a weight had been set upon her chest. "I detest the country."

"Is there anything you *do* like, besides courting scandal?" When she didn't answer, he stood and then resettled on the side of her bed. His shirt was open slightly at the placket beneath his messy cravat, and the glimpse of red curly hair on his chest made her catch her breath. Tremors of need made themselves known between her thighs. "We're both aware that I can't escape the title, but if you're adamant about it and truly cannot see yourself with me because of it, I can renounce the earlship. The outcry through the powers-that-be will prove enormous, and I'd be the first Worchester in history who couldn't come up to the mark." He looked a tad green about the mouth about it, but the determination in his eyes held her captive. "That would mean the responsibilities of the earl would fall to Trey, and I can't, in good conscience, give him that cross to bear after everything he's already survived in the war."

That's so much! For the second time that evening, Isobel's lower jaw dropped. She gawked at the man beside her. "You would give up the title for me?"

"I would consider it, of course, if that would sway your decision." A faint blush colored his cheeks. "Despite the scandal and the whispers that will surely follow, yes."

"I…" She what? Was that selfish? Would refuse to accept him as the man he was when every fiber of her being strained for him to accept her, flaws and all?

"I doubt our children would be able to live down that shame."

Dear God, he said children! Did that mean he truly wanted to build a life with her? Her heartbeat quickened. Everything was coming at her so fast she couldn't properly sort it. "That is probably true, and it wouldn't be fair to them to jeopardize their future and possibly put a rift in the Marsden family. I know what it's like to grow up with familial animosity and wouldn't wish that on anyone." *What if I unintentionally harm this child because of my inability to move through the world like a proper* ton *lady?* Responsibility pressed in on her, and she gasped from the magnitude of it.

And even more disturbing, could they survive on a physician's living? Without the title, they wouldn't have the coin needed to keep a house in Mayfair. She had no idea what his salary was, for they hadn't discussed anything of a serious nature during their affair.

He nodded. "However, despite the fact I was raised from birth to assume this very thing, I would do it for you. And God help Trey. He'll have a more difficult time of it than I would."

"Oh, Royce." For one wonderful moment, she teered on the edge of having everything she'd wanted from him—a man without a title, a man she got on with tolerably well, a man who made her fly with his touch and kisses, a man who would be the father of her children—but how heartless could she be if she asked all of that from him? Being the Earl of Worchester was his birthright. It was the connection to his family name. It didn't matter that he wasn't all too keen on holding the title himself, it was his, and even now he sought to protect his brother from it.

The longer she regarded him, the more tears filled her eyes, this time out of gratitude. Perhaps love. Her breath caught from the magnitude of that thought. *Did* she truly love him? And if she did, could she ask him to something so life-changing merely for her? Isobel trembled. He would come to resent her in a different way than he would have had he married her out of obligation, yet the willingness to forego the title had to mean something.

But at no time during this discussion had he declared himself. Her emotional upheaval plunged downward into the depths of despair. The tears started again, and this time they came with sobs that hurt her chest. In desperation, she reached for him. When he wrapped his arms around her, she melted into him with a sigh. "I can't let you do that. Not for me. Not for anyone." She clung to him, and her tears wet the superfine fabric of his navy jacket. "Marriage is one thing but giving up your whole history merely so I'll change my mind is quite another." Why did he have to feel so good and smell even better? Royce represented safety and excitement, protection and scandal, companionship but a loss of freedom.

Why can I not just be brave and demand to know he feels about me?

"Ah, Isobel." He pressed his lips to her temple. "You are a study of contrasts, and you've distracted me from the first."

What did that mean? She was too much a coward to ask.

"You're awfully certain *I* want to marry *you*. Obligation or not, title or not, stunning intercourse or not, perhaps I don't wish to wed you. It's bad form to assume, you know."

"There is that." He grinned, and she melted further.

She pulled back enough to stare into his face. But his wink slightly alleviated some of her worry. "Are you toying with me?" These newest changes in her life would soon carry her away on a tide she wasn't sure she could come back from. Not without him.

"Oh, indeed. How does it feel now that the shoe is on the other foot, sweeting?"

It was the second time he'd called her by the endearment. Did that mean his emotions had been engaged? "I think we should talk more."

"And I think you need to rest. I've given you much to think about, and knowing you as I do, it's all become jumbled up and knotted together until you can't make sense of anything." Gently, he urged her backward against the pillows, and for one brief second, his body covered hers, sheltered her from life's battery, but he merely brushed his lips over hers and then straightened. "When you're ready and have had time to sort everything, send for me. Then we'll talk."

She clutched his handkerchief tightly in her hand, but the deluge of emotions had exhausted her. Isobel nodded. "You won't leave me again?"

"I don't think I could even if I tried." The whispered words danced through her head as he slipped from the room and quietly closed the door behind him.

At least there was that.

CHAPTER NINETEEN

July 28, 1818

"NO, NOT THAT jacket, Vincent. The charcoal gray one," Royce instructed his valet that evening. "I want to look my best for the lady." He waggled his eyebrows when the other man looked at him with questions. "I intend to propose tonight."

"Ah, then I shall make certain you look the part of a hopeful suitor." Vincent whisked the bottle green jacket back into the clothes press and then soon returned with the requested charcoal one. "Let's have a look, then."

Royce slipped his arms into the sleeves of the exquisitely tailored garment. He grunted when the valet smoothed it over his shoulders. While peering critically at his reflection in the cheval glass, he did up the silver and mother-of-pearl buttons. "It goes well with the black cravat, yes?"

"Yes, but it would have gone even better had you let me dye a few shirts black too."

"There wasn't time." Speaking of which... He glanced at the carriage-style clock that sat on top of a bureau in the dressing room. Quarter to nine o'clock. Isobel's note said to meet her at the inspector's townhouse on the hour. "I need to go." Grabbing his black gloves from a table, he headed toward the door.

"Uh, Your Lordship, won't you be wanting this?" Vincent

held up a small, black ring box. When he flipped it open, a yellow diamond winked in the candlelight.

"As much as I would adore seeing that on my lady's finger, I fear she's not much impressed with gems and jewels." He patted the pocket of his black satin waistcoat. "I think she'll prefer this one instead."

"Hope springs eternal, my lord." The valet closed the ring box and replaced it in a drawer in the clothes press.

"Indeed, it does." Royce rested a hand on the door handle. "If all goes well, I shall see you in the morning. If it doesn't, I'll return within the hour."

One never knew if Isobel's storm hadn't yet blown itself out.

BY THE TIME Inspector Storme's butler showed Royce into an elegantly appointed parlor done in pleasing shades of cream and green, he had no idea what to expect. He'd assumed Isobel would still be in bed, resting, but of course she would go against the advice of her doctor. *Stubborn woman.* Two globe-shared gaslights flickered on one wall while a couple of candles in silver holders glimmered on small, ivory-inlaid tables that flanked a low sofa. There, lounging on the brocade cushions was where the lady had decided to hold court.

And there was no chance of him ignoring her.

"Isobel."

She reposed in an evening gown made of ivory silk so thin it was almost sheer—had she also dampened the skirting?—complete with a sheer overskirt that twinkled with golden embroidery. The low bodice and shoulders of the gown were trimmed in some sort of ivory gauze that drew his gaze to the tops of her breasts. The bruises on her arms did nothing to distract from her scandalously tempting image. Gone was the bandage from her head. Her glorious dark brown hair flowed down her back with the sides held up with golden combs. Gold embroidered slippers completed the picture, and he couldn't take his focus from her.

"You resemble a Greek goddess."

"That was my intent. I wanted you to think back to that poetry reading when we first decided to begin our affair, when I read those erotic verses."

"And you first captured my notice." He could only wonder why, for she largely remained a mystery to him. The soft click of the door being closed behind him jolted Royce from his silence. Did her family encourage this meeting, or did they not know of it? His throat suddenly tight, he cleared it and came further into the room, pausing at the edge of an Aubusson carpet in the same soothing green palette of the room. "Where is your brother?"

From somewhere within the bowels of the house, frantic barking from Ivan drifted through the air. Obviously, she'd also planned to have one of the servants watch the exuberant Corgi for this evening and the canine wasn't taking the news well.

"I believe he took Fanny to have dinner with Cousin Andrew and Sarah." She shifted her position to cross her legs at the knee, and her skirting rose up her calf. Like the other day, the only flash of color in her ensemble was the ruby ring on her right hand. "But then, you didn't come here to see them, did you?"

"No." The word sailed out, breathless. What the devil happened to all the words he'd wished to say? Suddenly, he felt at sixes and sevens much like he had the night they'd met on the shore of the Serpentine River. He waited, almost frozen to the spot, merely to see what Isobel would do next. The fascination he'd originally been caught with hadn't faded over the weeks. *Oh, no.* If anything, he was even more hooked and only needed for her to reel him in.

"Ah." Her grin held an edge of wickedness that went straight to his stones. "What *did* you come for, Doctor? Or should I call you Worchester?" Slowly, oh so incredibly slowly, she rose from the sofa, and once she was fully standing, the whole of her form was on display... and the gown was every bit as transparent as he'd thought, especially when she moved in front of a candle.

"At this moment, Royce will suffice. I'd rather not bow to ceremony just now." His voice was graveled with the myriad of emotions that bounced through him.

"Why don't you come closer so we can finish our talk from yesterday?" She gestured toward a matching chair near her vacated sofa, and every tiny movement had the folds of her gown clinging to various curves on her person. "Or does the cat have your tongue?"

He shook his head, determined not to let her waylay his purpose with her wiles. "I'm happy to do so, but it would be best if you'd cover yourself with a blanket. The last thing I want is for the inspector to swoop down on me and call me out for this latest scheme of yours."

"You worry too much." The huskiness of her laughter washed over him, and he stumbled toward her a few more steps as if she were a siren. "William is well aware that I've invited you here tonight. As for the scandal, well it's not as if I need to guard my maidenhead." She laughed again, and he was nearly lost to the sound.

"How does your head feel?" Royce finally blurted out, for what sort of physician was he if he didn't ask after the health of his patient?

Some of the naughtiness faded from her eyes. She touched a hand to the back of her head and winced. "The pain from the bump is still there, but my brain isn't pounding as much as yesterday. My vision remains clear, as does my speech."

"Good." He nodded as if he were a puppet on a string. "I'm glad to hear it." If they continued on in this vein, nothing would be accomplished other than him embarrassing himself in front of her. It had been much too long since he'd tasted her skin or buried himself in her honeyed heat. "Uh, what is the meaning of this?" He gestured at her to encompass her attire.

When she blew out a frustrated breath, she ceased to be the

alluring Greek goddess and had returned to the Isobel he knew and was coming to love with every breath that he took. "I am trying to gain your notice."

Not this again. He rolled his eyes. "You have it. There is no need for such theatrics." Though he appreciated the hell out of the gown, and if she'd give him half the chance, he would show her just how much.

"Do I?" Those sapphire eyes were wide as she approached him. "Can you swear that I mean more to you than the title?"

"You should know that by now. I would have given it up for you, Isobel." He'd been dead serious when he'd proposed the idea to her yesterday, but when she'd turned it down, he'd felt both elated and disappointed. And damn it all, he still had no idea what she wanted from him. "The title is something I am, but you are a woman I need."

A pout formed on her lips, and the hold on his control slipped. "Any man could say that."

"Yet any man hasn't." Thank every god in whatever pantheon he could find that she'd remained so aloof from the men in the *ton*, for his way to her heart was clear. Unable to be parted from her any longer, Royce crossed the room. When he cupped her cheek and she nuzzled into his palm, his chest ached with everything he wanted to say but couldn't find the words. "What do I need to do in order for you to believe me?"

"Tell me something no other man has."

"Gladly." He surprised her by maneuvering her about. When he sat on the sofa, he tugged her down to him, guiding her until she straddled his lap. The moment her warmth enveloped him, and she laid a hand on his chest, inspiration struck, and it would play on her wickedly romantic side. "You'd mentioned that erotic poetry."

"Yes? What of it?"

"Well, I think in this instance, the ancient Greek poet Sappho had the right of it when she wrote this bit from *The Anactória* poem:

>...the sweetness of your laughter: yes, that – I swear it –
> sets the heart to shaking inside my breast, since
> once I look at you for a moment, I can't
> speak any longer,
>
> but my tongue breaks down, and then all at once a
> subtle fire races inside my skin, my
> eyes can't see a thing and a whirring whistle
> thrums at my hearing,
>
> cold sweat covers me and a trembling takes
> ahold of me all over—"

He didn't have the opportunity to finish the part he'd memorized, for tears had welled in Isobel's eyes and spilled onto her cheeks. "Why are you crying?" Never would he understand why a woman's brain worked as it did. Not even Trey with all his knowledge in that regard would figure it out.

"That was beautiful, but you'll think I'm dense because I don't know what it means, for every moment I spend in your company lately clouds my mind until all I can think about is you." A wail followed the statement along with another torrent of tears.

"Oh, sweeting."

"I've been overly emotional for a while; I don't usually cry this much, which is aggravating in and of itself. I despise looking weak."

He quelled the urge to laugh lest she think he made jest of her. It probably didn't help that some women, once they began increasing, became watering pots. "Your reaction to everything just now isn't your fault. It will pass, along with certain other unpleasant symptoms of your condition." Royce held her head between his hands, caught the worst of the moisture with the pads of his thumbs. "The poet is talking about her love for another, of how she feels when they're having intercourse."

"It's wonderful." Her purr of laughter was no less erotic for her tears. "How clever too."

"Indeed." Perhaps it was time for him to seduce the woman in his lap instead of the other way around. In the world Isobel occupied, actions spoke louder than words, for she'd had enough empty promises from everyone to last a lifetime. He kissed her, drank from her lips again and again, tenderly, carefully, not yet wanting to push for deeper access. "My dear girl, you have distracted me in every way a woman can since I've known you."

"Until you took the title, right?" Though her eyes had gone soft and were luminous with moisture, the rest of her body was tense as if she expected bad news.

"Before that," he kissed her, "After that," he kissed her again, "Even now." He followed that up with another kiss. "It matters not. You hold the missing pieces of my soul, and I'm merely waiting for you to take the ones I'm holding to put into yours. Because I love you."

Dear God, there was truly no going back now, and he was at peace with that.

He loves me!

Isobel stared at the doctor, the man who'd turned her entire life upside down, and she hardly dared to believe what he'd just said. "Do you mean it or are you merely saying that because I'm potentially carrying your child?"

"It's how I feel; it's how I've felt ever since the night at the clinic before I ever knew of your condition." He rested his hands on her shoulders, and while he held her gaze with his, he slowly tugged the tulle down her arms, only stopping once her breasts were bared. "And I'm quite certain I'll continue to feel the same as time goes on and I spend it with you."

When he dipped his head and took one of her hardening nipples into his mouth, Isobel gasped. With each swipe of his tongue and every gentle suck on the bud, heat swept through her body. She took his hand and guided it to her other breast, needing to experience his touch, wanting to be claimed by this man who'd taught her that some men would sacrifice everything if it meant gaining love.

For long moments, he pleasured her breasts. Isobel squirmed on his lap, and unashamedly rubbed her lower half against the swollen length of him. Need circled with hungry intent in her lower belly, for it had been all too long since she'd been with him in an intimate capacity.

Royce lifted his head. He blew on her wet nipples, and the cooling affect sent a shiver down her spine. His eyes were dark with desire as he looked at her. "I can't help that I'm an earl, Isobel, but I'm also a doctor. You made me see that a healer is who I truly am."

"You mean to still work at the clinic?" Her hands trembled as she manipulated the knot of his cravat.

"I do, and I aim to find a balance between both sides of me." He took over the task for her, and once he tossed away the neckcloth, she pressed her lips to the newly bared skin of his throat. A half sigh half groan escaped him. "It was actually your cousins who inspired me. They all have very specific callings in their lives, yet the men they're becoming outside of that is astonishing."

Her chin quivered. "I suppose Stormes do make an impression on everyone."

"There are no arguments from me on that count." Royce claimed her lips again, but this time he treated her to a series of long, drugging kisses that made her head swim and sent tiny fires into her blood. If she wasn't careful, she'd ignite into an inferno right there on his lap.

What would William say then? He'd known she was to meet the doctor tonight in the hopes they'd come to an understanding, but her brother hadn't known about the scandalous gown she'd donned for the intent of seducing Royce.

But then she didn't care, for there was magic in those kisses, and his hands were seemingly everywhere as he caressed her, primed her, made certain she was well and truly heated before wrenching away again.

His breath skated across her cheek as he slid those elegant hands down the length of her body to grasp her hips. "I know you've been reticent on this stance before, but I'd like you to marry me." When she would have voiced a protest, he took it away with a fleeting kiss. "Not for society's sake, not for appearances, not because of the babe or obligation or guilt. I want you to marry me because I've fallen in love with *you*."

More dratted tears sprang to her eyes. "They're pretty words, I'll give you that, but I'm a mess, Royce. Even before my... condition, I wasn't exactly a diamond. I'm a Storme, and because of that, I'm far from perfect. I do many things wrong. I have a temper. My family is subject to destruction, and most days I fear I'm going down that path too because all my emotions are trapped inside."

"Dearest, there is no such thing as perfection. Even if there was, why would I want that? There's no challenge in it."

"Oh." She rather liked it when he called her by terms of affection. Tears fell to her cheeks, and she dashed them away in some annoyance. "I've never felt as helter-skelter as I have since meeting you, but I do know one thing for certain." She played with the open placket of his shirt. The skin beneath was hot, and it took all her willpower not to explore him with her mouth. There were still too many things unsettled. "When I'm with you, all those things don't feel as bad or overwhelming. You bring me peace."

"Are you saying that I'm the eye of your storm?" His eyes were bright with hope, and in that moment, he was the most adorable man that her heart fluttered.

"What a nice way of looking at it."

"I think so." Royce brushed his lips over hers. "Listen to me, Isobel. Every storm eventually exhausts itself of rain, but even if the sun doesn't immediately come out afterward, let me be there at your side to watch you do amazing things when it does."

She snorted. "What *can* I do? I'm not that talented." Though she did wish to explore writing down those old stories she used to tell Caroline, the ones of fairies and princess and knights errant that had calmed her sister when life grew overwhelming.

"The question is really what can't you do when you put your mind to it?" He kissed her again and slid a hand between their bodies to burrow beneath the rumpled mess of her skirting. "You're a Storme. I'm an earl. Those might be marks against each of us, but together I believe we'll make a good team, or at least the start of one. London will need to mind itself once we finally have everything sorted. Marry me."

"Oh, Royce." When had he become so romantic? Isobel laughed and for the moment it banished her maudlin tears. "Do I have a choice?" Her voice went up an octave when he slipped his hand between her splayed thighs and strummed those fingers along her sensitive flesh. "It's so much change in such a little period of time that I hardly know which way to go any longer."

"That's entirely your decision." There was a rather wicked glint in his eyes as he penetrated her body with two long digits while encouraging the tiny bundle of nerves at her center with his thumb. "Yes, life is constantly changing, but if it didn't, we wouldn't change into the people we need to be either."

Drat him for knowing exactly how she liked being touched and for telling her exactly what she needed to hear. He soon found a rhythm he liked while she gave herself over to the wild sensations coursing through her with each thrust and every circle. Pressure stacked and mounted in her belly as he varied the friction he used. Heat poured over her being the longer he worked. Soon she wriggled on his lap, pressing his hand closer to where she needed him to be.

All too soon fireworks exploded behind her eyes. The dull ache in her head temporarily ceased. She shattered in his hold. Contractions rolled through her core and waves of bliss shivered through her body. "Oh, I've missed that," she said on a whisper while her head lolled onto one shoulder. The delicious residual tremors only made her hunger for more of him.

The grin he gave her brimmed with smugness. He knew her all too well. "Our lives are at a crossroads. Be at my side with me at yours, or choose to go it alone, but that need for attention—for love—that drives you? I can give you all of that, whenever you want, just say you'll be mine, for I only want to see you happy. You at least deserve that."

How could she turn him down in the face of such a speech? "How can you know me better than I know myself at times?" She put a palm to the side of his head, traced a fingertip along his eyebrow, his temple, his cheekbone. "I thought all I wanted from life was scandal and a man to plunge into it with me. I'm angry and spoiled and lonely, yes, but then I met you and everything changed—again." She marveled over that fact. Perhaps all changes weren't necessarily bad. "As long as you're in the mix, I don't mind so much that my life is shifting into the unknown. With you I'm learning that it's nothing to be embarrassed about if I'm not like everyone else."

"Have you ever seen two storms that were the same?" When he fumbled at the buttons on his frontfalls, his knuckles brushed her sensitized nubbin, and a host of shivers erupted over her skin. "There's a reason for that, sweeting. Everything is beautiful in its own way. How dull life would be if everyone were the same."

Isobel rose up on her knees. She took his hot, hard length in her palm, and sighed from the pure wonder of it. Of him. Royce was just what she needed, in every conceivable way, and she'd nearly lost him because of immaturity and preconceived notions. With tears in her eyes and her heart on her sleeve, she guided his member to her opening and then, while holding his gaze, she slowly lowered herself down, down, down onto him until she was fully impaled.

Their moans blended and echoed in the silence of the room.

"I'll disappoint you. I'll make mistakes. There will be gossip." His girth filled her completely; his length rubbed comfortably along every sensitive spot she had.

"If I remember correctly, Hadleigh's wife is very fond of saying that is how we learn." He kissed her. "Society can go hang, for I'll have you… if you'd ever answer my bloody question."

"Patience, Doctor. You shouldn't rush these things." Perhaps she'd let him suffer a tiny bit more, for urgency compelled her to move. Isobel rose upward on his shaft and then plunged downward again for the sheer experience of feeling him fill her body. But her confidence faltered. "I'm not skilled in this position."

He growled. The man actually *growled* as he grabbed hold of her hips. "Come down when I thrust up." Then he moved, and she did too. They came together so hard and he was sent so deep that she cried out from the bliss of it.

Isobel rode him as best she could for as long as she could, and with each thrust her hold on reality slipped. "I'm losing it." She fell off his shaft when her concentration scattered, but instead of refitting himself to her body, Royce merely chuckled.

"Perhaps this will help." He wrapped his arms around her, shifted positions, and then laid her on the sofa, coming over her seconds later. "We'll have a lifetime to practice that particular feat."

"That assumes I'll wish to marry you," she said in a fair imitation of the line he'd teased her with earlier.

"Let me show you why you will." With one arm cradling her head and the other holding his full weight off her, Royce settled himself between her bent knees. A heartbeat later, he'd speared into her again, and when he moved, Isobel locked her ankles at the small of his back. She canted her hips to better receive his thrusts.

The pressure within built and stacked and coiled, but she didn't want this coupling to end. "More," she begged in a choked whisper. "I need more of you." Oh, her doctor was clever, for he took her instruction to heart. Over and over, he stroked. Again and again, he thrust. Faster and faster his hips moved until she moaned her approval and dug her fingers into his shoulders merely to keep from being shoved along the length of the sofa. "Oh... ah... yes!"

Sweat formed on his brow and upper lip. His eyes closed while an expression of fierce concentration lined his face. And still he worked to draw out her pleasure. He moved his hand to her hip, and when that apparently wasn't what he wanted, he found her breast, rolled the erect tip, squeezed it lightly. "I'm nearly done."

Isobel cried out. That prick of pleasure-tipped pain was all it took to smash through the dam holding back the insistent pressure deep in her lower belly. "Royce!" Her body stiffened before she shattered into a million pieces of light in his arms. Joy swept her into a tunnel of light and held here there, keeping her floating.

The doctor stroked once more before he, too, found his own release. His member pulsed and jerked inside her in a bid to match the fluttering contractions in her core. "Damnation, Isobel. You're amazing." His warm breath skated across her cheek. Then he collapsed onto her body, and she reveled in his unique weight, in his scent mixed with the more pungent scents of man and sweat and love-making. "Can you imagine thirty or forty more years of this?"

"I haven't said yes."

His sharp inhalation was the only response he showed. Carefully, he levered off her enough to hold her gaze. "You will, won't you?" Panic shadowed his eyes.

"If you'd asked me that a month ago, my answer would have been no."

He snorted. "I *did* ask earlier, in a roundabout way, and you did say no."

"Yes, well." Heat filled her cheeks. "After everything you've since told me, after everything you've done, after all that I've thought about, I've come to a decision." She held his head between her hands. Oh, he was so dear to her already it nearly brought her to tears. Silly, stupid tears she couldn't control, apparently. "Despite everything, no matter how many reservations or excuses I can invent, I've fallen in love with you, Royce Marsden."

His lips formed a perfect "o" of surprise. She lightly rested the fingers of one hand against them.

"Let me finish." When he nodded, Isobel dropped her hand to his shoulder. "Yes, these changes terrify me, and yes, the future baffles me, but somehow, if you'll be by my side, I know I'll be able to navigate my way through without losing myself in the storms of my own making."

"Does that mean you'll marry me?" Such hope rode on the question that she fell down, down, down deeper into love with him.

"Yes." She couldn't help the giggle that bubbled up in her throat. "Yes, I'll marry you—I love you—and I'll be quite content to do so, whenever that may be, for it's hardly a convenient time."

"Finn has given me a good plan." He struggled into a sitting position on the sofa. "And there's this." After digging into the pocket of his waistcoat, he brought forth a plain, slim silver band. "I didn't think you'd want gemstones."

"No." Tears gathered in her eyes. "It's perfect."

Slowly, he slid the band onto the fourth finger of her left hand. "You shine more brightly than any jewels, sweeting. But should you change your mind, I bought a different ring."

"I don't know what to say but brace yourself. I'm going to dissolve into tears again." What a maddening curse to have. "This isn't the kind of woman I am."

With a chuckle, Royce wrapped his arms about her and pulled her into his side. "I don't mind, my love. This has been a rather emotional summer."

CHAPTER TWENTY

August 18, 1818
Hadleigh Hall
Derbyshire, England

ISOBEL STOOD BESIDE Royce in the large drawing room at Hadleigh Hall as they listened to the clergyman with a ring of white hair around his balding pate speak the words that would join them irrevocably together as husband and wife. As the summer morning sun shone brilliantly into the room and a gentle breeze carried the scents of the country through the open windows and terrace doors, she trembled with anticipation.

Today, she'd chosen to wear a gown of pale-yellow silk, and because she always wished to be different and portray herself not like others, she'd added a long veil of delicate lace and embroidered along the edges with tiny pink and yellow flowers. Before she'd come downstairs, she'd left her mother's ruby ring on her bedside table. It might have once reminded her why she shouldn't marry a man with a title, but oddly enough, now that she was nearly wed, she no longer felt that way. It had been flawed thinking and a manifestation of her fears. As best she could, she would move forward into this new endeavor with her head held high.

And never in her life had she felt more beautiful or feminine, and certainly all eyes were on her.

Would they expect she'd fail in her new roles? Did they wonder if this was all a lark and she'd soon bring more scandal upon their heads?

As if Royce knew the direction of her thoughts, he squeezed her hand, and she stifled the urge to sigh. How did he know her so well this quickly? While she held his hand and the vicar spoke, she let her mind wander a tiny bit.

A little over two weeks ago, most of the Storme family made the journey from London to the Derbyshire countryside. Shortly after they'd arrived, everyone had gathered in the peaceful churchyard on the property to witness her mother's burial. Now she rested next to Isobel's father, and she wished them a peaceful eternal rest.

Now, that same family sat in the drawing room watching her marry Doctor Marsden, the man who'd sent her life tip over tail, the man who took the edge off her grief, the man who could calm her emotions when they felt overwhelming. Yes, the two events so close together would sound bizarre to most people, but she didn't much care.

When had anything the Stormes had done been proper or acceptable?

The vicar said something to Royce, and when the doctor shifted his stance to take the plain silver band, the clergyman said, "You may present the ring to the lady." With a faint grin and a deliciously wicked twinkle in his eye, the doctor slipped it onto the fourth finger of her left hand. Then the vicar spoke again. "Please repeat after me, Your Lordship."

A shudder went down Isobel's spine, for this was the most somber she'd ever been in the whole of her adult life with the exception of burying her mother. Though her throat was tight with unshed tears, flutters of excitement bounced through her lower belly. She met Royce's gaze. The abject joy in those hazel pools fed her own and soothed her frazzled nerves. *Please let us feel as happy years from now as we do today.*

Royce gently squeezed her fingers. "With this Ring I thee wed, with my Body I thee worship, and with all my worldly Goods I thee endow. In the Name of the Father, and of the Son, and of the Holy Ghost. Amen." And because her doctor had always been a gentleman, he raised her hand to his lips and kissed the back of it.

The vicar smiled. The gesture crinkled the skin at the corners of his eyes. "Please kneel, Your Lordship, while everyone is invited to pray."

As the words of the prayer flowed over her, Isobel dared to peek at her new husband. He looked back with a satisfied grin curving his lips. A shiver of anticipation went down her spine. For better or worse, they were wed, and soon she would have a husband as well as become the Countess of Worchester—and all that entailed.

Would she be good enough? Would she prove an asset, a support, to this man instead of a hindrance and an embarrassment? Only time would tell, but already she felt more accepted in his life than she ever had in the whole of hers. Beyond that, the urge to garner attention had receded somewhat. She didn't need attention any longer, not while Royce was with her.

Then the prayer was over, and Royce stood. He smoothly brought her to her feet. The warm clasp of his hand in hers sent trembles tumbling down her spine, and when he met her eyes and she caught that wicked twinkle, need throbbed between her thighs.

She gasped as a realization came over her. *I'm... happy.* Beyond that, she felt content. No longer did she want to lose herself in the emotional storms that had battered her for the last few months. Would it last? Again, she looked at Royce. With his help, she could learn how to live with them, and what a marvelous thing that was, this having hope.

The vicar closed his book. He beamed at the assembled company. "I'm pleased to say I now pronounce thee husband and wife. May the Lord smile upon your new life. If you'll step over to that table, my clerk will direct you to sign a few papers."

In a daze, Isobel followed Royce's lead. After she left her signature where indicated, her family surged around her, all offering hugs, kisses, and enthusiastic congratulations until her head spun and she wished she hadn't become temporarily separated from her new husband. But Cousin Andrew beamed at her as if he'd been the one to bring about the union, and William had suspicious traces of moisture in his eyes as he, too, smiled at her.

"I couldn't be prouder of you, Cousin Isobel," Andrew said as he engulfed her in a hug that had the power to rearrange her bones. When he set her aside, his wife Sarah came forward to kiss her cheek.

"Don't mind Hadleigh's excitement." Amusement danced in her eyes behind the spectacle lenses. She held her nearly four-month-old baby girl in her arms. "We are both beyond pleased at the match you've made." Once more she came close and said in a whisper, "If you should need advice on anything, please don't hesitate to come to me."

"Thank you." Then she accepted a hug from her aunt.

"You are radiant today, my dear. Your mother would have been so proud."

Tears sprang to Isobel's eyes. "I appreciate that. Somehow, I think she knew this would happen when I told her about Royce."

"I know she did." Her aunt patted Isobel's cheek. Fondness lingered in her eyes amidst grief. "She and I talked shortly before she passed. Oh, she was so happy you'd found a man who might accept you as you are and who might temper your emotions."

Isobel nodded. She wiped at a tear that fell to her cheek. "Royce—er rather Worchester—is surprising in every way."

"I'm glad, dear." Then she moved on to speak with the doctor. Lady Jane and Finn came to take her place.

Her new sister-in-law hugged her tightly. "Congratulations, Isobel. I couldn't have picked a better wife for my brother. You'll push him to become the man he was always meant to be, and he'll do the same for you."

"I hope so." She pulled out of Jane's embrace. "Everything is quite overwhelming, makes me want to run far away from it all."

Happiness sparkled in the other woman's eyes. "But you won't because he's the calm in the storms of life you've always sought."

"Yes." Was that what she was to Cousin Finn? Heat infused her cheeks. "I suppose this family is a lot to handle."

"Indeed." Finn rolled his Bath chair close and then tugged her down so he could buss both her cheeks. "Any person who is strong enough to stand up to a Storme and face them down has earned a place in our ranks." He laughed despite the shadows that lurked in his eyes. "Besides, Marsden is an honorary Storme anyway. This was bound to happen, especially after the way the two of you looked at each other during that Christmastide house party."

"Well, he did intrigue me from the start." Though when she'd set out to know Royce, it wasn't for a lifetime. Thank goodness fate sometimes knew what was best.

She smiled. Even though her family annoyed her at times, she couldn't ask for better people to have around her. "Will you stay in Derbyshire long?"

Jane shook her head. "Not more than a few days. Finn's mother and I will depart for Ipswich soon to help Elizabeth and Brand with their new baby. It will be a nice place to reflect on Papa's life and to relax from the rather hectic months we've all had."

"I'll miss you." Finn grabbed his wife's hand, and with a tug, he brought her into his lap, kissing her cheek despite the fact that Isobel stood there. Then he glanced at her. "Don't look at me like that, Cousin. Give it a few days and you'll do all this sickly-sweet romantic stuff with your husband."

Isobel snorted, but the heat in her cheeks intensified even though she and Royce had thoroughly and multiple times explored each other carnally during the course of their affair.

"Perhaps while Jane is away you and I can talk about book writing. I have a few ideas."

"Of course." Finn winked. "Two writers in the family? London will have to take notice."

Eventually, the merry making had the men passing around snifters of brandy. Isobel sat on one of the sofas with Andrew's baby daughter snuggled in her arms. Though worries and foreboding knotted her stomach as she wondered what sort of mother she would be with her own infant, she uttered a shuddering sigh. There was something nice about the smell of a baby that tugged at her heartstrings. When she glanced up and met Royce's gaze and he looked at her with such heat and pride, need shivered down her spine. Some of her anxiety faded. Whatever happened, she would have his support and encouragement.

Perhaps that's all anyone could ask for.

Later, after the wedding breakfast had been consumed and everyone had returned to the drawing room for cards and conversation, Royce pulled her off to one side of the room. "I can scarcely believe I have a wife."

"Neither can I believe I have a husband after years of promising myself I wouldn't."

"That makes me all the more fortunate." Emotions darkened his eyes. He lifted one of her hands to his lips and kissed the back. In a low voice he said, "Promise me you won't become a proper *ton* lady, even if you *are* a countess now."

"Oh, Royce." Flutters went through her belly. "I don't want to disappoint you. But I can only be who I am, and you're an earl and—"

He squeezed her fingers. "Promise me, Isobel." His eyes held such intensity it stole her breath. "I'm an earl, this is true. However, I won't give up my work at the clinic due to this change in status, so please don't change who *you* are either, for I fell in love with the wild, unpredictable woman, and I'd like to keep her."

Isobel's heart trembled. "I promise, as long as you bear in mind there might be the potential for scandal wherever I go because of it."

"We shall weather it together, no matter from which direction it might come." He took both of her trembling hands. "I love you. Every daring, maddening, outspoken, wicked, doubting part that makes you that woman. It's who I need with me in life so that I can have the courage to do what I must as well." When he grinned, she forgot how to breathe properly. Oh, he was so handsome in his formal clothes and with that love shining in his eyes. "I don't want to raise our children in fear of not being their true selves."

Another round of tears sprang into her eyes. "Oh, Royce." Would there ever come a time when she didn't marvel at the man who was now her husband? "Yes, I promise to remain true to myself."

"Good." He tugged her a tiny bit closer despite them not being alone. "I've found that when one has been touched by a Storme, one doesn't easily wish to let go of that power."

The remaining pieces of her heart flew into his keeping. Impulsive as ever, Isobel threw herself into his eager arms and shamelessly kissed her husband, so he'd know exactly how she felt about him. He apparently didn't mind, for he returned her embrace with enough heat that she wanted to drag him abovestairs or out to the maze on the property, whichever was closer, and do extremely wicked things to him.

When she finally came up for air, all of the Storme connection was staring, but not in shock or censure. They wore expressions of indulgence, happiness, and celebration. Finn gave a wolf whistle, which was followed with laughter and toasts. With heat in her cheeks, Isobel waved to them and then buried her face into Royce's shoulder as embarrassment swept over her.

Her new husband nudged her away so that he could peer into her eyes. "When you have a place where you know joy and peace and safety, you fight for it instead of running from it, yes?"

"Absolutely. That's what my family is to me… that's what you are becoming," she answered in a choked whisper. "Yes, the world is fraught with frightening things and uncertainty, but I have them and you."

"Thank goodness for that." Royce pulled her close and wrapped his arms about her, apparently content to merely hold her.

With a sigh, Isobel rested her cheek on his shoulder and let her eyes shutter closed. Life was a constant series of changes; one couldn't escape that fact. The key to a successful navigation of that life was to treasure the good when it came, proceed through the bad with determination, and always remember that the storm would pass and leave calm behind, especially when there was someone to walk beside.

The End

About the Author

Sandra Sookoo is a *USA Today* bestselling author who firmly believes every person deserves acceptance and a happy ending. Most days you can find her creating scandal and mischief in the Regency-era, serendipity and happenstance in Victorian America or snarky, sweet humor in the contemporary world. Most recently she's moved into infusing her books with mystery and intrigue. Reading is a lot like eating fine chocolates—you can't just have one. Good thing books don't have calories!

When she's not wearing out computer keyboards, Sandra spends time with her real-life Prince Charming in central Indiana where she's been known to goof off and make moments count because the key to life is laughter. A Disney fan since the age of ten, when her soul gets bogged down and her imagination flags, a trip to Walt Disney World is in order. Nothing fuels her dreams more than the land of eternal happy endings, hope and love stories.

Stay in Touch

Sign up for Sandra's bi-monthly newsletter and you'll be given exclusive excerpts, cover reveals before the general public as well as opportunities to enter contests you won't find anywhere else.

Just send an email to sandrasookoo@yahoo.com with SUBSCRIBE in the subject line.

Or follow/friend her on social media:
Facebook: facebook.com/sandra.sookoo
Facebook Author Page: facebook.com/sandrasookooauthor
Pinterest: pinterest.com/sandrasookoo
Instagram: instagram.com/sandrasookoo
BookBub Page: bookbub.com/authors/sandra-sookoo

CPSIA information can be obtained
at www.ICGtesting.com
Printed in the USA
LVHW040827310322
714909LV00008B/230